THE
NIGHT
BEFORE
CHRISTMAS

ERIN HEMENWAY

ECHO BOOKS

Visit us on the Web! www.eringowrite.com

LCCN: 2024919268

Paperback ISBN: 979-8-9915270-0-2

eBook ISBN-13: 979-8-9915270-1-9

Cover Design by Melody Simmons

First Edition

For my daughters,
who taught me what real magic is.

1

CHRISTMAS COOKIES

I'd had a hunch flying 3,000 miles home for the holidays was bound to get weird. I just didn't think it would be *this* strange. I didn't think I'd spend my first day back getting into fights with people from my past. I certainly didn't expect to get myself fired in the first twelve hours on the job. But here we are.

So, I sat alone. In a bar. On Christmas... Drowning my sorrows in tequila.

Fantastic.

"Nachos and margaritas at Christmas? Someone is having a tough day." A voice chimed like brass tea bells, somehow beautiful and, at the same time, grating.

"Honestly, nachos are great any time of year," I responded.

"That's very true." I turned to find what I can only describe as a matronly rockstar dressed like Santa's 'little helper' smiling at me. "Mind if I join you?"

Without waiting for an invitation, Mrs. Claus slid down the bar, collecting her rocks glass and cradling it like a lost kitten. I shook my brain, demanding it come back online. I've always been pretty good at noticing my surroundings, but had she been there a minute ago? It felt like she just appeared out of thin air.

How much have I had to drink?

The woman was easily seventy years old, evidenced by her soft powdery cheeks and delicately veined hands. Her intense eyes were the blue of a winter sky just before twilight, glittering with mischief. Perfectly coiffed snow white hair drifted in loose curls down her back. Her surprisingly lithe body was wrapped in a bright red lace over black satin sheath. The garment accentuated her pleasantly firm curves in all the right ways. Even the gaudy gold reindeer belt matched her sleigh-bell earrings.

I have the perfect shoes to go with that belt, my brain mused admiringly. Meanwhile, my nose crinkled in distaste even thinking about my own outfit. I was fashionably challenged in well-loved work boots and soggy snowman socks. All of which complimented my *just-fired* ensemble of black slacks and a buttoned-down white collared shirt. I positively reeked of popcorn and I'd bet good money my red curls had escaped my careful ponytail. I was too afraid to look in a mirror. Little Orphan Annie had gone wild.

It had been *that* kind of day.

"What's a girl like you doing in a place like this?" Mrs. Claus slurred. She'd clearly indulged in generous libations herself before she had started chatting me up. *Aren't we a fine pair of misfits on this Holy Night?*

"Nowhere to go," I admitted mournfully.

A dull ache somewhere between brain freeze and migraine began to thrum at the base of my skull. I ignored it, licking the rim of the bubbled blue margarita glass. Salt and sour mix burst over my tongue. I made the involuntary and unpleasant expression I always make whenever tequila is involved.

"Me neither," Mrs. Claus sighed, smiling warmly as she raised her rocks glass in salute. "It's my one day off a year."

"What made you pick this dive?"

"I spin a globe, point, and go. Here we are," she said with a flourish, settling onto her barstool like a freshly pressed tablecloth. She clutched her beverage to her chest with one hand, offering me her other soft snowy hand. "My name is Mary, Mary Christmas."

"You're serious?" I just managed not to laugh as we shook hands. It was entirely possible I'd had way, *way* too much to drink. "Mary Christmas?"

"That's my name. Don't wear it out." Finding herself terribly amusing, Mary broke into a fit of giggles. Gin and tonic sloshed onto the copper bar top as she tittered.

"You really are Mary Christmas?" I chortled right alongside her.

"At least fifty women named Mary have married a man with the surname of Christmas over the past 170 years," she declared hotly.

"Why would someone know that?" I asked, incredulous.

"Parties. And bars. And because nosy gingerbreads like yourself always ask." She finished her drink and rattled the ice at the bartender. "Another round, if you please, Gerry."

The bartender was already ferrying a plate of nachos to the bar. *Rude!* He'd ordered it before asking me. *Or did I order and forget?* Honestly, I didn't know. But it was nachos. *Who am I to complain?*

"Just tequila this time, please. I don't need any more sugar," I said.

"Oh, tequila! Forget the gin, love. I'll have the tequila, Gerry!" Mary exclaimed excitedly, rapping her knuckles on the bar for emphasis.

Gerry-the-Bartender, a trim, well-groomed gentleman, narrowed his eyes. They were kind eyes, the shade of fresh muddled cider. His face was round and jolly, accustomed to laughter, with deep creases by his eyes and around his mouth. His smile was not intended for us girls. For me and Mary Christmas, he glowered like an ogre, giving us a critical look as he delivered the nachos and collected our used glassware. He suffered a sigh, tilting his head skyward in exasperation as he walked away.

Priorities. Food. I pounced on the nachos, and Mary Christmas joined me. There's comfort in the unabashed confidence of a stranger who had zero issues sharing food she did not order. I munched on a sinful bite of cheese, olives, and tortilla chip before saying: "I'm Zoë by the way."

"Well, of course you are, my girl. Look at you." It was difficult to tell if the British accent was legit or affected. I swallowed more nachos as Gerry-the-Bartender delivered our next round of drinks, shaking his head. Of all the watering holes in all the world, the two of us had to wander into his pub on Christmas Eve. I giggled, blowing my nose with my cocktail napkin.

"Goodness, me. You're a wreck, child!" Mary brushed loose hair out of my eyes with manicured fingers. "What was it, some bloke broke your heart? I can curse him for you if you like."

"What? Oh, no. Thank you. I mean, there was a potential... something. But it didn't work out."

"That's unfortunate."

"It *is* unfortunate. No, I'm upset because I... I was fired tonight."

"Fired?"

"Fired."

"Dashing girl like you? Whatever for?" Mary talked through a mouthful of cheese and toppings. Somehow, it looked delicate and demure on her. I probably looked just this side of feral, wolfing down nachos like a famished goblin.

"Stealing a copy of *Titanic*," I mumbled between bites.

"Oh, I've always wanted to see that film. Is it any good?"

"Um, yeah. I guess." Did Mary live under a rock? Or in some never-never land? I knew I was a bit fuzzy. But how had this woman *not* seen *Titanic*? Hasn't the entire planet? It's on the second… No, third theatrical release?

"Wait, how did you steal a copy of *Titanic*? Is it even in theaters?" she cut off my runaway brain-train and turned toward me with equal parts excitement and confusion.

I shrugged. "It is. I didn't. But a few careless mistakes later… The results speak for themselves."

"Mistakes happen!" Mary cried at the injustice. "I make them all the time! I just go back and fix them. That's the magic of mistakes. You can fix them."

"God, I wish. I wish this whole day never happened. I wish I could just…" I sighed, dropping my head onto the bar top and wrapping my arms around my throbbing skull.

"Sounds to me like you need a do-over, love," Mary soothed, rubbing my back.

"Yeah, well… that's not a thing. Otherwise, I'd take it," I leaned into her touch, grateful for her kindness and warmth. "What I wouldn't give to go back in time."

"Well, you have had a rough go of it. Here I thought I needed a vacation." Mary Christmas licked the last of the salt off her glass, sucking on the neon straws until she slurped the dregs of sour mix and tequila hiding between the squares of ice. I started laughing uncontrollably, doubling back on my stool until I nearly fell off.

"What in the world could be so funny at this exact moment?"

"Oh, Mary. Mary Christmas. Just... Us." I grinned like an idiot. "Just look at us."

Mary Christmas raked her gaze over me from top to bottom, like a judgey grandmother. She then appraised her own polished holiday attire in the slice of mirrored wall behind the bar before returning her attention back to me.

"Speak for yourself, little gingerbread. I quite like the way *I* look," she replied tartly, smoothing the fabric of her lace dress, then fluffing her snowy hair.

"I mean this," I waved a hand at our empty glasses and the devoured plate of nachos. "Two skirts drinking themselves stupid on Christmas."

"Well, I don't know. I enjoyed the nachos. And the company." She dabbed a gob of beans and salsa away from her signature Chanel red lipstick. With a flick of her wrist, she signaled for Gerry-the-Bartender. "Another round, if you please."

Gerry-the-Bartender approached slowly, exhaling through his nose. He set calloused palms firmly on the bar top, an eyebrow arched at each of us in turn. "I think I'm going to have to call it, ladies."

"What?" I half laughed. I'm the great descendant of a Viking warrior. At least, that's what my untamed mop of curls—which would not have been out of place at a Weasley family reunion—told me. And, at nearly 5'9" with 140 pounds of lean muscle earned through years of disciplined workouts, I was no wilting flower.

A few margaritas are not going to kill me, Gerry. Maybe just make the drinks and don't give me any lip.

I kept those last thoughts to myself.

"Oh, we're calling it, are we?" Mary cooed, cackling at the absurdity of being cut off at her age. I had to agree. We collapsed into a fit of hysterics. Hot tears streamed down my cheeks, my belly aching. I couldn't remember the last time I laughed so hard. Gerry-the-Bartender shook his head, refilling our waters before abandoning us to our mirth. Mary paused to look at me sideways. Her blue eyes gleamed with a shameless twinkle.

"Fancy a cookie?" she asked quietly.

"A what?" I wiped saltwater from my eyes with the back of my hands. The gesture streaked flaky black eyeliner into geometric patterns on my cheeks. Mary Christmas howled with laughter, amused by my unfortunate Picasso face-scape. Still giggling, she dipped her napkin into water, dabbing at my face as though I were her toddler.

"A cookie, dear. Would you like a cookie?"

"A cookie?" I repeated through hiccuping giggles.

She finished cleaning my face, discarding the crumbling napkin on the bar top. From a green, fur-lined, suede coat pocket she withdrew a box. The lid was embossed with a cartoonish Santa, his sleigh ready to take flight. It glowed when she unclasped the latch, the brass interior refracting the twinkling lights of Christmas. A handful of shortbread cookies lay on a red velvet lining, cut into perfect snowflakes, and dusted with a sprinkle of rock sugar.

"A special cookie," Mary's manicured fingers plucked a single, glittering cookie from the box. "My very own recipe."

"A 'special' cookie?" I chortled. I just bet it was 'special'.

"Magic," Mary whispered. "I promise... You have never had a cookie like this before."

Mary Christmas grinned like a naughty queen of the Keebler elves, popping a cookie into her own mouth. Sublime delight spread across her wintery face, traces of rock sugar clinging to her rouged lips. She licked it off with a swipe of her pink tongue. *Of course, Kris Kringle's crazy ex-girlfriend has a cannabis dispensary in her coat pocket.*

Somewhere, in my tequila-mush-addled brain, I remembered something my mother once told me: *Don't take food from faeries.*

No. That wasn't right. Strangers? Yes, that's the one. Don't take candy from strangers. But Mary Christmas wasn't a stranger. Was she? She cleaned my face with a wet nap. Strangers don't do that.

Oh, why not?

I accepted her offered cookie and popped it into my mouth. The soft buttery confection melted in bursts of home and the pleasant sweetness of Christmas. I had *never* tasted a cookie quite so indulgent. The sensation bordered on magical. My blood warmed, my toes curled, and my fingers tingled.

Maybe it wouldn't be the worst Christmas after all.

2

WAKE UP IT'S CHRISTMAS

The ear-shattering obnoxiousness of the Nokia "Jingle Bells" ringtone cut through the morning silence like a katana. Never mind that Nokia was from Finland and the katana was from Japan. It was far too early for this. And who the hell programmed my phone with "Jingle Bells" anyway?

I opened my eyes and immediately regretted my life choices, snapping them shut decisively. A yawn escaped my mouth in a growl I was not entirely sure was English.

Or human.

I ran a hand over my face and racked my brain for clues. It was a strange dream, full of Christmas and sparkling lights. Even Santa and Mrs. Claus had been there. No, that was the bartender. What bartender? Merry Christmas?

Where am I?

The complex primordial grey matter known as my brain supplied absolutely nothing useful. There was a shrouded fog bank where memory should be. I stretched my stiff muscles to discover myself tucked, rather neatly, under a coffee table. As if someone lovingly and tenderly took the time to make sure no one would step on me.

What. Just. Happened?

My head throbbed with pain and fear. I felt like I was suffocating under the table. I wrapped my fingers around the table legs to pull myself out. A shocking electric pain forced me to retract my hand.

Ow! Was the damned thing made of iron? No, that wasn't right, either. Iron is a terrible conduit for electricity. So, why did I think it was iron?

Well, that's a strange thought first thing in the morning.

"Jingle Bells" trilled again, and I cracked open my eyes. Except for one blinding light nearby, my surroundings were completely dark. A darkness so crushing that the only safe place to stash me would have been under the iron table.

So, why does it feel like a trap?

A thought, somewhere in my mind, reminded me iron was dangerous. A cage, a prison. Slowly, very slowly, I blinked away the cobwebs of my mind and wiped my mouth with the back of my hand. There was drool on my chin.

The digital beep-beep-beep, beep-beep-beep, beep-beep-beep-beep-beep of "Jingle Bells" continued to pierce the air. It grated my nerves. My lungs constricted in panic. I fumbled blindly, trying to retrieve my phone before another chorus could assault me. My fingers finally landed on the vibrating, singing banshee posing as a cellular device.

"Yeah?" I croaked. My tongue had the dry sour taste that comes when you know you drank too much. *I swear, I don't remember drinking...*Then again, I didn't remember much of anything. My pounding headache argued there may have been drinking.

"What do you mean, yeah? Where are you, agent?" A valid question, if I knew the answer. I wiggled out from under the table to get better data. And air. I needed fresh air. Badly.

The anger-bear on the other end of the phone was my nemesis, Mike Cassidy. Another word for him might be boss man. Another word for him would be inappropriate, insubordinate, and grounds for termination. I kept that word to myself.

"Where do you think I am?" I snapped back. It felt like I was swimming through a dream. A memory? What's the difference, honestly?

I blinked some more, willing my brain to function. *He sounds grumpy today.* Not that I was much better.

"You're supposed to be at the Cineplex for a staff meeting in an hour!"

There it is.

I was at the movie theater. My brain processor was back online. Let's recap before the spiraling red wheel of death forces me to reboot completely.

Number one. I work for the FBI, and I'm on an undercover mission.

Number two. My plane landed at Seattle International Airport late last night.

Number three. I drove straight north for an hour to get to Skagit Valley.

Number four. I dropped my bags at my best friend Halia's place… and ended up at the theater.

Why did I go to the theater?

"I'm getting to it, man. I'm already there." I struggled to sit up and look around. I really was at the theater. I couldn't remember how. I barely remembered the drive.

I must have rushed right over after Halia's party, or maybe before I even made it to the party? I must have snuck inside before the last showing. There was no other logical explanation for how–or why–I was at the theater.

"Bly, if you fuck this up, you're done," Mike warned.

Such a gentleman. Mike was the clean-cut, no-nonsense kind of guy the FBI traditionally loved to put in positions of power—whether they deserved it or not. He was the type of guy who despised young agents like me because I possessed a particular set of skills he did not. Skills I used to hunt things down. Skills I used to… I'm just playing.

Seriously though, the FBI did not hire USC summa cum laude nerds like me because we're cute. They hired us because we're just this side of hackers ourselves. We understood the digital world. We move within the expansive gateways of information without training wheels. The ones and zeros mean something to us. They mean something to me.

All the weapons, training, and pushups did absolutely nothing against hackers. And it was quickly becoming frighteningly apparent law enforcement, not to mention our laws, were woefully underprepared for the digital age. Catch up, congress. Seriously.

Anyways. Mr. Grouch Monster, Mike Cassidy, was mad because even with my particular set of skills, we were nowhere closer to finding our unsub—that's Fed speak for unknown subject—*Key$troker.* Yes. It was and remains a *very* stupid name. I suppose we can't all be Deep Throat or Jason Bourne.

Like all responsible hackers, this clown shoes was using an online alias. Something they felt captured their essence. Don't ask. I don't know, either. *Key$troker* belonged to a troublesome digital pirate somewhere in the Skagit Valley, nestled in Washington state.

Mike and his Seattle agents *should* have been able to handle *Key$troker* and their shenanigans. Especially with all the Amazons, Googlers, and Softies. Side note: Microsoft has the *worst* nickname in tech if you ask me. My point is, they have plenty of talent in the Pacific Northwest. Plenty of capable people ready and willing to gobble up a good mystery.

But, unlike Mike's male-dominated-middle-age-neckbeard crowd, I fit the skill set *and* the social profile for this particular undercover role—twenty-something, female, computer literate, and, most importantly, passably local. A person on the ground who wouldn't scream FBI when I walked through the door.

Yesterday, I'd been sent to my hometown to do just that.

I hadn't been home in ten years. But sure, let's head home for Christmas. *Surprise! Did you miss me?* Sounds delightful. Yay… Right.

I'd once done hard time working at this theater when I was a teenager in high school. I knew the job, the expectations, even the building inside and out. It should be a total cakewalk.

Although…

Anyone who has ever worked a day in customer service will tell you that was a big fat lie. Customer service will always be one of the most abused industries on earth, even if service is the backbone of most modern economies. No matter how fun working at a movie theater might be, it will always be a public facing service job. Let's just be honest. Customers are assholes. And no, you are *not* always right. In fact, you are most definitely wrong about at least one thing in your argument. And don't get me started on the robots.

End rant.

"I know what's on the line, Mike," I sighed in resignation. The theater would be my second undercover op. My first solo mission. Until recently, I'd been the youngest desk jockey in my division at the ripe old age of twenty-eight. It was hard to be taken seriously when you were a computer nerd with boobs. Every woman everywhere knows exactly what was on the line in this position.

"Good. And it's *sir* to you, agent. Because, unless you want to spend the rest of your life working at that shit-town theater, I suggest you find a solution. Yesterday."

I let the obnoxious Nokia brick drop to the floor the second the connection ended. He knew I'd only been on the ground for less than twenty-four hours. *What a punk.* It was just dumb luck I was already at the theater. I would never have made it on time if someone hadn't stashed me under the coffee table.

Some soulless cretin in corporate decided Christmas Eve would be an *excellent* day to have a staff meeting, rather than *any* other day in December. And, because we can't have nice things in the service industry, the staff meeting was also at 7:30 a.m. My first day on my new-fake-job, and there was a bloody staff meeting. Before sunrise. A guttural growl is how I feel about that.

"Uuuugh!"

At least drunk me was mindful enough to set up my laptop and jack it into the hardwiring in the wall, thank god. *How was drunk me able to get a plugin into the wall?* It didn't matter. I wiggled all the way out from under my iron prison and stretched until my spine popped, settling my meat puppet back over my weary bones with some satisfaction.

"Ow!" I yelped.

A low-hanging garland of Christmas gnomes caught me right in the eye. I hadn't noticed the haphazard decorations strung by Santa's minions in the crushing darkness of the booth. No normal sized person would hang decorations that low. I pressed a palm to my right eye and glared at the festive trolls.

They bobbled indifferently.

I stumbled onward, focusing on the soft green glow of ones and zeros from my computer. Its rhythmic pulse was far easier on the eyes than the blazing ball of flame posing as a ghost light. Elbows propped on the desk, I shielded my eyes with my hand as I watched code scan and file into folders. The visual scroll was therapeutic and comforting. Something familiar while I pondered how all of this fit together.

Then, I spotted it. An empty bottle of tequila was in the trash beside the work desk. Don't worry, I didn't drink it *all*. I'd have woken up dead. But it was most definitely why I woke up under the godforsaken iron table in a dark corner.

Somewhere between the drive and the empty bottle, I... lost track of everything. *When did I drink tequila?* Was it yesterday? It felt like it may have been yesterday.

My profound sense of déjà vu was interrupted when the overhead lights suddenly blazed to life. Spots of red and orange seared my brain in strange shadows. The projectors shimmered like hulking metal ogre in my blindness.

The managers must have arrived. Their first order of business would be to warm up the building, starting with the projectors. The booth operators would be minutes behind them.

A loud *creak, thunk, thud* echoed down the hallway as a heavy door banged open somewhere in the darkness. My heart leapt to my throat, and I spun around. To my undying relief, whoever entered the projection booth entered by theater six, not by theater three. I exhaled swiftly.

They have not seen me. Not yet.

My vintage Ms. Pacman wristwatch blared a warning. *6:25 a.m. I can make it.* I fumbled to silence it, looking around frantically as I slammed my laptop shut and yanked the cord free from the wall. There wasn't time to worry if my computer had finished any decryption. If I was very, very lucky, I might be able to sneak out of the booth and into the locker rooms without being noticed.

I shoved all of my belongings into my shoulder bag, whipping the strap over my head then bolting for the door. Heavy boots stomped on the linoleum like a heartbeat.

Opening procedures were headed my way.

3

STINK, STANK, STUNK

I can make it.

I quickened my steps, bursting through the door in a rush, barreling into an unseen person who bellowed in alarm. I shrieked in reply. We both stumbled backwards in surprise. Shallow gasps burned in my chest, my pulse ricocheting through my veins. It took an insidiously long moment to register that I ran into a person and not a monster.

"You gave me a heart attack!" I wheezed, a hand pressed to my sternum in a futile attempt to calm myself down.

"What are you doing here?" a deep velvety voice asked.

"I was…" Our eyes met. I found myself drawing a blank on things like words, my brain a mash of alphabet soup. Slack-jawed, I gazed upon the most beautiful mortal I'd ever seen.

He wore his night-dark hair combed neatly behind his ears in casual waves. A day-old beard scraped over his marble-cut jawline. His flawless bronze skin positively glowed. Michelangelo himself has chiseled this man's face.

Tailored black slacks and matching gothic black shirt cut neatly across his broad shoulders before tucking into a trim waistband. Corded muscles and solid legs stretched as he stood to his full height, 6′5″ at least. His eyes were pools of Cognac that sparked with delight. An amused smile tugged the corners of his mouth. He smelled like orange blossoms and cinnamon. A soothing scent that settled my roiling stomach. I wondered if he would taste the same.

What? Who said that. Oh, wait, it's me.

"Did you get lost?" he asked, head tilted to consider the pitiful creature in front of him.

"I've been here before," I managed in a whiny protest, blinking stupidly at him. "I need…"

I needed to sober the hell up before I made a complete damned fool of myself. I shook my head, attempting to shake my muddled brain back into alignment.

"I'm Malachi," he said, hand extended in greeting.

"Please don't tell the managers," I begged, completely ignoring his proffered hand. "It's my first day. I would really like to not get fired on my first day."

"Alright," his mouth quirked into a wry grin and he tucked his hands into his pockets. "How did you get in the booth?" he pressed again.

"Oh. I worked here ten years ago. As a projectionist."

He remained unconvinced.

"Y'all haven't changed the code."

His eyes tracked to the keypad then back to mine. I really hoped it was the same code. Cause I still have no good reason for how the hell I got into the projection booth in the first place. *Must. Find. Coffee.* I gave him a winning smile, hoping confidence would counter my woke-up-hungover condition, and ducked past him. His gaze lingered, a warm tingle on the base of my neck.

"Thanks for not ratting me out," I saluted before shoving into the women's bathroom.

I hissed at the blinding white lights, shielding my eyes to take a good look in the bathroom mirror. *Why are all the lights in this building so damn bright in the morning?* Inquiring minds must know.

My appearance elicited a sigh of distaste from the depths of my soul. My Celtic skin was sallow in the harsh tungsten light. Yesterday's tattered FBI t-shirt was drunk-girl wrinkled. My green corduroys smelled of stale cheese puffs and disappointment.

I cringed when I considered what Malachi might have thought at the sight of me. Or the smell. Oh no. He smelled like a fresh cup of muddled cider on an autumn morning. I smelled like that afterbirth of a rave concert. *Gross.*

Thank god my past self was mindful enough to tuck fresh clothes into a go-bag along with my computer. I snapped out a *Christmas Things* t-shirt with a glittery graphic garland of *Disney/Stranger Things* ornaments. I didn't remember packing it, but FBI training was always good for one thing: preparedness.

Muscle memory did the rest for me. I plunged my face under the faucet, the icy water sluicing away the last dregs of sleep. Droopy red curls, smeared day-old eyeliner, and faded red lipstick were beaten into submission with paper towels and an iron will. It was a botch job at best, tidying my face and rage brushing my gums until they bled.

Yesterday's clothes were stripped, bagged, and tagged. Standing in my underwear and bra, I cracked my neck just as the door swung open.

"Heavens to Betsy, Zoë!" Bette exclaimed. Bette, short for Bethany, was the most beautiful and vivacious black woman I ever had the pleasure of knowing. It was Bette, more than anyone, who encouraged me to leave this small town after my mother died.

Life is what you make of it, girl. Your life is waiting for you somewhere else. Go find it," she'd told me after graduation. Bette and my mom had been church friends when I was little. Before everything changed. Bette knew the real me. She had accepted my pathetic plea to have my job back, no questions asked.

"Just come home," she'd told me.

I really loved Bette.

Unfortunately, she was also the infuriating sort of woman who was completely put together at 6:25 a.m. on a holiday, ready for her day. Her hair was perfectly styled, the makeup effortlessly flawless. It was enough to make a grown woman cry.

She took a long hard look at me in my underwear. Comparatively, she wore a well-cut violet blouse over her buxom frame. It shimmered like satin but probably breathed like cotton. Bette was a practical woman. It got hot at the theater.

"Sorry, Mama B," I smiled broadly, unashamed. Modesty and I weren't the best of friends. And, Bette wasn't one to judge. Mostly.

Just seeing her beautiful face again felt like a warm hug. I felt better than I had all morning.

"What are you doing in your skivvies, Zuzu?" she demanded.

"Just changing before the meeting." The cold cotton t-shirt and clean jeans felt like silk as I pulled them on. I shuddered in pleasure.

Bette eyed me suspiciously, the universal look when mama catches her kid with their hand in the cookie jar. She strode toward me, one fist planted firmly on her hip.

"You been drinking?" She hooked a finger under my chin, forcing eye contact between us. I had the good sense to appear sheepish and felt my cheeks flush with embarrassment.

"Not since last night."

"I should send you home."

Her soulful brown eyes were full of warmth and wisdom. And more than a little bit of judgment. Totally deserved. I gave her my best impression of abject failure, hoping I projected pathetic burnout enough she would take pity on me.

"I suppose that wouldn't be the same kind of punishment as making you work a double shift on Christmas Eve, now would it?" she clucked at me with satisfaction.

I hadn't thought about that. Being sent home on Christmas Eve sounded like Christmas morning. Her smile was smug, sauntering down the row of toilet stalls for her morning business, whistling "Twelve Days of Christmas."

Damn.

For the record, Bette was not usually a villain. Working the Christmas holiday double was the price she had demanded when I called and begged for my job back. She told me I'd better be here at 7:00 a.m. the next day, neglecting to mention the staff meeting. She had me by the ovaries, and she knew it.

I would be working an *entire* double shift.

Double damn.

"And brush your teeth, child," Bette hollered through her closed stall door. "Your breath is foul."

Cheeky old crone.

4

CUP OF CHEER

After I put on pants… and brushed my teeth… again… I headed for the lobby to get my bearings. My black Airwalks padded silently over the squishy polyester carpet one only finds in casinos and movie theaters. It always smelled of melted butter, warm bodies, and putrid sugar at the theater. The scent immediately assaulted my system the minute I rounded the corner for the lobby. I braced myself against a wall rather than find out just how hungover I might be.

It sure as hell wasn't cinnamon and orange blossoms.

I sucked in a determined breath of air and gagged on the scent of burnt oil and sugar. If I didn't get real food and caffeine in my system stat, I would be making an unfortunate imitation of Linda Blair. I closed my eyes, focused on the grounding aroma of coffee, and followed my nose.

Like every native Pacific Northwesterner alive, I personally have a one-track mind when it comes to coffee. No, your single venti non-fat Starbucks milkshake does not count. We're a pot a day people. We are coffee snobs. Coffee is the lifeblood which must be consumed before any rational things could happen.

I directed bad thoughts to whoever's idea it was to have a staff meeting on Christmas at the crack of dawn. It would be nice if they at least let us wake up first. Though, I suppose you couldn't exactly shut down a theater for something as trivial as a staff meeting at Christmas time.

The hamster wheel must turn.

Mercifully, Bette always bought the good coffee, local donuts, and fresh bagels for the industrious among us. There was also orange juice to pacify the health conscious crowd. The delicacies were generously laid out on twin folding tables across from theater seven, where the meeting would take place. People were already helping themselves.

I made straight for the caffeine drip, snagging a maple bar and stuffing the donut halfway into my mouth. I began to doctor my coffee. And by doctor, I meant drown the caffeine in sugar and milk. Pros like myself avoided the bottle of powdered shame that some people use for creamer. Bette, the queen that she was, provided us with fresh half-n-half.

Thank you, Bette.

"I take it you like coffee with your cream and sugar," teased a familiar gravelly voice from behind. I choked on the donut in my mouth, half of the sugary pastry falling back to the table. The same tall-dark-and-mysterious man from earlier was grinning at me with his perfect porcelain teeth. I stopped breathing until my brain remembered oxygen was required for life. Forgetting the donut, I sucked in a breath and promptly began coughing like a barking seal.

"Are you okay?" he asked. I sputtered and choked, struggling for air. I managed to swallow, washing down the last chunks of fried dough and sugar with a swig of coffee. I wiped salty stinging tears from my eyes with the back of my hand.

Mystery man soothed my choking with a gentle pat on my back, his brows knit in concern. He was several inches taller than me, bending to examine my face, his eyes sweeping up and down.

My primitive body betrayed me. Blood rushed to my cheeks. My pulse began to thunder in my throat. It had been ages since anyone triggered such a magnetic reaction in me. *Danger, Will Robinson! Danger!*

"Just peachy," I managed to croak out.

His hand lingered delicately on my spine. I gulped, begging my heart to return to normal. If he were some preternatural creature, I'd have been toast. Predators sense these things. Thank the stars, he was just a regular hotblooded male. He sensed none of my roiling emotions.

"Zoë!" Halia shrieked.

Malachi quickly withdrew his hand, sucking away his warmth with him. A flash of guilt washed over me, as though I had been caught playing five minutes in heaven. My system was about to crash from overstimulation.

I stepped on my own foot in an attempt to ground myself. I barely gained my balance as Halia, my best friend since we were eight, threw her arms around me in a crushing embrace.

"I missed you too, Halia," I laughed, fighting a surprise rush of tears. I didn't expect to feel sentimental today. I had not seen her in ten years. She smelled like mangos and vanilla, her favorite lotion. I inhaled deeply, a twinge of longing piercing my heart. Halia smelled like home.

How she managed to pull herself together at this unholy hour of the morning, I'd never know. I was suspicious dark magic may be involved. Halia and Bette may very well be in a coven.

Halia was effortlessly festive in a purple sweater of dancing gold snowflakes. The bold color set off the lustrous glow of her chestnut skin. Her fawn-like brown eyes were set in the perfect oval of her face. Her black and burgundy hair was pulled between a dozen bands. The effect created a crown weave of silky locks before cascading down her back.

God, she's stunning. It simply wasn't fair how gorgeous my best friend was.

"Morning, Halia," Malachi said, his face brightening at the sight of her.

"I see you've met my roommate, Malachi. Our newly minted manager." Halia smiled at Malachi in a familiar playfulness. I scolded myself for the twinge of jealousy that twisted into my soul. *Remember. Your prime objective is find the unsub, Key$troker. Gather evidence. And go home.* Getting caught in this Malachi's bewitching presence—especially if Halia had already claimed territory—would only end in fireworks and tears.

Not. Enough. Coffee. Do not engage.

"You're a manager?" *Thanks, brain, I thought we agreed not to speak.*

"You asked me not to tell the managers. I didn't." Malachi shrugged. The mischief in his tone set my temper on fire. He let me make that ridiculous show of myself. Twice. I didn't know if I was embarrassed, angry, or both. *Both. Definitely both. Congratulations, brain. We're back.*

"Well, thanks for that," I glowered. Halia raised an eyebrow with a knowing feline smile as she glanced between us.

"See you inside, Zuzu," she gushed, abandoning us to our awkward standoff.

"Your name is Zuzu?" Malachi asked, eyes twinkling. He tilted his head in delighted curiosity.

"Only my mom calls me Zuzu," I waved a hand dismissively, then spotted Halia loitering near the theater door, still watching. "Mom and Yente over there."

He laughed and offered me his hand. "I'm Malachi."

"You said that already," I said, taking his hand. It was warm and strong. A strange familiarity to his grip, like I was still dreaming. *Have we met?* "I'm Zoë."

"Zoë," he said my name quietly, sending a shiver down my spine.

"Shit!" someone shouted, breaking the spell and drawing our attention to the concession stand.

A dark-haired Clark Kent lookalike had knocked his till off the counter, sending loose currency flying. An unremarkable boy around eighteen with forgettable brown eyes and a shy smile rushed to help. The boy dropped a bag of popcorn seeds in the process, spilling kernels everywhere.

Chaos erupted.

"Excuse me," Malachi said with a grimace, marching to rescue his staffers.

Man, I am glad I am not over there this morning. I shuddered and shuffled after Halia to wait for the meeting.

5

BABE'S IN TOYLAND

The staff meeting was so mind-numbing and long I blacked out. Can't remember a thing.

I did know I spent a large portion of it glowering at our dark and mysterious overlord, Malachi. Then I scolded myself thoroughly. Uncanny handsome managers would be nothing but trouble. I simply could not have any distractions if I wanted to get out of the theater by New Year's.

Those of us working the morning shift booked it upstairs to change as soon as the meeting ended. The lucky bastards who did not work the matinee, hightailed it out of the building as fast as their feet could carry them before Bette had finished saying, *"That's a wrap."*

In the lobby, a gaggle of staff congregated around the manager's station by the time I made it back downstairs. Bette was studying a paper schedule, checking it against faces. It was her best guess which staffer would survive the holiday onslaught in any given position. Today was going to be a shit show no matter what Bette did.

There were three possibilities: concessions to shovel popcorn, usher on the floor to clean popcorn, or in the box office to sell tickets to buy popcorn.

My stomach and I grumbled at the memory of my lost donut and coffee this morning. But popcorn sounded completely unappealing in that moment. I sighed and dug in my pockets, hoping I'd left a Snickers or granola bar. I discovered a half-eaten package of gummy bears and chuckled to myself. Gummy bears made everything better. I popped one in my mouth, patiently waiting for my next instructions.

"Boo!" Halia blurted, gripping my shoulders with both hands. Everyone around us jumped in fright.

"Christ Almighty, Halia!" I shrieked, damn near choking on a gummy bear. I was going down by snack food today. "Was that absolutely necessary?"

"Yes," she answered primly.

Bette gave us both a disapproving look as she called out placements. "Thor, you're my usher. Check the men's restroom. The janitors have been avoiding it again."

The forgettable young man with the mousy brown hair cringed as she handed him a sheet of paper. It was a list of movies coupled to their start and stop times. He lumbered away, reading the sheet and eyeing the balcony with distaste. *Good luck, buddy.*

"Consider us even, after you bailed on me last night," Halia said, handing me her Salvador Dali's *The Persistence of Memory* tie.

"Appropriate," I said.

"I thought you'd like it," she mused. We'd already changed into the uniform. Halia made flawless work of her own. She was always one of those infuriating women who made anything she wore look better. And I do mean *anything.*

Everyone but managers wore the same thing: white collared shirt, black vest, black slacks, black shoes. The staffer's getting to pick of a unique tie was some corporate stooge's idea of individuality. A way to tell the customer, *hey, I'm a person too.* Insert eye roll here.

"It smells like popcorn." I frowned and cringed, slipping the tie over my head.

"Just be grateful you're skipping training since you've been here before. You can do videos later," she whispered.

Yuck. Training videos. Every corporation has them. And we all goof off and catnap through the sham of a liability shield. They only force us to watch the nonsense so they can point and say, *see, we made them watch the videos. They should know better than to do whatever it is we're being sued for. It's the staffer's fault.*

Corporate, please.

"You're welcome." Halia crossed her arms, waiting for me to acknowledge her gift.

"Thank you?" I asked with a tone of ingratitude, popping another candy in my mouth. She rolled her eyes and I ate another gummy bear.

"What are you eating?"

"Gummy bears," I offered her some.

"How old are you?"

"You're never too old for gummy bears," I said cheerfully. She retorted with another eye roll.

"Hey, can I have some?"

It was the Clark Kent guy who had dropped his cash till. Up close, the resemblance to Superman was even more striking with his cobalt eyes, jet-black hair, and comic book chin dimple. Unfortunately, he had a painfully soft voice that did *not* match his exterior. He sounded like a kindergarten teacher who sucked in a helium balloon.

The Almighty lost a bet when they made this one, I mused.

Clark Kent stood uncomfortably close behind us, his muscled arm extended between Halia and me. I noticed he was more George Reeves desperately trying to be Henry Cavil and missing the mark entirely on both. This was the sort of guy who worked out because he *wanted* you to know he was strong. The ugly bulge on his bicep suggested juicing may have been involved.

He wiggled his fingers, his greedy beefy palm open between us. He fully expected to get what he wanted. Not a lot a girl wouldn't do for Superman—just don't let this one talk.

Before I could stop myself, I poured a handful of gummies into his presumptuous little palm.

"Thanks, you're a peach," he cooed. He was far too close for comfort. I suspected he was about to kiss my cheek and leaned away from his twitchy lips. He winked. I nearly growled.

"Pecks! Go drool on someone your own age." Halia smashed his face in a practiced face-palm to shove him back. She's been dodging unwelcome male advances since we were twelve.

"Pecks?" I asked in a whisper.

"Isn't it obvious?" Halia shot him a look to kill. Pecks was completely unfazed by her venomous glare. He blew her a kiss, and she stuck out her tongue at him.

"How old are we?" I teased. She stuck out her tongue at me, and we giggled. Honestly, if you are the age you act, Halia and I were still fifteen and not closing in on thirty.

A door opened on the balcony above. Malachi shoved a cart loaded with metal boxes out of the projection booth. Malachi's doppelgänger balanced the other end, grunting and steadying the tower with one hand. He wore a faded hoodie over an untucked, unbuttoned, and generally disheveled, uniform. Except for the just rolled-out-of-bed part, they looked like brothers.

A buzzing in my head flit around this thought. *Are they brothers?* I gasped when I recognized the second man. *Wes Jones.*

He'd started at the theater the same summer as I had. Which was when I learned we also went to the same high school—go Bulldogs! We were nearly the same age, both juniors heading into senior year. I didn't know him well, but I remembered his extreme dislike of my ex, and by association, me. *Just swell.* I fussed with my tie to give my hands something to do.

"I know you like 'em brooding," Halia interrupted my musings. "But good luck with the Grady Twins."

"I wasn't!" I protested.

I was. I am. Tall dark and brooding was a type, and Halia knew it was mine. Sometimes, it was hers too. Luckily, we never actually crossed into the love triangle because our friendship was always more important to both of us.

"Kimber, Xan, you're in the bar with Halia, tills three and four. Amanda, box," Bette said firmly, another side eye for Halia and I. We were smart enough to cower and huddle closer to keep talking as two blonde girls made their way to concessions.

"You were," Halia whispered, batting away my hands to fix the tie for me. "Besides, the brooding one is mine."

"They're both brooding, in case you hadn't noticed," I laughed.

"Yeah, but the booth troll is all Halia's," Amanda, a pixie-haired girl with fierce brown eyes teased before she flounced into the box office and disappeared from sight.

"Which one's the booth troll?" I asked.

"Wes. He doesn't come down except to refill his soda," Halia explained.

"But does he know the airspeed velocity of an unladen swallow? Is that why you call him a troll? Please tell me that's why you call him a troll."

"African or European?" Halia replied without missing a beat.

"You two are weird," Pecks chirped.

"Yeah, but she's my kind of weird," Halia replied, setting the knot in my Salvador Dali tie with delicate fingers. "Malachi is your kind of weird, in case you're wondering. He transferred from Virginia about six months ago. Something to do with the computers, I think."

"Ladies, please!" Bette snapped.

Halia dipped her head close, choking off a laugh with her hand.

A pit opened in my stomach, my mirth swallowed in its depths. Malachi transferred six months ago. Six months ago, we started seeing the watermark. It could be a coincidence.

Something to do with computers, Halia's voice repeated in my mind. It could be nothing... *Unlikely...*

"Yeah, the Dark Lord is our new drill master," Pecks laughed, leaning into our conversation like a meddling neighbor, an arm draped over each of our shoulders.

Nope, don't punch him, I reminded myself. *Punching civvies is bad.*

"The Dark Lord?" I asked. I supposed Malachi did give off a gothic Egyptian Prince sort of charm.

"Whadda you bet it's his code name, like he's special ops Black Hawk or something?" Pecks whispered in our ears, his whiny little voice ringing like a buzzing electronic.

"Go away, Pecks," Halia batted at him like a fly.

"I hear he served in Nam," Pecks was completely undeterred. "Some regular double-o shit, I'm telling you."

"Black Hawks are helicopters. And, he'd have to be at least seventy to be in that war," I said flatly. Working with civilians was going to take an earth shattering amount of self-control.

"See, now shuddup, Pecks!" Halia pushed him away playfully. *Oh… Oh, I see. Halia has a crush on Superman*, I chuckled. *Helium boy is all yours, Hali. I'll take the Dark Lord, thank you.*

"Greg, concessions," Bette said, louder than was strictly necessary. Pecks sauntered away, unfazed by Bette's tone.

"Zoë, you're my floater today. I'll need you for breaks just about everywhere. Let's start you in concessions," Bette continued.

I had an internal sigh of relief. There was a walk-in freezer behind the bar where one could scream in peace if you needed a minute away from people. I'd be just fine disappearing into its arctic embrace when my anxiety kicked in.

Halia must read minds because she gave me an unexpected hug. It had been far too long since I'd come home. I'd never did have a great poker face for people who knew me like Halia did. She squeezed my arm again. I leaned my head on her shoulder, tears beading in my eyes.

Maybe that's why this assignment was so hard. These people *knew* me. Undercover with people you know… It just wasn't done, for a reason. They would know who put one of them behind bars. I didn't even want to consider it might be someone I cared about.

"Come on, I need help with theater checks. You take one through five and I'll get the rest," Halia said, pushing me down the hall.

6

STEALING CHRISTMAS

You would be surprised how often something was "found" in a theater from the night before. Once, it was an actual real live person. At least, I think they were alive. It could have just been a dead body.

The point is one body was all it took for morning checks to become a *priority*. Every. Single. Day. Someone must physically walk through all fourteen auditoriums to make sure there were no surprises.

So, I headed for theater five. It was clear at the tail end of the hallway, right before the glass exit doors. Emergency floodlights burned through the night to help the janitorial staff *see* the goddamn mess customers left behind. Seriously, people. Do you throw the popcorn and soda on the floor at home, then leave it? What's wrong with you?

Four hundred seats were arranged in fifteen stadium rows, making it the largest auditorium in the building. The check sheet waited patiently, mounted at the bottom of the steps near the fire exit.

I took them at an easy gate, stretching my legs. The movement was invigorating, my body finally starting to wake up. I didn't even mind the blinding floodlights.

Mostly.

I stopped at the landing. Black walls stretched 100 feet high and bordered a large silk screen the color of starlight. When the Balrog challenged Gandalf and blew out everyone's hearing four states away, it was the base speakers curtained off beneath the screen in theater five that did it.

This morning that curtain was askew.

A cardboard box of DVDs, shrink-wrapped in glassy plastic, peaked out from under the heavy fabric. *Someone must have been rushing.* The disks were thrown in the box haphazardly, sharp angles jutting into the spines and covers of other DVDs. I grabbed one. A rosy-purple picture of Leonardo DiCaprio and Kate Winslet, poorly Photoshopped over a small boat. *Titanic in 3D*, it read in bold type.

"Seriously?"

I jumped as a loud clang echoed through the auditorium. In the blinding flood lights I could barely see. A dark figure stood ominously next to the projector behind a small window. They were completely shrouded in silhouette. It was impossible to tell who it might be at this distance. Curious about my discovery, I returned my attention to the DVD in my hand. The break I needed and it was only the first day. *Hot damn!* I could call Mike Cassidy tonight and report I found *something*.

The emergency lights suddenly blacked out. Panic surged, and my breath burned in my chest. I could hear nothing but rushing blood in my ears as my pulse raced in the darkness.

"Deep breaths. They're just threading the film. Just getting the auditorium ready for the day," I reassured myself. Wes... or Malachi... or whoever... just happened to kill the lights in the theater... at the exact moment I happened to find a box of contraband. *Just a coincidence.*

I waited for my eyes to adjust, the gentle track lights set into the floors warming to a soft glow and banishing the crushing darkness that blinded me.

The projector stood alone, a shadowy sentinel watching over a sleeping valley of upholstered seating. Whoever had been there was gone. My eyesight and heart rate returned. I took another calming breath before I started walking.

In my right hand, I was still holding my evidence. I weighed my options—go straight to Bette with my discovery or save it for the FBI. If I went to Bette and she knew… I shuddered at the thought. Agent Cassidy was my best option to not get anyone I cared about in trouble without a damned good reason. If I skipped morning checks, I might have just enough time to hide it in my locker. I tucked the DVD into my waistband under my shirt and ran.

I was eager to call the Mike and report my discovery. Unfortunately, I had misplaced my phone. It wasn't anywhere in my locker or bag. I would have to retrace my steps. Probably in the projection booth since that was the last time I used it. I filed it away on my to-do list and rushed back to the lobby before anyone noticed I had gone rogue.

7

NO SLEEP 'TILL CHRISTMAS

The tight quarters of the concession stand, also known as "the bar," lead to feelings of claustrophobia. I didn't have claustrophobia, but I did feel trapped as we all shuffled through the narrow corridor. Halia didn't seem to mind as she lead a group of new staffers, myself included, into the bar. Other staffers crammed around me, oblivious to my aversion to crowds.

To my right, an industrial sized kettle for popping corn sat inside the plexiglass box. It would not be out of place at a carnival with its bright red trim and shiny steel base. Three matching metal baskets held folded paper bags in various sizes. Gliding metal doors hid the oil supply and the steel drawer holding the popcorn seed.

A sweeping arm rotated around inside the popcorn cauldron, continually churning the uncooked kernels of corn. A bright red button stimulated the mechanism to dump oil directly into the drum. A steel basin caught the corn as it began to pop and overflow out of the mouth of the kettle.

The lights dimmed, and a spotlight lit Halia. I was the only one who seemed to notice her caress her fingers across the overly happy yellow words 'FRESH HOT POPCORN!' like a horrifying impression of Vanna White.

This day is a god damned twilight zone.

Halia dumped the finished batch of popcorn with practiced ease. She refilled a large steel box with seed, throwing one scoop of suspicious orange powder in with the kernels. She returned this entire concoction to the kettle, pressing the red button for oil, before turning to me with a murderous grin.

"Popcorn is the bread and butter of the theater. We make most of our money off of concessions, so this is where we make the big bucks," she informed our group in a sultry mezza voce. She turned a critical eye on the new blonde girl, gesturing to the orange powder.

"Don't give customers *this* salt under *any* circumstances. Like, ever."

I grinned, recalling a time when a customer insisted the regular table salt option we offered simply wasn't enough. He wanted more. Halia, in a moment of rage, had scooped not one, not two, but three of the industrial grade popcorn seasoning directly into the man's bag. An ambulance had to be called. Halia had nearly been fired. Nearly.

As if someone had cut a film reel, our training group was suddenly passed along to Pecks. His smile was nearly as maniacal as Halia's when he grabbed a stack of thirty-two-ounce cups from the red cupboard behind him. He suggestively stuffed the flimsy paper cups into a rubber holder beneath his cash register. In a fluid single motion, he slipped the last cup off the end with a disturbing *pop* and ripped away the plastic wrapper like a discarded prophylactic.

"Each beverage should be served ice cold. They're on a sensor so they will stop filling on their own automatically," Pecks grinned. He used the cup to scoop ice directly from the bin by his elbow. He smiled and thrust it under the Coke dispenser.

"Watch out for foam. It's like beer. You'll need to ease down the head." He slapped a lid on the beverage before sliding it smoothly across the counter with a mischievous wink.

Gross.

In a flash, our lesson had moved on again. A woman with white bouffant hair and thick pancake makeup smiled alluringly.

"Hot dogs should be cooked to 140 degrees," her southern lilt cooed at us.

Rosemary, my muddled memory supplied. The mousey retiree turned supervisor had forgotten she was no longer in a 60's sitcom. Sexy was not the word anyone would use to describe her. But that smile was positively risqué.

She traced a finger down the red label on the hotdog rollers as glossy pink links rolled in piping hot rows. Air conditioning blasted through vents and made the hotdog sign shimmy. She shivered in delight and opened a steel drawer beneath the rollers. Steam dramatically billowed into the air, fogging her glasses into strange mirrors.

I could see myself in their reflective surface but not her eyes. The people standing right next to me were missing from the reflection. I spun around in alarm. The lobby was empty, black as the pitch of night.

What is even happening? I could *not* be this hungover.

"Buns should always be nicely warmed," the woman drawled. Her porcelain smile was disturbing. "Careful now. Don't let the dogs sit too long. You want them nice and firm. No one likes a wrinkled dawg."

It occurs to me the sexual innuendos border on inappropriate for routine training.

A smash cut, then the room went dark. A spotlight came on over the work desk. Wes sat hunched, cutting and splicing together film reels like he was Tyler Durden.

I blinked. How the hell did we make it into the projection booth? I finally found my voice. "Am I the only one confused how we got here?"

Wes whipped film around on a reel-to-reel machine until the canister was spinning like a moving vehicle. Malachi stepped out of the darkness and into the light.

"Jesus, where did you come from?"

Malachi crossed his arms, leaning against the worktable beside Wes. The noir lighting transformed his smile into something positively sinful.

"In old theaters like ours, movies don't come on one giant reel," Malachi rumbled. "Wizards like Wes here splice them together and incorporate them on our platter system."

As if on cue, Wes stretched a line of film to the full length of his right arm. A cigarette burn popped above Malachi's head for a moment then disappeared.

"Never mind cigarette burns, that's just a myth," Malachi assured me with a mischievous wink.

Wes halfway turned to face us. His smile was serpentine, a cigarette dangling precariously from his lips. He had never looked more like Brad Pitt than he did in that moment. And Wes looked nothing like Brad Pitt.

"What in ever loving hell is going on?" I demanded.

The whirling projectors buzzed like a cat's purr. Film scratched across the table. Tape snapped with a zip as it stretched. A choppy *thunk* of the splicer joining celluloid coalesced in the air. The cacophony snapped with electricity.

"Wake up, Zoë. Wake up," I muttered to myself. This video, or daydream, was getting seriously out of hand. To be honest, it wasn't the worst dream I'd ever had. But it certainly ranked in the top five weird.

I suddenly found myself waiting inside of a theater as customers slowly filed out like zombies. An older gentleman with white hair and a neatly kept mustache waited impatiently beside our group of trainees.

Gene, my fuzzy brain supplied his name. He gestured me forward. Mechanically, trainees began to sweep up spills with a push broom. Others collected used cups and bags into an overturned booster seat. Gene leaned against the wall his attention on me.

"Guests exit the theater in a disorderly fashion, trashing the place as if they were at a frat party," Gene said.

For good measure, a pair of bros dumped their popcorn by attempting a three-point basket shot. They missed by a mile but congratulated themselves with a chest bump. They didn't even notice the wallet falling behind out of one of their pockets. Gene scooped it up.

"Be sure all lost items are properly cared for. They might be important to someone." He stuffed the wallet into his own pocket and continued cleaning, whistling "All I Want for Christmas" as he waltzed into the distance.

"Are you ready, Zoë?" Halia asked. I blinked several times.

I was standing in the concessions with a vacant expression on my face counting down my till. Halia looked like she may have repeated herself several times and might be annoyed with me. She dumped the popcorn from the kettle and reset it for another batch. "Count your till, remember?"

Did I just hallucinate an entire training video?

From here on out, I commit to eating healthy, and no more tequila. I vow to sleep before my shift instead of dredging through the dark webs... For once in my life. I promise.

I groaned and finished counting my till.

8

EX MAS

Christmas was on a time-loop.

Every thirty minutes, eight god awful songs piped through the building. Eight Christmas songs no one liked very much. Eight Christmas songs peppered with ads for movies and popcorn, as if you didn't know exactly what you were there for in the first place. *What MBA thought of that genius idea?*

The music had already cycled twice before the staff meeting even started. It was well into its fifth cycle by the time we'd opened the doors. The insanity was starting to set in. The only thing drowning out the repetitive music was the din of customers.

The very moment we opened the doors, the flood gates of Christmas shoppers infiltrated the theater. The demand for popped air, fake butter, and sugar water outweighed the quality of our instructions. The training wheels came off. New hires and seasoned pros alike were shoved onto tills unsupervised.

Nothing like trial by fire.

Straight down the concessions line, the pitch was the same.

"Hi, welcome to—"

"…Cascade 14. Would you like to try—"

"…a Super Combo?"

The words tumbled out without thinking as a grandmotherly type stepped forward. She paused to look over the soda choices. We only had Coke products, but for some reason, everyone still needed to think about it. I glanced down my line to see how long before I could hide in the fridge.

I froze when I spotted him.

The ex-boyfriend.

Jake Landen had been my high school sweetheart. Hair the color of an island sun, eyes the sea green of a raging ocean, the Talented Mr. Ripley and Dickie Greenleaf in the same body. Jake's golden boy charm left a string of broke hearts in his wake, myself included.

He liked shiny broken things.

"Zoë? Zoë Bly?" he asked.

"Yeah?" Pretending I didn't recognize him wasn't an option. But if someone ran out of the back screaming, "FIRE" right about now, I'd be okay with it.

"Holy shit!" he shouted, detaching himself from the girls on either arm to lean across the counter. "It's me! Jake, Jake Landen!"

"Oh, I remember." *How could I forget?*

"You look exactly the same. How long has it been, three years?"

"Ten. It's been ten years, Jake," I replied sardonically. He knew it'd been ten years. Was he trying to make the girls think he was younger? *The crows' feet are taking care of that just fine, buddy.* Frantically, I scanned the sea of people for a savior. *Get me out of here.*

Like a dark knight, as if he sensed a disturbance in the Force, he raised his eyes to meet mine. *Malachi.* Just the sight of him calmed my panic. I held his gaze long enough to be pleading. His brows narrowed, and his mouth thinned into a frown. With long lanky strides, he began crossing the river of customers blockading the lobby.

Oh, there is a god! I sighed internally.

"Man, just like yesterday," Jake continued to jabber, completely unaware. "We were high school sweethearts!"

His dates wore their battle armor of pouty lips, crossed arms, and sour expressions. Light glinted off their sharp polished nails like Krampus fangs gorged on blood. If we had been in school at the same year, I'd have been their seek-and-destroy target.

Halia had been my friend before we entered the Gladiator ring of high school, thank the stars. Life would have been miserable if she hadn't already been my life-sister. She always treated me as though I mattered. I smiled down the bar where she trained the new blonde girl, Kimber. Halia grinned and pointed at her trainee before she rolled her eyes.

"What a life, right? I was the football star, Zoë did a few plays," Jake explained to his dates, indifferent to any of the cues from the females in his radius.

"I did more than a few plays, Jake," I sighed through my nose in frustration.

"Your name is Zoë? That's a little girl's name, isn't it?" one of his dates chimed in.

I can curb stomp you with my barefoot, you prepubescent donut. It's good to have an inner monologue. I'd get myself into a lot more trouble if I had an outside voice.

"Little girls grow up," Jake said, his voice low. A crude smile played across his thin lips as he raked me with the assessing superiority only an ex is capable of.

I nearly vomited. Which, at this point, would actually work in my favor. Quick, brain, think of something vile, and vomit.

"Hey, we should get coffee. What's your number? Do you still live with your dad?" I cringed. The very idea of spending time with Jake and his family very nearly did the trick of inducing projectile stomach contents.

"Jake, I'm kind of working here," I said.

He straightened up as if realizing this was not how adults spoke to one another. "Right. Hey, we'll take the combo thing. Coke and butter."

I turned to fill his order. I could feel his eyes burning into my back. Suddenly I was extremely conscious of how terribly my uniform fit. I glanced to my right.

Malachi had made it to the end of the bar but was caught in a traffic jam. A wild box of candy had spilled. The new girl, Kimber, was sobbing on the floor. Malachi, Dark Knight that he was, stooped to save her. His eyes flicked to mine.

"*Are you okay?*" he mouthed, sweeping Skittles into a dustpan. What was he going to do anyway? I didn't need saving. I needed a psych eval. I offered him a grim smile and turned away.

"Do you still like gummy bears?" Jake asked in a whisper. "I'll take two."

"Thirty-seven, seventy-five," I spit the price with acid, slamming candy on the counter, spinning away to fill the rest of his order as quickly as I could manage.

The fountain shut off the soda at the exact moment I returned. With one hand, I transferred the massive thirty-two-ounce container onto the counter, pressing the lid down as I slid everything forward. My register screen was suddenly very interesting. *I think I'll just stare at it for a while.*

Jake held two twenties crisply between his fingers. He tilted his head, a smirk on his annoyingly handsome face, despite his obvious aversion to sunscreen.

He slid the bills slowly across the counter. I reached for the money, but he snapped it back in a round of tug-of war. Not willing to play his stupid game, I let go. He grinned and offered the money again. I ripped the bills from his fingers.

It took me much longer than it should to enter the cash and produce change. When he made to play tug-of war again, I dropped the money, withdrawing my hand and letting the bills and coins crash to the counter. Jake didn't even move to collect it. He just grinned in an uncomfortable game of *Don't Blink.*

"Mr. Landen." Malachi slipped behind me. He was close enough to feel the warmth of his body. A gentle hand pressed against my waist, a quiet request for permission to touch me.

Years of self-defense training, combined with a healthy dose of trust issues, would have me throwing other men over the counter. If it had been Jake, I'd have broken his arm in the process. Malachi's touch sent ripples of pleasure down my spine.

Permission granted.

I leaned in, covering his hand with my own. He instinctively laced fingers with mine.

"What can we do for you, Mr. Landen?" Malachi's voice was deep, a velvety bourbon sort of sound. I practically swooned in relief.

"Seeing double-oh-seven. Ladies dig an action flick," Jake answered, a tense timber to his own voice. *Is he jealous?*

Malachi certainly was. His fingers flexed, gripping my waist protectively as he drew my back against his flat stomach. My heart stilled. *Is this what safe feels like?* The sensation was strange, my head spinning with conflicting desires.

"Perhaps you should get to your theater, instead of holding up my lines," Malachi replied, his voice taking on a tone of warning.

"I'll call you," Jake laughed with one last wink in my direction. He slipped his arms around his dates, allowing each girl to carry his popcorn or soda. I scrunched my nose in disgust.

9

FROST SPRITE

Malachi chuckled softly behind me, unlacing fingers. It felt suddenly cold. By some black magic, Bette appeared in my line, directing annoyed customers away. She turned to face me, my line empty behind her. "Take your ten."

"Thank you, angel of mercy." I turned and ran smack into Malachi, my nose smashed into his well-muscled chest. He steadied me, a firm grip on my arm, gentle fingers resting on my back. A fire raced through my blood, dread ratcheting my nervous system into fight or flight.

Flight. Definitely flight.

I needed to escape before something stupid came out of my mouth. I slipped from Malachi's grasp, my gaze on the popcorn laden floor, refusing to make eye contact as I evaded my emotional hurricane. I weaved through the crowded bar and disappeared into the back room.

The stainless steel tomb that doubled as our massive walk-in refrigerator was built right into the wall. A frigid blast of air blew my hair back as I wrenched open the heavy door to submerge myself in its arctic embrace. I stepped inside and yanked the door closed, a whomp of silence in the cradle of freon and steel. I sank onto a bucket, gulping breaths of cold air, counting backwards from twenty-five.

Peace.

Quiet.

Calm.

And cold.

My burning cheeks began to cool, my shoulders relaxed. I recognized it as a little absurd, but this had always been my sanctuary in the chaos. In a building bursting with people, the walk-in was as close to a sensory deprivation tank as I could get. Just breathe with me, alright?

The door cracked with a sucking sound as the foam seal broke cold against warm air. The two temperature fronts swirled in an invisible dance as Halia closed the door behind her. She held a small bag of popcorn and a cup of Sprite. Her lips were pursed somewhere between frustration and sympathy.

After a moment, Halia threw the soda into my face.

"Jesus, Hali!" Lemon-lime zest soaked into my hair, sticky sugar water running down my face. "What the fuck?"

"If you get back together with him, I will never forgive you."

"What?"

"You've been acting weird all day. Then, the prince of flowers comes waltzing in, and you're a god damn mess!"

"Excuse me for having a visceral reaction to the asshole who cheated on me during my mother's funeral—"

"I know, Zoë! I was there! I was always there for you! I love you, Zoë. I always have."

"I know—"

"No, you don't!" Halia sniffed, wiping her nose with the back of her hand. "I watched him break you into smaller and smaller pieces until there was barely anything left of the Zoë I love."

"Halia, I didn't... I didn't mean to..." I reached for her, but she cut me off, holding a hand up for silence.

"Do you even remember the last Christmas we spent together?" she asked quietly, leading me toward some cliff I didn't want to go anywhere near.

My mom had been cancer free for nearly ten years. Then, a dark blot appeared on one of her bone scans just days before Halloween. By Christmas, she'd had lost her hair to chemo again.

"Mom... relapsed. I didn't take it well." I shivered, the cold dregs of Sprite swirling with my memories and making my body shiver.

"I know," she said softly. Then, a thought seemed to occur to her. "That's why you agreed to the party at Jake's house... isn't it?"

I remembered the party, but not because of anything in my brain. I remembered it because of what happened after the party. The party itself was a muddled knot of filmy memories that didn't make sense. I stayed silent, waiting for her to speak.

"I guess it doesn't matter," Halia said. "You weren't going to listen to me. You never listened to me about Jake." She laughed bitterly, wiping her nose with the back of her hand again. "I was the one who called your mom."

"You called my mom?" I demanded.

"I had to do something. You were my ride, but you were beyond wasted. And you wouldn't give me the keys. You told me to leave. I was worried. Your mom was worried," Halia's voice quivered. She took a slow deliberate breath as though preparing to dive into deep water. The very idea made me take my own breath, holding it until it burned.

"It was late. It was only a few miles home… I figured I could walk. But the city hadn't cleared the sidewalk, so I used the road. Your mom… she tried to stop when she saw me. It's just so slick on the bridge around Christmas. She couldn't stop in time. The car went spiraling by me into a pylon. She just… couldn't stop." Halia raised her wet eyes to mine. "Zoë, I'm sorry. It's my fault she's gone."

The ice on my skin melted into my marrow and froze. Somewhere in my bones, I knew my mom had been on her way to pick me up from the party. Why else would she have even been on that bridge? Jake's family had a huge property right on the river. We lived up the hill near the elementary. What no one could understand was how she'd lost control, even in the dead of winter.

"Zoë—"

"No. Don't. Not right now." I pushed past Halia. The snap of the door opening was met with a burst of hot salty air. It burned my eyes.

"I was just coming to find…" Bette trailed off when she saw me. "Everything alright?"

I had no idea what I looked like from her perspective. Probably a drowned rat covered in Sprite. I wiped my face with my fingers, reaching for a paper towel to finish the job. There was nothing to be done with the sticky wetness in my hair. Maybe it would dry into a cute curly hair product. Unlikely with the day I was having. I'd end up looking like Cameron Diaz in *Something About Mary* with my luck.

"Everything's fine." I forced myself to smile at Bette. I knew it wouldn't reach my eyes.

"Alright. Zoë, you can break Thor, then. He's at the door stand."

I nodded and brushed by, refusing to meet Halia's eyes as I rushed out of the concessions and into the chaotic lobby. I'd been faking it all day.

I was very good at pretending everything was fine.

10

BOXING DAY

It was only half a dozen strides or so from the concessions to the door stand where Thor, the not-Asgardian surfer guy, was tearing tickets. I told him to take his break and he happily dance-skipped away. Breaking Thor for his lunch was Bette's way of isolating me to the door stand where I would be restricted to customer interactions only.

Bette was smart like that.

Customer service could be dull and repetitive. You were usually stuck in one place for long periods of time. Tearing tickets was about as interesting as a toenail. But the droning work was exactly what I needed to simmer down and process what had just happened.

Deep breaths, Zoë, I reminded myself, as I directed another customer to their theater. The breathing exercise cooled my temper from blistering anger to a dull ache. Rage and sorrow often feel the same in the soul. As the two emotions warred for control the only thing I could do was breathe and wait it out. Maybe think. A little logic to cool my temper and soothe the pain.

I *knew* it wasn't Halia's fault. An icy road and suddenly there's a person. What choice was there to make? An impossible choice, and no time to decide. My mom had avoided killing my best friend by simply reacting.

She saved a life.

Lost her own.

Malachi's voice thrummed under the whine of electronics and popping corn. He was busy at the hulking L-shaped managers desk behind the box office. He spoke quietly on a phone hooked into at nest of cables that snaked behind the computer.

"No, no sign of the carrier yet. Yep." He sighed, replacing the receiver in its cradle before sweeping his attention over the lobby. His gaze fell on me and stopped. The ferocity of his blazing eyes softened to a warm glow, giving him the impression of a vigilant dragon considering his prey.

I sucked in a breath and looked away, stewing in self-loathing. Even Malachi's piercing gaze was not enough to numb my pain. My mom had been sick. Maybe she could have fought it. Maybe she would have made it if she hadn't been on that bridge. Maybe she could have won against the cancer one more time. Halia had called her because she didn't—couldn't—trust me to take care of myself.

I shook my head. It was an accident. Whatever force of nature aligned all the wrong things to take my mom from me, I knew somewhere in my heart, none of it was Halia's fault. I couldn't help but be angry, though. We had never really talked about *that* day. That fight. And now, to learn my mom had likely died because she'd been avoiding hitting my best friend? It was really too much to process.

I didn't care how long ago it happened. I didn't care how irrational it was to be mad. Sometimes, the body feels what it feels. And yet... It wasn't Halia's fault. If anyone's, it was mine.

I am such an idiot.

"It wasn't her fault," I repeated, to myself more than anyone within hearing.

"Are you alright?"

I practically jumped out of my skin at the rumble of Malachi's voice over my left shoulder. I could feel my eyebrows trying to hide under my scalp from surprise. I took a settling breath and shook my head. I was not okay. But it wasn't his job to fix it. It was mine. The sooner I did, the sooner I fixed all of this. The sooner I could go home.

"I'm fine," I said, turning back to tearing tickets for customers with a firm crispness. Malachi made a sound that could have been a laugh, could have been a grunt. I don't know, I wasn't looking at him, alright? I sighed through my nose and reached for a stack of tickets.

"Theater nine is to your right," I told the family. They slipped by us and meandered on their way.

Malachi's calming presence lingered near my hip. He leaned in, propping his elbows on the ticket stand and stretching out his long limbs.

"I was thinking," he said, tilting his head to look up at me through dark lashes. His eyes burned with something I couldn't quite name. My stomach did some interesting acrobatics.

"Well, that can be dangerous," I replied without thinking. Because my brain was not connected to my mouth at all.

Malachi smiled. "I was thinking that you have had a tough first day," he continued. "And, I would like to take you to lunch on your between shifts break. If you are willing."

I smiled, anticipation coursing through my body until I felt warm and tingly from head to my toes. "Lunch would be wonderful."

"Great." He straightened to his full height. I was not a short woman at 5'9", but Malachi made me feel delicate and small. The foreign sensation took my breath away. "How does sushi sound?"

"Great!" I replied, again without thinking. *Brain, please catch up, would you?! We hate sushi!*

"I'll come back and get you as soon as Thor gets back. Sound good?"

I nodded and watched him stride away.

"What a handsome man," an old woman's voice warbled.

I reluctantly pulled my eyes away from Malachi's muscled backside and turned to help my guest. If Rainbow Bright had a grandmother…

"Uh, yeah. He's pretty nice," I said, dumbly.

"Nice is how we describe children and puppies, dear. Specimen like that are Christmas morning. Get yourself a bite, or I will!" The woman grinned, blue eyes bulging behind bottle glass spectacles, lips in Barbie pink pulled tight in a toothy grin.

I blinked in shock. *Did she just… Yes, she did.*

"Theater nine, on the right," I clapped back with an irritated glare, as the squat little toad of a woman sauntered away to her movie. My traitorous hormones needed to simmer down and take a seat. I sighed in frustration, trapped in my thoughts, stuck at my podium, wishing for anything more interesting to happen.

As if on cue, a bulky man with thick hands and bulging muscles dragged a cart loaded with three gunmetal grey boxes through the carpeted lobby. The studio's courier escort had arrived, at long last.

Most modern films are screened digitally, projected in the latest format available. But some die-hard cinema directors insist on real film. Some of the studios still humored them, sending film reels in large metal containers with giant FBI warning labels in bright red.

Really big movies like *Star Wars* were likely to show up with an actual FBI escort. Lucky me, the FBI figured it was better to have an inside man. Girl. Woman. You know what I mean.

"You're new," the courier said, wheeling his boxes past my podium. *Thank you, Captain Obvious.* He parked his cart beside the manager's desk, unloading the awkward metal boxes. "I'm looking for a signature."

I glanced around the lobby. Where the hell had Malachi disappeared to? Or Halia? Or Bette, for that matter? There wasn't a manager or supervisor in sight. From this angle, I couldn't even see anyone in the picture window hiding in the managers office. *Just my luck.*

"Can you wait?" I asked.

Captain Obvious fiddled with his scanner, grunting before he proceeded to ignore me.

"Thanks," I grumbled and looked around for anyone who might be able to help. I spotted a young blonde man in a staff uniform lingering near the box office. I couldn't remember his name from the meeting. Chad? Maybe Kevin? With his shaggy blonde hair, untucked shirt, and sallow skin, he could easily be confused with Kurt Cobain. Until properly introduced, he was going to be hereby named Nirvana whether he liked it or not. I grabbed him by the arm.

"Hey, man, can you watch the door stand for a minute?" He pulled his head back in surprise at being touched, looking around as if uncertain I was talking to him. "I gotta find a manager to sign for the film prints."

After a moment of consideration, he gave me a greasy smile and nodded, waltzing to the door stand. I rolled my eyes and rushed to the manager's desk.

I tried the phone, dialing the direct code for the office. No answer. I opened the box door. Amanda—I think it was Amanda—thumbed through a wad of twenties, her lips silently counting until she reached $500.

"Hey, I'm gonna go find a manager," I told her. She snapped a rubber band around the bills, dropping them in a security box. She nodded absently as she greeted the next customer. I wasn't entirely certain she'd heard me, but I abandoned her anyway, racing up the stairs.

11

CHRISTMAS WITH THE KRANKS

The manager's door was a muted red with a stainless steel handle, sandwiched between giant movie posters from the 90's on either side of the door. I rapped my knuckles on the expanse of drywall to the left, knowing about the hidden cash room beyond the wallpaper and poster. I repeated the knock after a minute, just to make sure they truly weren't there.

Where is everyone?

I looked over the balcony and scanned the lobby again. I saw no sign of Halia, or Bette, or Malachi. There wasn't much of a line. Amanda had it handled. Nirvana was chatting up the courier.

Without a manager on hand, my best guess was I needed to find Wes. He would be responsible for assembling the film. Of course, the only way to get to him was to venture into the projection booth, again. Which was technically off-limits. Technically. I mean, I had already violated this rule… Like, a lot.

I dashed for the projection door with a built in key pad and jammed in a four digit code, crossing my fingers no one had thought to update it since my morning excursion. The light blinked green as I turned the handle. "Victory!"

The whirring sound of projectors swelled and fell on the linoleum floors. The sound dampening walls swallowed what bounced back. Calling for Wes would be an exercise in futility. With fourteen screens, it was almost impossible to guess where he might be. I checked around the corner where Theater 6 was tucked, hidden behind the manager's office. He wasn't there, so I made the trek down the dark hall toward the other screens.

I ended up by the projectionist desk, again. It was littered with discarded scraps of film and a box of rolled trailers. Art I hadn't noticed earlier was taped to the walls, creativity born from the projectionists boredom. The booth log lay open and inviting. The garland of Christmas gnomes that had tried to kill me earlier had been rehung. I scowled at them as I thumbed through the logbook.

"How did you get in here?" Malachi's voice was surprisingly stern. I dropped the booth log and spun. Malachi and Wes stood shoulder to shoulder, dark and ominous.

The Grady twins.

"I was looking for a manager. The print arrived," I said cautiously.

"But how did you get in here? The door is locked," Wes demanded.

"Oh… You still haven't reset the code." I smiled at Malachi in an attempt to make it not seem weird. But it's weird, isn't it?

They both stared, the awkwardness growing. My intention had been only to talk to Wes. I wasn't expecting to see Malachi before lunch. My cheeks flushed hot, and I just knew they were burning pink. The trouble with being a ginger was we wore our emotions on our skin.

"Right. Well. I guess you gentlemen have it handled. I'm gonna head back." I felt their eyes on me the entire walk back to the door.

Back downstairs, the lobby had turned into a retail war zone in the five minutes I'd gone. Lines stretched from the concession stand to the butter-bar, from the box office to the street. Halia stood impatiently at the podium, tearing tickets with a frustrated look on her face.

"Where have you been? You know you are not supposed to leave without permission."

I am a grown ass adult, I thought in defiance before silencing the retort. I worked for the theater. Even if it was temporary. Even it was fake and undercover. Even if I was still upset about what she had told me. It was all 100% irrelevant at the moment. *So, keep your big mouth shut, Zoë.*

"Sorry, I was looking for a manager," I mumbled, moving to take up my post. Halia held up a hand to stop me.

"Zoë, I know you don't want to be here, but you asked to come back. So you have to show up, okay?" she said, earnestly. I blinked several times, processing her words.

Her expression was tired, sad, more than a little hurt. There were so many more layers to what we needed to say to each other. I didn't have the time or energy. Not to mention, I was still rattled from our little ice-capade in the fridge. I was pretty sure there was still Sprite sticking my bra to my shirt. I ground my teeth.

"I didn't abandon the door stand because I was bored," I said coldly, turning on my heel and storming away. If she thought I had abandoned her, she could rot right where she was.

"Zoë, wait!" Halia shouted, but I could barely hear her over the rage in my head. All I wanted to do was to escape this nightmare and go home. But no, I had to go through the motions. Solving this case and getting gone was officially my top priority.

I didn't need any friends.

12

IF WE MAKE IT THROUGH DECEMBER

"I hate Christmas," I finally admitted to myself. Christmas had not done anything for me lately. If it was going to treat me like a Scrooge, I might as well be one.

Malachi and Bette huddled, Wes trailing closely behind them as they rounded the corner. They were fervently discussing a matter, gesturing between themselves furiously. I stalled at the sight of them.

It hadn't been more than five minutes, and they were all in some sort of panic. Malachi was the first to notice me and beckoned for me to join them at the manager's desk with a wave of his hand. *What now?* I wondered sourly.

I looked to Bette. She was frazzled, her beautiful coiled hair frizzy, sweat beading around her temples. Malachi frowned, the crease giving him a sour expression. Wes sank into the chair, a scowl plastered on his face.

This can't be good. I cautiously approached them.

"Did you sign for the film print before you came upstairs?" Malachi asked.

"No, I did not. I came to find you, remember?" I said, as calmly as I could manage.

"Are you sure, Zuzu?" Bette asked softly. Warning bells sent my adrenaline into full blown panic. *Just breathe, Zoë.*

"The courier showed up. I grabbed a kid from the staff meeting to tear tickets, then came up to look for you in the projection booth. I've been away for maybe five minutes," I pointed out in clipped tones.

"What kid?" Malachi asked, eyebrows shooting up in alarm.

"I don't know. The Kurt Cobain lookalike." Was it Chad? Jerry Garcia? Kevin? I racked my brain, trying to remember more details. Clearly, they were going to be important. "Blonde, maybe seventeen. The giant lip tie with the tongue lolling out. Like Rolling Stones. White shirt, black vest... Just like everyone here."

"Shit," Bette swore.

"We don't have any blonde males on staff at the moment," Malachi explained in frustration.

"Unless you count Jake," Wes growled, shooting me a venomous glare. He had been here last time, when all three of us worked together. And Wes had been on shift the day Jake and I had an explosive fight at work.

I gaped at them. No one had told me Jake still worked here so it was news to me. But it would explain why he and Malachi knew each other. *Fantastic.*

"If you weren't batting eyes at that worthless piece of trash, we wouldn't be here right now," Wes snarled.

For the record, I had not been batting my eyes at anyone, save possibly Malachi. Certainly not when the print had been delivered. And certainly not when Wes and Malachi caught me in the booth.

"I–I didn't… I don't… what happened?" I stammered.

"You let someone take a fucking print," Wes bellowed, a mixture of fury and disgust on his face.

"That's enough, Wes," Bette scolded. "No one did anything on purpose."

Wes clearly disagreed. He yanked the remaining reel off the ground with brutal force before marching off in a huff. He paused just long enough to shoot me a final scowl before rounding the corner and disappearing.

"I'm–I'm so sorry. I didn't… I didn't know." The disappointment on Bette's face barely outweighed my fear. Somebody was getting fired. Or going to jail. The way my day was currently going, it was very likely going to be me.

"Why don't you take your lunch, Zoë. We'll sort out this mess while you're gone," Bette offered quietly.

Thirty minutes would not be enough time to sort out anything. She was stalling to make the worst phone call of her life, deciding if I was getting fired or not. How the hell I was going to explain getting fired to Mike Cassidy was beyond me.

13

SCAMMED BY A KINDERGARTNER

I stood listless in the food court. Hundreds of shoppers packed tables beneath garlands of twinkling rope lights. Christmas music chimed in unheard tones above the noise of conversation and food vendors shouting customer's names.

I was dazed, trapped in the middle of holiday chaos. The lines were, predictably, longest at the pizza shop. Ivar's Clam Chowder was just a breath less busy. Both sounded entirely unappetizing at that particular moment. And I loved pizza. Only a monster didn't love pizza. Though, pizza did sound a lot better than questionable mall fish.

Why not?

The line moved quickly. I placed my pizza order, lingering near the display case to wait for my food. Dark swirling thoughts needed to be chucked right into the fires of Mordor along with the rest of my day. I people watched to distract myself.

A dozen or so parents were herding family groups through the chaos. One small girl bounced across the food court in her best Christmas dress, squealing in excitement about Santa. Dad did not look optimistic about his chances for whatever she had wished for.

A dusty group of grannies wearing red aprons covered in flour lumbered to their feet. They hustled their trays to the garbage and shuffled away down the main thoroughfare just as an announcement for a gingerbread house competition warbled through the speakers.

Teenagers loitered near Orange Julius, a perfect impersonation of holiday Mall Rats. They were the kids who never seemed to leave the mall, rebels without a cause. Their idea of edgy was Zumiez corduroy and a mass produced Clash t-shirt from Hot Topic. They found no irony to it all as they snuck smoothie samples off the counter when the managers turned their back.

"Zoë?" The boy behind the pizza counter called my name. I took two steps toward him before a flurry of activity near Orange Julius captured my attention.

The manager had finally caught the teenagers. He was screaming at them. The girl behind the counter melted in mortification as her friends scattered like cockroaches, fleeing in every direction. I recognized an obnoxious tie with the giant red lips and lolling tongue as a blonde boy speed checked my right shoulder, grinning like a moron as he ran.

Nirvana.

Probably on his way to work. I could see now he was not wearing *our* uniform. Not exactly. But it was similar. Some corporate nitwit considering themselves fashionable and edgy only to be foiled when every other service worker had on the exact same thing. I didn't have time to rage how I'd been tricked by this little shit.

He was getting away.

I abandoned my pizza and followed in hot pursuit. I considered yelling the kid's name, Kevin, maybe. I honestly didn't know. Plus, shouting at a random teenager was more likely to get me into trouble. I was gonna lose him to the Christmas hustle if I didn't run too, so I did. With a little luck, I would pass for an aging teenager late for her shift and not an adult tailing a kid.

Nirvana was surprisingly fast. He didn't slow at all as he sprinted right on by the rent-a-cop flirting with a barista at Thomas Hammer Coffee. Nirvana flew by cranky parents and hopeful children snaking around Santa's workshop in an Ugly Sweater Christmas conga. He nearly knocked over the group of grandmas clustered around a table supporting a giant cookie castle. I zipped through them as they fanned out to protect their creation.

I nearly missed it when he ducked into the Suncoast Video as I dodged a particularly festive caroling group, dressed straight out of a Charles Dickens novel. I was both surprised there was a Suncoast still in operation and relieved Nirvana had stopped running. I paused to catch my breath, watching through the display windows.

Inside Suncoast, a Metallica looking groupie with shaggy brown hair and guy-liner impatiently tapped his wrist the minute Nirvana burst through the door.

"Missed the plane again, Kevin?" Metallica asked sarcastically. *What are the odds his name was actually Kevin?*

"Whatever, man. Crystal's working. I had to get my juice on." Nirvana threw his hands in the air before barreling into the back room.

I breezed in, making a show of looking at a collector's edition *Home Alone* toy. About a minute later, Kevin returned to clock in.

I flipped through the display case of movie posters, pretending not to listen. Why were there always posters of girls in red bikinis on motorcycles stacked in with the movies? *Sigh.*

"Don't count on me to cover for you next time, alright? I'm already on thin ice with Doug," Metallica warned, shaking his shaggy brown head and disappearing into the back.

"Find everything you're looking for?" I was genuinely startled to find Kevin at my elbow.

"I... Um, maybe?" *Pretty eloquent for an ace detective,* I chastised myself. "Hey, do you have any *Titanic* stuff?"

Kevin eyed me up and down. My aesthetic was more Shirley Manson than Rose Dawson. He rolled his eyes and gestured for me to follow anyway. I was downright shocked by the number of trinkets, sold by one out dated store, for one twenty some odd year old movie. James Cameron really knew how to make a dollar.

"Yeah, the anniversary release means they pretty much made everything you can think of. Keychains, posters, they even made a Jack and Rose doll set." He pointed at box holding a Victorian Barbie with red hair.

"I am actually looking for something more functional. Any copies?"

"We stopped selling movies a while ago," he laughed. "You could try the theater. I hear it's playing to sold out crowds." I wondered if he was toying with me. *Boy, are you in for it.*

"Funny you should mention that," I said, turning to face him. "I work there, and it's my first day. Wouldn't you know it, some sucker stole a film reel."

"They did?" His face fell, a sickly green cast washed over his cheeks. Kevin abandoned me, slinking away for the safety behind the counter. He raked a nervous hand through greasy blonde hair. I followed him.

"Bummer for whoever took it, though," I continued casually.

"They've only got one of the prints. It'll be pretty easy to track if they go to sell it. They only have part of a movie." I leaned on the counter and Kevin glowered at me in agitation, occupying himself with price checking items around the register.

"And with the new piracy law that just went into effect, when the FBI catches them..." I let out a dramatic whistle with a shake of my head. "They are looking at $200,000 fine or ten years in prison."

"Prison?" He swallowed hard, his lips almost disappearing in his anxious grimace as his eyes snapped to mine.

"It's a federal crime," I cooed. "Of course, if it magically reappeared before the FBI gets here..." I shrugged a dismissive shoulder. Kevin stared apprehensively, his eyes searching. I glanced at the gigantic wall clock and made a big show of surprise.

"Yikes! Break's over. I'd better get back." I dragged my feet, waiting, hoping, praying. Three steps toward the Christmas chaos, I wasn't sure he'd do the right thing.

"Wait!" He yanked me back before I could leave the store.

"Yes?" I blinked at him innocently, as if I hadn't just hooked him on my line. *Gotcha.*

"How would someone go about returning a thing like that? If they knew where to find it, that is." He swallowed again, like he was choking down a bad idea.

"I mean, the dumpster behind JC Penny is exclusive to the theater. If it were to suddenly be discovered in... twenty minutes? No one would be the wiser." I gave him a leveled look, doing my earnest best to appear more friend than big sister about to rat him out to Mom.

"Yeah, that... that just might work," he agreed and disappeared from sight. I crossed fingers and made my way back into the mall to wait and watch.

Nirvana didn't notice me as he rushed by, bumping kids in the Santa lines with the film canister clutched in his hands. I could only imagine the conversation he'd had with Metallica, trying to explain why he needed another ten minutes. *Hey, man, I sort of took this from the theater. Mind if I run it back real fast?*

I lost sight of him and decided to walk the rest of the way. Nirvana needed time to return it properly. I'd already decided not to throw him under the bus, no reason to embarrass him further. I sighed, content to have solved one problem for the day.

14

JINGLE SMELLS

Malachi, Bette, and Halia congregated in a semi-circle around the manager station when I got back. I could see them before I hit the first step, though their attention was focused inward. Malachi held a Styrofoam container with my name in bright red letters on the top.

Well, aren't we the gentleman?

"I went to look for her, and the pizza guy called her name just as I was getting to the food court. I don't know if she saw me, but she bolted down the mall at a full sprint," Malachi explained, genuine hurt in his eyes.

"She just ran off? What is going on with her?" Halia seemed confused. Bette looked equally troubled. It wouldn't be the first time I'd ran away from a problem. My heart fractured to know I'd hurt them. Again.

"Hi, guys," I said, loud enough to alert them to my presence. They clammed up immediately. *Nice.*

"You forgot your lunch," Malachi said, handing me my boxed pizza.

"Thanks," My stomach grumbled. "I'll just put it away and, uh...

get back to the floor, I guess."

No one argued or tried to stop me. Concessions was not technically where I should put my food. I figured they could scold me later. It was clearly the least of my sins today. I tossed the food in the walk in, not bothering to clock back in before I headed for the dumpsters.

The exit hallway reeked of old sugar and crushed dreams. The smell never really went away. The gangway ramp was carpeted for some reason. It made it squishy after ten years of garbage runs. I flung open the steel door, a blast of winter fresh air clearing my lungs of the putrid stench.

The parking lot was packed with vacant cars waiting for their shoppers. Some had thin coats of snow. The weather report predicted a massive storm tonight, but at the moment the skies were silvery blue with wispy clouds. It was peaceful, in a frozen sort of way.

The trash compactor's whine pierced the quiet. Someone was currently using it. I aimed for the buzzing sound only to skid to a stop as Jake stepped out from behind the concrete wall. Some survival instinct had me diving behind a sad little tree. It did nothing at all to hide me. But maybe if I held perfectly still, he wouldn't notice me.

Jake was in street clothes, a cigarette in hand. There was a smugness to his stance as he gestured with his cigarette hand. A second voice berated him in hushed tones. Wes stepped forward to blow smoke in Jake's face. Jake laughed, a sneering chuckle as he blew smoke back at Wes.

He pulled a wad of cash out of his pocket, holding it out like he might drop it. Wes snatched the papers, stuffing the cash into his pocket. Jake clapped him on the shoulder, a seemingly friendly gesture. It was more of an intimidation tactic, coming from Jake. Wes shook him off, tight lipped and anxious as his gaze darted around.

That's not suspicious, not at all.

Jake laughed again, swaggering toward the theater. My tree was a lousy place to hide so I stepped out, walking with intention toward the dumpster. Jake smiled, surprised but pleased to see me.

"We have to stop meeting like this. People will talk." He grinned and grabbed my wrist. I grimaced, wrinkling my nose in disgust.

"I'm just here for the garbage, Jake," I broke his grip.

"Let Wes handle it," he suggested, reaching for my hand again.

The hair on my neck stood up and a shiver walked down my spine like a spider. A nervous feeling swelled in the pit of my stomach, as though I'd been caught in the act of something horrible. I turned my head to find Wes standing with a sour expression a few paces away. He shook his head in disgust.

"Un-fucking-believable," Wes spat, rushing by in a frustrated tunnel vision, muttering to himself. He kicked the door open, not bothering to make sure it didn't lock behind him.

"Now that we're alone…." Jake tried to pull me closer. "I've been thinking about you since I saw you this morning."

"Let. Me. Go." I firmly removed Jake's hands from my waist, digging my finger nails into his skin until he relented and stepped back. "We're done here, Jake."

I left him standing there, disappearing behind the dumpster. I heard him growl in frustration, his boots scuffing the icy sidewalk as he went back inside.

It took me longer than I am comfortable admitting to get my heart rate back to normal. I was a federal agent, and this asshole got under my skin. It was an embarrassment. I hated how tied up in knots I got over this moron.

Irrational rage knots, but still… Knots.

An eternity later, I'd calmed enough to gather my wits about me. *I couldn't have beat Nirvana, could I?* It had been at least ten minutes since he'd run past me. Maybe more. Or maybe he saw Jake and Wes and changed his mind. And what was *that* all about, anyways? Something significant was definitely going on with Jake and Wes. I'd have to investigate it more thoroughly later.

But first, I had to resolve the matter of this stupid kid stealing a damned print problem. I started looking around the dumpster. There were only so many places it could realistically be. After five minutes of searching, I reluctantly conceded he wasn't coming. Plus, I needed to get back before the managers saddled me with even more guilt and mistrust. I needed to get out of this cold.

15

CHRISTMAS CATCH

It had turned into the strangest Christmas Eve I'd ever had. Not the worst, not by a long shot. But the whole day felt like a hangover. I know a lot of jobs feel that way, but this was my first day. It shouldn't have felt like I'd already lived everything. Déjà vu was a real bitch. I grumbled with irritation as I hefted the big wheel barrows back into the lobby.

"There you are!" Halia called as soon as she spotted me. She half jogged over to catch up. "Bette was hoping to talk to you. They need you in the office."

"Now?" I asked.

"Now," Halia confirmed.

"Did they find the print?" I asked, hopeful that Nirvana was stupid enough to bring it directly back. Maybe save me all the trouble of sweet-talking myself out of this impossible day.

"Dunno." She shrugged and put her hands on the wheelbarrow as we rounded the corner. "She just asked that I send you straight up when I see you. I'll take it from here."

"Fine," I grumbled.

"We still on for tonight?" she asked, a nervous smile on her beautiful face. I sighed. Maybe spending a little time with her outside of work where we could just learn to be friends again would be good for both of us.

"After the day I've had, I plan on waking up drunk tomorrow." I smiled, though I wasn't sure it reached my eyes. She squeezed my arm affectionately and took off with the empty wheel barrows. I wiped my hands on my pants and headed up the stairs.

The office was surprisingly cold, despite being on the second floor. Despite the constant wave of heat rolling up against it from bodies and the concessions stand. A shiver shot down my spine as Bette held open the door for me when I knocked.

"I'm sorry, Zoë. It's been a doozy of a first day back," Bette began. "But we've got to have some paperwork settled before we go any further."

"Write ups run the world," I joked.

Bette raised a perfectly penciled eyebrow as she lead the way into the space, claiming her chair with a sigh. She rubbed her eyes, looking even more tired than the last time I saw her. The last few hours had been an absolute dumpster fire for everyone. I didn't know why I expected the rest of the night to be different.

"When the print got stolen, it triggered some internal protocols we have to follow," Malachi explained, holding a chair for me.

I plopped down, cautiously sweeping my eyes between them. A legal looking affidavit was waiting on a long desk overlooking the lobby. I reached for a pen to write my statement. Then, I saw it.

A letter of termination.

"What's this?" I asked, bewildered. *I'm getting fired?* I was rendered absolutely speechless, my entire body locked. My brain short circuiting at the unexpected twist of fate neutralizing any possibility of salvaging this terrible day.

"I was really hoping it wouldn't come to this," Bette murmured, a sick cast to her beautiful brown skin.

"But then I found this." Malachi lowered himself to sit beside me. Out of his pocket he pulled my Nokia phone and placed it on top of the letter. His hand came to rest lightly over the electronic brick.

"I don't understand, you have my phone?" It took me a hot minute to recall where I had dropped it. The projection booth. In my rush to escape discovery, I'd completely forgotten my phone call in the dark beneath the iron coffee table. I hadn't even thought about the damn thing until this very moment.

"Zoë, if it had been just one thing, it would only be a write up and we go on with our day," Bette said, rubbing her temples as if she had a migraine.

Malachi studied me in earnest, pausing as though he wanted to say more. Instead, he bent to retrieve my bag from under the desk, setting it beside the letter. On top of the bag, he placed the pirated shrink wrapped copy of *Titanic*.

My sopping oatmeal bag of brain goo solidified. Clarity hit me like a punch in the gut. He'd been in my locker. He'd seen my phone, my computer, and the evidence I found in theater five. The combination pointed to one thing. Nothing but a confession of guilt or blowing my undercover mission completely would clear the air. And neither of those was an option. Not when I couldn't be sure they weren't involved somehow. The investigation had to continue even if my cover was blown.

"We had to search you," Bette murmured. "I can only give you one more chance. What were you doing in the booth this morning when Malachi found you?"

Guilt washed over Malachi's face. Of course he had to tell the managers. He *was* a manager. He avoided my gaze, jaw tight and eyes shadowed.

A pounding at the office door made me jump. Malachi raked a hand over his face in frustration. He shot Bette a grim look. She nodded crisply. Malachi grimaced before opening the door.

"Am I interrupting?" Jake Landen sauntered into the office like Wyatt Earp at the OK Corral. *What in the fresh hell?* He stopped in genuine surprise when he spotted me. He recovered quickly, his breezy demeanor transitioning from shock to noxious glee.

"We had to call him in, Zoë," Bette said.

"I'm sorry, what? I'm so confused."

"Jake's a cop," Malachi grumbled as he banged the door shut in irritation, glowering as he ushered Jake inside. He plainly disagreed with the proceedings. That or he had a distaste for Jake. Could be both. Probably both. It would be both if it was me.

"Lieutenant Deputy," Jake corrected hotly, slipping one ass cheek onto the desk, tipping his knee at an angle to brace himself and lean toward me. "I work undercover over the holidays in case they need extra hands around here."

I noticed what I hadn't bothered to earlier in the day. His hair was Semper Fi short, cropped high and tight to his ears. His True Religion jeans were a half a size too large, hiding military grade steel toed boots. His black bomber jacket barely concealed a bulge under his right arm where a concealed carry holster would be.

Holy shit.

"I hope you have a damned good explanation for why you recorded and stole a copy of *Titanic* today, Zoë," Jake drawled. "Otherwise, I'm going to have to arrest you." He sounded delighted by the very idea of putting me in handcuffs.

"Enough, Jake," Bette warned. "Zoë, it's me, now. Tell me what's going on with you."

No explanation was going to exonerate me in any of their minds. *Oh, I'm sorry. You and your theater are currently under investigation by the FBI for copyright violation, and a myriad of other IP related charges. Please don't arrest me. I haven't made my case yet...* Let's watch six months of work get flushed down the drain. Mike Cassidy would let me rot in jail just to be spiteful.

Jake took my silence as an omission of guilt, satisfied he'd lassoed me in his cowboy web of justice. He leaned close, a malicious grin thinning his lips until they disappeared behind bleached white smokers' teeth embedded in pink and grey gums.

"We may have to involve the FBI if—"

Hysteric laughter erupted from my soul, which startled Jake into silence. I couldn't help it. I chortled like a dying cat, wiping away hot tears with the back of my hands. My cheeks were flushed, hiccuping giggles bursting uncontrollably from my mouth.

"By all means... call the FBI, Jake. I beg you!"

"This is serious, Zoë," Jake scoffed, displeased with my amusement.

"Serious as a car wreck," I laughed harder. "This whole day has been a complete dumpster fire since the minute I woke up in the booth."

I realized, belatedly, this admission would sign my arrest warrant. But I just didn't care. Too many things had gone so horribly wrong. At this point, I was convinced it was all just a yuletide nightmare. The only thing missing was me dancing in my underwear down the concessions bar. I was just waiting to wake up for real.

"Quick," I cackled through tears. "Someone pinch me."

"I'm sorry, Zoë," Malachi said, a light touch to my hand. An electric charge shocked us both into looking up at one another, but neither of us let go of the other's hand. He squeezed gently and my mirth simmered into a low boil. I gave him a smile that under any other circumstance would have been my best come-hither invitation.

"It's alright, Malachi. I'll be okay," I told him, truthfully. He didn't know I had a get out of jail free card. But I didn't want him hurt. This mess wasn't his fault. "You were the only fun I've had today."

A bemused smile pulled at the corners of his mouth, light dancing in his amber and whiskey eyes for a heartbeat. Then, shadows crashed back in, wrapping the Dark Lord in dark thoughts.

"These things are protected under federal law," Jake interjected, bruised ego and jealous temper getting the best of him. My chest heaved as another burst of laughter shook my body.

"Oh, for fuck's sake, Jake!" I raked a venomous glare over his cowboy bravado. He balked as though I slapped him. "Arrest me, or call the FBI. I'm so over this day. Get me out of here."

Absolute dumpster fire.

16

KISS, KISS, BANG, BANG

The holding cell Jake gleefully threw me into smelled like bleach and urine. There were a dozen or so other overnights and low-priority first timers. I mean, it was *my* first time being arrested, too. I wondered absently how long it might take to get a phone call. Mike Cassidy was going to have roast Zoë for Christmas dinner.

"Never thought I'd see the day," Jake drawled in a strange southern accent, considering he'd never left the Pacific Northwest. "Can't say I'm not enjoying myself."

He took his time unlocking my cuffs, his hands lingering. I felt his hot foul breath on my ear as he loomed over me. I nearly bit his face. "Miss perfect Zoë Bly, behind bars. And, I'm the one to take you in!" Jake released me with a light push into holding before closing the barred door.

"You know I didn't do what they suspect I did, right? I'll be out of here one, maybe two days tops?" I taunted him, hands on hips as soon as they were free of the cold steel cuffs.

"A lot can happen in two days," Jake said smugly.

"You're gonna eat crow. I'll serve it up on a silver platter."

"You can't talk to me like that. Not in here," he snapped, fingers gripping around the bars so tight his knuckles turned white.

"I'll talk to you any way I want, Jake. You've already arrested me. What else can you do?"

"Why don't you ask your little friend over there," he growled, pointing into the crowded holding cell behind me. "He's the little shit that pinned you. Made it so easy for us."

I turned and nearly died of shock to find Nirvana sitting unhappily next to an elderly woman with silvery hair repetitively muttering to herself about wishing she could skate on a river. Jagged mismatched pieces fell into place in my mind. I'd given the ungrateful POS an opportunity to do the right thing. But, being a selfish opportunist, the little sociopath tried to exonerate himself in the process. Kevin must have been arrested minutes before they'd taken me to the office.

"I'm gonna kill him," I huffed, stomping over in a rage.

Kevin pressed away as if the wall might swallow him. "The cops were already there!" he whined, holding up his hands defensively. "I thought if I gave them you they'd let me go!"

"You idiot!" I hooked my fingers in his vest, jerking him to his feet and slamming him against the wall. I was tall enough I could glare into his mousy blue eyes. He cringed, as if there was anywhere to go to escape my wrath in this cell. "You. Ruined. Everything! You stole everything!"

"Zoë, stop!" Jake commanded. I could hear the clang of a metal door and stomp of boots as he rushed to get back into the holding cell.

"I didn't think they'd take both of us!" He was practically sobbing. "Should have just kept the stupid thing!"

I shook him, his back cracking against the cold concrete wall. I didn't really want to kill him. Just scare him a little. Some people need to get their fingers burned before they learned not to play with fire.

My whole terrible day, I had tried to do the right thing. I gave this idiot a chance to undo the damage he'd done. He threw me under the bus. My fingers were thoroughly burned.

I changed my mind. I did want to kill him. He was a dead man walking. A bellow of fury ripped from my throat in a war cry.

Whoops of excitement and juvenile calls for, *"Fight! Fight! Fight"* rang in the cell. Two powerful hands grabbed me at the elbows, tearing my hold off Nirvana's pathetic greasy frame.

Without thinking, I pivoted and ducked, breaking Jake's hold by raising my knee and snap-kicking my leg. My boot connected. Jake went down clutching his hands over his groin.

I spun and reached for Nirvana. The slippery little eel was already across the cell, back against a different wall. Our other cell mates smartly dove out of my path. I charged for him, only to be restrained by more hands on my arms, my waist, my legs.

My brain didn't register the police officers were just doing their job. My fight or flight instincts, carved like a knife by the FBI, wrapped me in a battle armor of adrenaline, fueled by blind rage. I clawed and kicked and twisted.

The officers tackled me to the ground, squatting on me like toads on a log. My arms were wrenched behind me as I tried to lift my head from the wretched stinking floor. A massive palm shoved my skull down with a disturbing crack.

17

CHRISTMAS CHRONICLES

The excruciating chime of the Nokia "Jingle Bells" ringtone shocked me from unconsciousness like a war siren. My heart leaped to my throat when I realized I was under a coffee table. Again.

I was not at all clear how I would manage that particular magic trick two nights in a row. Unless *Inception* was real, and I just leveled out of a nightmare. *What a horrible dream.*

The incessant beep of "Jingle Bells" continued. I rolled out from under the table, shaking my head. It throbbed as though someone clocked me with a billy club. My mouth felt scorched by a thousand suns.

Closing my eyes, I blindly fumbled on my hands and knees to find my phone. The smell of the concrete was earthy, cold and solid against my burning skin. I wanted to lay down and rest on its chilled surface, thankful it didn't smell like last night's floor.

What floor? What happened?

My fingers landed on the vibrating appliance I'd mistook for a cellular device. I lifted the thundering brick to my ear and pressed answer, sitting up to look around.

"Yeah?" I asked. *Am I at the theater?*

"What do you mean, *yeah*? Where are you?" Mike Cassidy barked.

"I honestly have no idea," I said, rubbing my eyes and trying to get my bearings. If I wasn't hallucinating, I was in the projection booth. Granted... I didn't really recall getting here yesterday, either. I was beginning to suspect foul play.

"You're supposed to be at the cineplex for a staff meeting in an hour!"

"Wait. Mike, what day is it?" I scanned my surroundings, looking for anything that might help me figure out how I got here. My brain was so fuzzy. Nothing made sense. *Was I in a fight last night?*

"Bly, if you fuck this up, you're fired," my boss threatened.

Fired. Which meant I hadn't been fired yet. Why was I fired?

Was it really a horrible rotten dream? All of it?

"Seriously, Mike... what day is it?"

"It's Christmas Eve, you worthless piece of shit. So, unless you want to spend the rest of your life working at that shit-town theater, I suggest you find a solution. Now."

The line went dead. Mercifully, there was no dial tone. Just absent silence.

It's Christmas Eve.

I sat in confusion on the cold floor of the empty projection booth contemplating how exactly I'd come to this crossroads. The last thing I remembered was... *Nothing.* I remembered exactly... nothing.

I tossed my phone onto the couch so I had both hands free to massage my temples. The projection booth was completely dark except for the retina-searing ghost light. My computer gently pulsed green lines of code on the work desk.

"I don't like this dream," I mumbled. "It can stop now."

I dragged myself to my feet, ducking just in time to avoid a garland of wicked looking Christmas gnomes. Their pointy hats glittered and winked. Their cherub faces bobbed up and down as I bat them aside.

I knew they would be there. *How did I know they would be there?* I slumped into the projectionists chair, pressing my palms to my eyes until I saw orange splotches. I was exactly where I was yesterday. Or was it today?

What in fresh hell happened last night?

I blinked until my eyes adjusted to the light. There was an empty tequila bottle in the trash can beside the desk. I didn't remember drinking it. I mean, I remembered drinking. There had been lots of tequila. But unless I was completely out of my mind that was at a bar with Mrs. Claus. Yesterday. Two nights ago?

How did I get here? And then a second thought occurred to me: *What did that witch do to me?*

Which was completely unreasonable. Mrs. Claus wasn't even real. It was a strange dream, about a nice old lady with magic cookies. But it was just a dream, nonetheless. Which meant the whole day had been a dream. Beginning to end.

It just felt so real.

My Ms. Pacman watch screamed in alarm just as the lights flooded the booth with high voltage luminescence. A familiar creak, thunk, thud echoed down from the far hallway.

6:25 a.m.

Well, if today was Christmas Eve, then it *was* a bad dream. Which meant I had absolutely no time to waste. I slammed my laptop shut, yanking the cord from the wall. I shoved it all into my bag and ran.

I reached the heavy metal door at speed, throwing it open as I burst on to the balcony. Malachi and I collided. We both shrieked, bouncing apart like magnetic opposites.

"Malachi! Jesus, you gave me a heart attack!" I shouted, gripping the railing for balance.

"What are you doing here?" he asked in bewilderment. Our eyes met, and I found myself slack-jawed. "Did you get lost?"

"I was… I need…" The scent of orange blossoms and cinnamon caressed my senses like a silk blanket. *I know this smell.* "You smell nice."

His mouth quirked into a wry smile. "How'd you get in the booth?"

"It… was unlocked. I thought it was the bathroom."

With an arched eyebrow and a puzzled expression, Malachi jerked his thumb over his shoulder. "First door on the left."

I rushed by, barreling through the swinging red door. The women's restroom was as bright as flash bang at a rave. I covered my eyes with both hands and made a mad dash for the sink, dunking my entire head under the tap.

My brain was swimming, my stomach threatening to return whatever might be in it. Nachos, if my memory served. But if today was yesterday, then nachos and tequila never happened. Cheetos and despair? More likely. Not any better.

Was it really all just a dream? The biting cold water ran over my scalp and through my curls, rivulets of water soaking into my t-shirt. My tattered, dirty, FBI shirt. And cheese stained corduroy pants. How pathetic.

"Today is going to be a very strange day," I whispered to myself.

"Déjàvu is a real bitch."

"You're here early," Bette's voice passed behind me as she made her way to a bathroom stall. The distinctive clunk of the door latching was followed by the specific sound of a morning pee. "You been drinking?"

"No, Mama B. I'm clean as a whistle."

"Good, 'cause I was fixing to send you home if you had."

"You can send me home. I won't complain," I replied.

Water gargled in a circular torrent as Bette flushed. She exited her stall and shuffled to the sinks. She focused on her task, a plop of soap into her palms and a rush of water accentuating the quiet.

"Now, that wasn't the deal, was it?" She asked quietly as she ran her clean hands through the Dyson wind tunnel they called a hand dryer, shaking the last stubborn droplets free. Her eyes flicked to mine in the mirror.

"No, it wasn't," I agreed.

"Good. Brush your teeth first. Your breath is foul," she said before strolling out of the bathroom. I sighed in resignation, stripping to change right there in the blazing spotlight of the bathroom.

"I'm telling you it can't be done," a male voice fumed, the loud baritone rumbling through the wall.

"And why not?" a second voice demanded. They must be in the mens room. I pressed my ear against the tiled wall, trying not to think about when the last time anyone washed them as I listened.

"I don't have the capacity," the first voice explained.

"I have your money. Don't be a douche." The second voice was obnoxious, grating my nerves. I couldn't put my finger on why.

"I'll have something for you today. The usual spot." The door thunked open. They were on the balcony, if my ears weren't deceiving me.

Standing like a statue in my underwear, I was barely breathing. In all probability, these were the clowns pirating movies. That conversation was just too suspect not to jump to conclusions.

Modesty left the building, right along with my sanity this morning. It could blow my cover... But it could make my case. *Fuck it.* I ripped open the bathroom door.

"Man could you guys be any–" I was speaking to dead air, the balcony abandoned. Whoever they were, they were gone.

I lingered in frustration, debating whether I would get fired for racing around in my underwear or not. My coworker Pecks answered the question for me when he stepped out of the staff room to witness me in all my Victoria's Secret glory.

At that exact moment, Malachi returned to the balcony. He froze in his tracks, eyes tracking from my exposed body to Pecks and back. He tilted his head ever so slightly, slipping his hands into his pockets. Fire raced along my skin, though out of embarrassment or the thrill of Malachi's gaze, I truly could not tell.

"Nice. I didn't know it was gonna be one of those staff meetings," Pecks squawked, swaggering as he looked me up and down. A disturbing smile transformed him from Clark Kent into the Norman Bates. Gross. Just gross.

Malachi's eyes narrowed to a dangerous glint as he turned his attention to Pecks fully. "Gregory, didn't you need to be downstairs five minutes ago?"

"On it, my liege," he said. With a double thumbs up in my direction, Pecks disappeared down the stairs. Malachi angled his head, a crisp nod as if he were tipping a top hat in greeting. Mortified, I slithered back into the bathroom to pull on some clothes.

By the time I made it to the lobby, the scent of burnt popcorn saturated the air. My stomach lurched. I needed to get food and caffeine in my system ASAP.

I rounded the corner, beelining for coffee and donuts in time to watch Pecks knock his till off the counter, sending currency flying. An unremarkable young man, *Thor,* my brain supplied, dropped a bag of popcorn seed, scattering chaos in his wake.

Impossible! I'd seen too many repeat movies not to be suspicious.

Mortified and confused, I needed quiet to puzzle out what was happening. I swiped two donuts and a coffee I hosed in cream, intent on disappearing into the stairwell by theater six to get my bearings.

Time travel wasn't real. Magic wasn't real. Quantum entanglement... Well, that was a thing, wasn't it? The door to the stairwell banged open in front of me just as I stuffed the maple bar in my mouth. Malachi yelped in alarm as he careened into me at full speed.

"Zoë!" Halia shouted in warning. Malachi's paperwork went flying. My donuts flipped into the air as coffee arched in a murky shower. I dropped firmly on my ass, the breath whooshing out of me in a choked rush as my head cracked back and slammed against the ground.

Irrational rage filled every fiber of my soul as "Jingle Bells" wailed like an air raid warning a split second later.

"Zoë, can you hear me?"

The voice was warbled, an echo of some distant past I couldn't quite recall. It was warm, full of love and concern.

Malachi? I wondered. *I must have slept in today. No, that can't be right. He never reaches me before I hang up on Mike. And why is it so bright in the projection booth?*

"Where am I?" I croaked, managing an excellent impression of a dying cat. The wailing continued, smoothing from the staccato of a Christmas carol to the steady howl of a siren.

"Zoë, honey, can you open your eyes?" A deep rumble of a voice. My eyelids felt like someone superglued them together, bright orange spots blotted my vision. With considerable effort, I managed to break the seal and blink. I hissed in pain. Such excruciating pain in my head as light met my eyes.

"Zoë," there was relief in the voice I couldn't understand. A face swam into view. For a moment, I thought it was Malachi with his dark hair and deep brown eyes. My focus adjusted to Kelly green eyes, a salt and pepper beard, round cheeks, and deep laugh creases at the corners of his mouth. The lines were pulled tight in concentration.

"Dad?"

"Lay still. You had a pretty significant head trauma." He swept a flashlight across my vision. I flinched away in surprise. "Your manager found you unconscious."

"What?" My arms and legs wouldn't move. My head lolled back and forth. There were straps restraining me against a spinal board. *I'm in an ambulance?*

"There's a gash on your head. Luckily, you have your mama's thick curly hair. Helped it clot," my dad said, a grim smile behind the flashlight, his eyes searching. "Guess Mom is still looking out for you."

The wail of sirens and beeping called out in warning as the ambulance made an extreme left turn. The doors burst open in a flurry of activity as the ambulance came to an abrupt stop.

Meaty hands and strong arms jostled my board out the rear of the ambulance and onto a gurney. We rushed through sliding glass doors. A part of me was dimly aware of an EMT—my dad—rapid firing vitals to an intake nurse.

"Female, twenty-eight years old. Head trauma and loss of consciousness."

"Dad?" my voice came out a squeak.

I didn't realize how afraid I'd been until I saw his face. I didn't realize how much I missed him until he was handing me off to a hospital stranger.

"Dad!" I screamed, panicked I'd lose him if I fall asleep again.

"It's alright, Zoë. I'm here," he soothed, tucking hair behind my ear. There were people rushing about everywhere in a chaotic dance of urgency as I was rolled into the hospital.

"You're her father?" An authoritative man in green scrubs waved a light in my eyes, holding my lids open with a thumb and index finger.

"Dad!" I jerked my face away from the nurse.

"Yes, I'm her father," my dad said, following along. "It was just dumb luck I got the call."

"Dad!"

"Good luck, if you ask me," the nurse agreed. "Take her to trauma four. We'll get some vitals and a CT. Any idea what happened to her?"

"Zoë, do you know what happened to you?" my dad asked.

I stared blankly. *Haven't a clue dad, 'cause I should have 100% ended up under the coffee table again. But, here I am, with you lovely people.*

"She fell and hit her head. She can't make coherent sentences," another voice, also warmly familiar. "She's been talking about fairies and cookies and nachos."

I strained my neck to look behind me. Malachi, striding behind the gurney like a valiant dark knight. "Were you in the ambulance?"

"Rest, Zoë," my dad again. He wore a white collared shirt. A navy blue embroidered patch with a red cross was stitched on his left shoulder.

"When did you become an EMT?"

Gentle hands positioned a plastic mask with tubes over my mouth and nose. It faintly smelled of salt and tropical fruit.

Nitrous oxide.

"No! I can't go to sleep!" I thrashed as best I could. I had to get away from the mask. Firm hands stabilized my head while another pair held the mask in place.

"We'll take care of you," the doctor, this time. Their voices bounced back and forth as they discussed my condition, confirming their assumptions with one another.

"It'll start all over if I sleep…"

"Rest, Zoë," my dad and Malachi said in unison. They exchanged a look between them before the doctors wheeled me through the double security doors. Their faces were grim and anxious, like my own personal sentinel statues.

Then, my conscious mind faded to nothing.

18

REPEAT THE SOUNDING JOY

"Dad!" I shouted, convulsing to sit up only to slam my forehead into something solid. I was alone, jammed under the coffee table from hell. "Dad…"

I choked on tears, a fissure cracking in my chest. I hadn't seen my dad in such a long time. We'd barely spoken, and yet… I was in his ambulance. It had to be a dream.

"I miss you." The sound of my own voice nearly broke me, tears welling in my eyes. "I miss you so much."

It *had* to have been a horrible dream. A terrible, visceral, dream.

But it wasn't. It was all happening again. All of it. I was about to have a really shitty Christmas Eve. For the third day in a row. I rolled out of my prison and struggled to get my bearings just as "Jingle Bells" began to scream into the void.

Nightmare before Christmas would be a lot more accurate.

Stumbling to my feet, I was snared by the garland of gnomes as I struggled to silence my phone. I ripped the gnomes from their bow, throwing the cheerful little gremlins into the darkness as I fumbled with my computer cord. My shrieking banshee of a phone bleated again.

"Absolutely not." I pressed the power button until the screen went black, chucking the brick into the bottom of my bag. *No one's home today, sir. We are not doing this again.*

I burst onto the balcony. I had to get the hell out of this building. Maybe schedule an emergency session with a psychologist. Or a neurosurgeon. Maybe a witch. Honestly, any would do with the luck I was having. I bolted for the exit.

"Zoë!" Bette shouted in surprise, the two of us narrowly missing a collision at the top of the stairs. Apparently, this was what I did now. Collide with people. "What are you doing here so early?"

I stumbled back, whirling around chaotically. Across the balcony Malachi paused, a curious glance in our direction before he slipped into the darkness of the booth.

Nightmare before Christmas, indeed.

"I'm having a very strange day," I muttered, pressing the heel of my palm to my pounding forehead. She hooked a finger under my chin, lifting my face to see it more clearly.

"You been drinking?"

"Not that I recall." I sighed through my nose.

"I should send you home." *God, yes! Please send me home.* "I suppose that wouldn't be the same kind of punishment as making you work your double shift on Christmas Eve."

Fuck. I should have said something. *How have I lived this day twice already?* Three times? *Damnit.* I'd definitely done this more than once and was still making a complete mess of it. I gestured vaguely toward the bathrooms, turning on my heel before panic could consume me.

"Brush your teeth at least. Your breath is foul," Bette hollered just before the door to bathroom closed behind her.

I growled and followed her into the restroom. Submerging my head for five minutes straight in biting cold water did jack-all to stop the spinning. My brain was scrambled eggs. The runny kind that needed to go back in the pan.

I'm losing my goddamn mind.

"It's just not possible, Zoë," I scolded myself in the mirror once I was dressed. "It's simply not possible to live a day twice." *Let alone three times.*

My wardrobe change would not have been out of place in the Best of a Broadway quick changes. I was clean and relatively calm before the first staffers trickled in. I bolted down the stairs. *Must find coffee, before anything else can go wrong.*

I sank into the lone chair at the manager's station determined to enjoy my caffeine drip, for once. Determined to watch and mark patterns. *It's just not possible.*

"Just one more. I'm done. Understood?" a male voice drifted over the balcony.

"That's what they all say." A second man laughed.

All I could see was a set of ratty black All-Stars. *Wes.* The other man ducked into the booth, trailing Wes closely. I considered running after them.

"Nope, not enough coffee yet," I decided.

"Girl after my own heart," Malachi chuckled beside me.

I practically jumped out of my skin. "What?"

"Coffee. Must have coffee to function, right?" He gestured to my cup, my greedy amount of foiled topped creamer cups, and three empty packs of sugar carelessly discarded on the desk. "I take it you like a little coffee with your cream and sugar."

I had to crane my neck to see all the way up to his eyes—startling eyes of gold and brown. Eyes like a polished tigers eye, cracking with lighting. Eyes that continued to suck out any reason from my soul. Eyes I had *absolutely* seen before. My pounding head started to spin again. I stared blankly.

"I'm Malachi," he said, casually perching on the desk, extending his hand in greeting.

"Zoë," I managed in a tight voice.

He nodded. "Bette told me you were starting today." His smile was genuine, entirely for me. *Gulp.*

I looked away, focusing my attention on the clock. He noticed my concentration and tried to follow my eye line. From the corner of my eye, I watched him tilt his head, considering the expanse of glass and wall I seemed to be absorbed with. "What are you looking at?"

"The clock."

"It's not going to move any faster."

"I am having a very strange day."

"You're at a staff meeting on Christmas Eve, I'd say that's strange enough," he laughed.

"Yeah," I replied with a nervous chuckle. "Whose bright idea was that?" I caught myself tucking hair behind my ear, flirting as if this was the first time we had this song and dance. *What is wrong with me? I have shit to do. Get your head in the game, Zoë.*

"Definitely not me," Malachi chuckled. "There is not enough coffee in the world where I would make this choice willingly."

"Zoë!" Halia screeched. "There you are!" The roller chair collided into the desk as she hopped into my lap, snagging my coffee from my hand before it could spill. I let out a guttural *oof* as the air escaped my lungs momentarily.

My initial response was to dump her beautiful butt on the floor. To yell at her for throwing Sprite in my face. But, I quickly realized that was an irrational response to something that clearly only happened in my mind. Instead, I wrapped my arms around her, the scent of mangos and vanilla filling my nostrils and tugging at my heart with a flood of emotions. Panic. Calm. Fear. Confusion.

Home.

I inhaled deeply and hugged her tighter. She laughed.

"You do like it sweet," she grimaced handing back my coffee. "I thought you'd come by last night."

"I didn't?" This was actually news to me.

"No. I even waited up till two a.m. Thanks for that."

"I never made it…" *So, where did I go?* The answer was obviously the theater. But why?

"You could have called, you know," she chided me.

"I'm sorry. I didn't mean to abandon you," I replied truthfully. Really, in more ways than she knew. She seemed to understand what I was not saying and wrapped her arms around me.

"I see you've met Malachi," Halia continued, unfazed. She shot Malachi a conspiratorial wink. "He's also our newly minted manager."

"Morning, Halia," Malachi said, a tone of irritation in his voice.

Cold fear shivered down my spine drawing me to my very present reality. We'd had this *exact* conversation. In multiple locations. It *had* to be a bad dream. There was no other logical explanation for this. Because the alternative was I was stuck in a time-loop. And there was no easy way out of those. Ever. I've seen the movies.

Bill Murray had to live like a bazillion years and have a perfect day where he was nice to absolutely *everyone*. George Bailey had to see what a world without him might look like. Emily Blunt helped Tom Cruise kill a bunch of aliens. That one chick had to solve her own murder.

All of them involved at least several gruesome deaths and more than a little magic to get out. How the hell was I supposed to escape the most magical time of the year without a drop of magic or physics to help me?

"Zoë, are you okay?" Malachi asked.

"Hey, what's wrong?" Halia soothed, holding me and searching my face as she brushed away tears. "What happened?"

I watched as if in slow motion. Pecks carelessly knocked his till off the counter, again. Currency went flying. Thor dropped a bag of popcorn seed in his enthusiasm to help. The bag burst, showering kernels everywhere.

Nope, hard pass, my brain chimed.

I could not do this another god forsaken day. I bolted upright, dumping Halia unceremoniously out of my lap and onto the floor, running across the lobby. There was zero chance I'd make it up the two flights of stairs to the bathroom so I aimed for the concessions stand.

I barreled past staffers, claiming a garbage can to vomit in. Halia was behind me moments later, waving off the others with orders to finish setting up. She held out a cup of Sprite, and I flinched away.

"Please don't throw it at me!" I begged, warding her off with hands crossed in front of my face.

"What? Zoë, are you hungover?" she demanded, shoving the cup into my hand. I gingerly accepted.

"God, I wish," I moaned, trying not to think too hard about my dreams. I would be *very* hungover after the night Mary Christmas and I had. The drinking or her stupid special cookie would have knocked anyone on their ass. But this was something else entirely.

What is happening to me?

"Did you get any sleep, or were you up all night on the computer again?" Halia demanded, unsympathetic. It would not be the first time I'd disappointed her because I'd been lost to the dark web for untold hours. I shook my head, melting to the floor, taking deep breaths.

"No," I said firmly. "I'm just... I'm having a very strange day." I didn't know any other way to put it.

"Are you on your period?"

"No."

"Are you pregnant?"

"God, no. Look, I'm really sorry. I just had a super weird dream."

"A dream?" Halia remained unconvinced. She folded her arms across her chest, popping a hip and plastering a stern look on her face.

"I..." *I feel stupid even attempting to explain myself. Here goes nothing.* "Okay. Okay... I need you to stay with me for a minute, alright?"

She blinked, her brown eyes full of hurt. "Zoë, I've always been with you."

"Alright. Okay, then." I took a deep breath. "Two days ago, I woke up and came to the staff meeting. The one about to happen. The first day, I made it to the end of the day but got fired—"

"You what?"

"Then yesterday, yesterday, I did it again. Only, I didn't make it past coffee. I fell and hit my head running smack into Malachi when he came down the stairs. Today, I am convinced I'm in some sort of weird time-loop."

"Ten years. It has been ten years since I've heard from you, and this is the first bull shit you say to me?"

Resentment surged through me. My lips thinned as I bit down on my own tongue to keep from lashing out. Halia was clearly not buying what I had to say. I wouldn't buy it, if I was being honest. It was bananas.

"Halia, I know it sounds crazy," I said, dangerously quiet as I wrestled for control of my temper. She must have noticed because she crossed her arms and tilted her chin in defiance as she waited. I took a steading breath. "It's crazy, but I have repeated the same day for three days in a row now. I don't know, maybe more."

Halia's face went through several expressions while she calculated the odds of me being hungover versus telling her the truth. It may have been ten years, but she'd never known me to be a liar. Erratic and emotional, sure. But never a liar.

"All right, I am waiting. Let's have it," Halia said, firmly planting her hands on her hips.

"What?"

"Prove it."

I didn't know how to prove it. All I had was a bunch of jumbled memories that were completely out of order. I sighed and looked at the floor. "This all happened already. All of it. The meeting, being here… I don't want to relive this day again. But I'm trapped."

And that was the root of this episode of *Zoë makes a hot mess of herself*. By some trick of luck or fate, I was back. Back to feeling trapped. Back to living a life on repeat in my hometown. It was why I fled. Why I went to school and took a job three thousand miles away. Yet somehow, I was back.

Popcorn. Soda. Rinse. Repeat.

I might vomit again.

Halia softened, uncrossing her arms and crouching beside me.

"I know it's hard being here," she said gently. "It's not going to always be the same. You won't be here forever."

She'd understood why I had left. Even if she was secretly thrilled to see me, she would rather I was off doing the things that made me happy. Halia was always a good friend like that. We should all have one friend who wished us nothing but the best, like Halia. If I had a sister, I would hope she would be like Halia.

"Can you manage the day?" she asked softly. "Or do we need to send you home? I mean it, Zoë. Be honest right now."

It was tempting. God, it was tempting. Christmas Eve off? Who wouldn't take it? But I heard my dad's disappointed voice in my mind. Calling my dad and making it right would be my only option if I left. I had no where else to go. It wasn't like the FBI would put me up in a hotel because I'm having a déjà vu day. I shook my head.

"No, I'll be fine. This helped." I finished off the Sprite.

Malachi snuck through the door, leaning against the frame as if waiting for an invitation. I smiled weakly at him. I didn't have the energy for more. Today was just too damn weird.

"Everything alright?" he asked.

"Yep, just some girl trouble. We're all stocked up on pads, right?" Halia asked.

Malachi stiffened. I met his eyes, absolutely mortified. He nodded once, turned on his heel and retreated back the way he came. If this was any indication how the rest of Christmas was about to play out, I should take Halia up on her offer and go home.

"Girl trouble?" I demanded. I mean, I knew my unspoken attraction to the Dark Lord was back burner problems, at best. But did she have to be so crass?

"If there is one thing I know, men are terrified of a woman on her cycle. Even the thought of tampons and sanitary napkins sends them screaming for the hills. If you need space, just fake cramps."

Fantastic.

19

BLUE CHRISTMAS

My upchuck reflexes convinced Bette to put me on the floor rather than in the concession stand. It was a healthy spot to put someone having a mild mental breakdown. I wasn't in denial or even a rage any longer. I skipped right to acceptance and spent most of the morning tearing tickets to avoid trouble. It took some effort, considering I teetered on the edge of panic anytime I thought too hard about my current situation.

Escape a time loop.

Solve the case.

Don't fall for the Dark Lord.

I started organizing the events on my timeline. Paying special attention to what happened and in what order. I even snagged a notepad from the managers desk to write everything down I could remember. Organizing data like a computer calmed my brain.

First, wake up in the booth. Second, Mike Cassidy calls to yell at me. Alternatively, I ignore the call completely, which I thoroughly enjoyed today. Next, the Christmas gnomes may or may not try to gouge out my eyes as I leave the booth. Malachi and I nearly collide if I'm not fast enough, then Bette and I head to the bathroom where she chastises me about my breath.

After that, a whirlwind of a morning that included coffee, donuts, gummy bears, and saying good morning to Halia. That idiot Pecks drops his cash drawer, and Thor makes a bigger mess trying to save him.

All of this happens before 7 am.

The day got a little muddy after that. Yesterday, I hadn't even made it past donuts, opting instead for an ambulance ride and a CT scan. At least one of the days, I had lunch with Malachi. Wait, no. We never made it to lunch because of that shit head Nirvana.

Malachi had *invited* me to sushi, and I'd accepted. Even though I hate fish. But he had such a great smile, and I didn't have the heart to tell him. If this worked out in the end, I'd have to tell him. I'm not about to commit to fish long term.

I was relieved when Thor finally returned to claim his throne as the ticket tearer and sent me to clean theater five. *Damn.* I forgot about the giant box of DVDs in theater five. And the ominous shadowy figure leering at me from the booth when I found them. And, let's not forget, my ex-boyfriend showed up to argue with Wes near the dumpsters.

"I really need to figure out what the hell *that* is all about," I said.

It wasn't Jake with Wes this morning, though. Someone, who had a reason to be here, was arguing with Wes. Someone Wes would actually talk to. That narrowed the list significantly.

I was loathe to admit it, but it kept circling back to Malachi. Something about our interactions sent my personal detection system into overdrive. Something I couldn't quite pinpoint. I lamely went through the motions, rolling ideas around in my mushy brain. I tried, and failed, to find someone else to blame. Someone else who could be my unsub, *Key$troker*.

I really wanted it to be someone easy to dislike. Like Pecks. Or Jake. I'd take anyone at this point. Anyone other than where my wayward heart was taking me.

Malachi was a manager. He had access to all the places. But every time I'd run into him, he was on the floor or concessions. He was a fully present manager. So, how was he doing it?

He would need to be in the booth a lot more during business hours. Which made me think maybe Wes was his accomplice. It certainly would explain the altercation before the staff meeting. Because you didn't get dubbed the Booth Troll or the Dark Lord for nothing. Those titles had to be earned.

I huffed and busied my brain by floating around the floor. Instead of exit greeting movies, I searched each auditorium for more clues, more evidence. Hoping for anything to turn me onto a different path.

I found a second box of DVDs and, surprisingly, hard drives under the screen in theater thirteen. It made a lot of sense when I thought about it. Keep the goods in two places in case one was discovered. Theater five and theater thirteen were the auditoriums closest to the exits. And neither of the fire exits had alarms or cameras.

It was an excellent location to move merchandise.

I toed the box back under the curtain. I needed something more than just the contraband. All the evidence did nothing for me without a suspect to point to. We already knew someone was pirating movies.

The obvious next step was to search the booth. The trouble was if Wes was in the booth, I didn't want to twist into a pretzel explaining myself to him. But something in the booth would point me in the right direction. I was sure of it. I just needed to gird my loins and get back in the there.

20

ENEMY OF THE STATE

Lost in thought, I popped out of the auditorium and ran smack into Halia. "There you are!" she said, her tone exasperated.

"Where else would I be?" I asked.

"Bette would like you to check the restroom," Halia said mildly.

"*Bette* would like me to clean the restroom?" I asked with a twitch of my lips.

Halia absolutely *hated* bathroom checks. She'd been pawning them off on subordinates for as long as I could remember. Today, I was as subordinate as it got. Not to mention my odd confession she hadn't taken seriously put me squarely on her shit-detail list for the day. I was sure of it when she tossed her shiny black hair over a shoulder, her lacquered lips pinching in a pout.

"Bette wants you to take a lunch so you can break box in an hour," Halia replied tartly. "*I* want you to clean the restroom before you do."

I checked Ms. Pacman and was startled to realize how late in the day it was. Food sounded like a grand idea. I barely remembered the morning. Had I eaten anything other than gummy bears and coffee again? *Stop doing that.*

Down the hall, Wes shoved an oversized wheelbarrow loaded with garbage in front of him, towing the second behind him. It seemed weird that the Booth Troll would be moving garbage at all. Maybe it was an excuse to take a smoke break. Smokers *loved* doing garbage runs because they could disappear for twenty minutes at a time and no one noticed. Wes was definitely a smoker.

My little hamster kicked up the pace, my hindbrain sorting through all the facts I had thus far. It wasn't many, but whoever was responsible for this Christmas suck fest had been in the booth when I found the DVD copies. They had definitely seen me. Of all the people who had access to projectors to make clean copies of movies, the Booth Troll topped my list.

"I should go," I said. Even ten years ago, Wes despised helping anyone ushering on floor, even if it meant a smoke break.

"You have to do the work, Zoë," Halia interrupted, a sharper tone this time. I stopped and pivoted to face her, my shoulder tense with the rage I'd been containing since this nightmare before Christmas started. She crossed her arms, her eyes narrowed in a glare. She was definitely mad at me.

I laughed. "Believe me, I am doing the work." I raised a hand to stop her before she could clap back. "I got it, Halia. I'm on it."

I felt her eyes follow me as I shuffled down the hall, dropping the garbage can and brooms at theater six before slipping outside after Wes. I raced down the hallway after him. I reached the exit as the door clanged shut behind him.

Outside, I shivered a little in the chill air. It would snow again soon. Two sets of footprints tracked beside the wheelbarrows in the light dusting of snow. One set was made by heavy boots, one by tread bare All-Star Converse. I aimed for the far side of the compactor, determined to get close enough to hear over the buzzing.

"I told you what I wanted," Jake's voice carried. I could see him through the iron gate, though I was pretty sure he hadn't noticed me. He was the epitome of smug, gesturing with a lit cigarette toward Wes, who was still behind the concrete wall. "It shouldn't be that complicated."

"I don't take orders from you," Wes snarled, blowing smoke into Jake's eyes. He sounded a lot like Malachi when I couldn't see his face. No wonder Halia dubbed them the *Grady Twins.*

Jake's laugh was callous, sneering as he blew smoke right back at Wes. "You need the money, and I'm a paying customer." He pulled a wad of cash out of his pocket. "I'd hate for mommy dearest to find out what you're hiding in the booth."

Wes snatched the papers, stuffing the cash into his pocket. Jake clapped Wes on the shoulder, fingers digging ever so slightly into the fabric of Wes's hoodie. Wes flung him off, tight-lipped and anxious.

"I knew you were a team player," Jake laughed, swaggering back into the theater.

"Un-fuck-ing-believable," Wes growled, rushing by in frustrated tunnel vision, muttering to himself. He kicked the door open and disappeared inside. Jake chuckled and followed close behind him. The compactor stopped, and I realized Wes had abandoned the wheelbarrows. Again.

I sneered, hauling the Rubbermaid carts back inside. The door thwacked open hard enough I winced. The people in theater six most definitely heard that.

"What happened?" Malachi balked in surprise as I rounded the corner and headed for concessions. I shrugged but Malachi followed.

He must have seen Wes take a smoke break, then not return with the garbage bins. He was plainly annoyed with Wes as he hurried to help me.

"I can manage an empty wheelbarrow," I dismissed.

"I realize that, but he just left you to it?" Malachi frowned as he held the concessions door for me. His strong hand pressed back the steel with ease as I passed under his arm hefting the cumbersome plastic bins.

"I'm alright. He had things to do," I assured him. I held up my hands to indicate I'd like to wash them and he followed me to the sink. I needed him to stop fussing so I could abandon work and go explore the booth. Whatever was going on upstairs, money was being exchanged. I had a solid lead. More importantly, solving my case could help me go home... Maybe escape this nightmare repeat.

"He shouldn't have just left you. It's ungentlemanly," Malachi insisted.

I stopped dead in my tracks and blinked several times. Then I threw my head back and laughed. A hearty laugh that started in the depths of my soul.

"I didn't..." Malachi sputtered, flushing red.

"No! It's okay." I wiped away tears. I was miles away from the Anger Bear I woke up as. Fathoms away from suspecting Malachi. He was just too damned *nice*. Even if some small voice in my head said being a nice guy didn't make him a good guy. *Shut up, voice. He is a good guy.*

"No one has ever insisted on that level of chivalry for me. I'm grateful," I said with a genuine smile. The first I'd given him that day.

"I guess I just wouldn't have abandoned you like that," he concluded. So, it was less that Wes had abandoned a girl, and more specifically that he had abandoned me. How sweet.

"I'm perfectly capable of a little hard work," I grinned, taking his hand in my own (freshly cleaned) ones. It seemed to draw him out of the darkness that threatened to rain down on him.

"I know you are," he returned my smile. "Doesn't mean I can't hold a door for you."

I didn't need to get trapped in another spellbinding goo-goo eyes moment with the Dark Lord. I looked down, squeezing his hand for emphasis. "Thank you."

"My pleasure," he said, voice whisky thick and rough around the edges.

"I have to take my break," I told him softly.

"Right," he nodded, withdrawing his hand. "I should go too." Malachi quickly returned to whatever it was managers do. I ran as fast as I could to follow my intuition into the booth.

21

WASSAILING

I zipped up the stairs, rounding the corner to head for the entrance closest to the manager's office. It was a risky entrance to take, but it had to be done.

I fumbled the code the first time, punching 1-2-2-4 before realizing Christmas was not the code. I entered the correct code, 6-9-6-9 because someone in the last ten years thought it was funny. The lock clicked and I slipped inside.

As usual, it was dark as night except where projectors threw light in shimmering veils toward their screens. The whir of machines and the whine of electronics purred like wild cats. When my eyes adjusted, I looked around to see what I could find.

There were any number of places Wes could hide things. I started by snooping around each projector, careful not to disturb the mechanisms running film. It would be a poor place to hide things since Wes was far from the only person who worked in the booth. But it was a solid place to start snooping.

A light flicked on several projectors away and I ducked behind the one I'd been investigating. Wes began threading a film through the sprockets. His fingers deftly moved from reel to reel, popping film strips free and feeding them back inside the projector.

When he finished, he secured the end to an empty reel on a platter tower beside the projector. He ran several frames of film through just to make sure it was tight enough to run, nodding in approval at his own handiwork.

The light flicked off, and I waited.

If he held to the same schedule as the ushers did, he would be on his way to theater seven to thread the theater I'd missed completely for exit greeting. But he wasn't. Instead, he made for the back end of the booth.

I did my best to melt into the shadows and crossed my fingers he wouldn't notice me crouched by the projector. In the dim lighting, I could see him fussing over a large silver canister. I heard a hissing sound followed by a metallic pop. There was more clinking and rattling as metal scraped against metal, the dull thud of the whole thing shifting against the concrete.

A full minute later, Wes lumbered back in my direction, hefting the heavy canister over his shoulder. He muttered and swore under his breath before stalking out of the booth.

As soon as the door snicked shut behind him, I made a mad dash in the opposite direction. I hadn't rounded the corner to the workstation yet when I tumbled into a stack of boxes I hadn't previously noticed. The boxes were tucked in an awkward dark corner, a place other booth ops would just walk by, barely noticing. One box shifted, and I barely caught it before it tumbled to the ground.

Shit, shit, shit! I hoisted up the heavy case, glass clinking inside. I held my breath until the tinkling stopped. I exhaled slowly as I settled the box back on its stack, unfolding the stiff cardboard to find capped bottles. Each bottle had a home pressed label with an AFK in large red ink blocks. The letters crossed each other to form what looked like a Viking rune.

I blinked, rummaging through the boxes to find they were all identical in shape and size, glass bottles neatly arranged in six pack crates. Beside them sat two rows of six silver barrels with the same red rune painted on their tops. Plastic tubes snaked from pot to pot, a white gauge with a black needle carefully measuring pressure.

Beer. Homebrew craft beer bottles. It actually made a lot of sense, when I thought about it. Wes would be the kind of guy who got into homebrew.

Maybe he was the sort of guy who was *really* good at it. The gamer guy who spent enough time at a console to use 'Away From Keyboard' as a Viking rune. The sort of guy who maybe turned his hobby into a side hustle to bring in extra cash. Didn't Jake insinuate Wes was cash poor for some reason?

So, Wes started hustling, selling his homebrew to people he liked. If the beer was any good, and the volume he was making indicated it was good, people would start to share with their friends. Eventually, word got around to people Wes didn't like. People like Jake, who always had to be the first 'in' on anything.

Wes was not my hacker. I mean, he *was,* in a technical sense. I'd bet money any homebrew boy using nerd speak like Wes was on his beer had at least some passing familiarity with computer coding. But this was a full on side hustle. I wasn't sure he'd have time for both projects. Wes was not *Key$troker.*

I sighed, considering my next options. After a moment, I snagged the darkest bottle in the first case I could reach. I popped the cap off on the steel reinforced work table and sank onto the booth couch. I tipped the top toward the garland of gnomes.

"Cheers, boys!" I saluted and took a drink. It was, after all, my lunch break.

I practically melted. Wes' homebrew was rich and full bodied without being so hoppy it triggered an instant headache. It was like a perfect cup of coffee with hints of caramel and chocolate. Only it was beer. If Wes was looking for investors, I'd happily throw down. I tipped my head back and savored the most tranquil moment I'd had in days.

It was a short lived, though. Not halfway through the beer, I heard the ominous whoosh of air and clang of the booth door opening and closing. I grudgingly rallied myself into an upright position, depositing the half full bottle in the trash, careful to make sure it was hidden from view.

"You know you can't keep it here, don't you?" Malachi was saying. *Damn.* I was out of time to hide. I dove under the coffee table just as Malachi and Wes rounded the corner. With a little luck, they wouldn't notice me. I tried to take shallow quiet sips of air, willing my racing heart to settle before they could hear it thundering in my ears.

"I'm not stupid," Wes snapped. "I just needed somewhere cold where I can keep an eye on it until I'm ready to sell."

"You gonna make the deal with golden boy?" Malachi asked. Wes snarled something inaudible as they brushed by the coffee table. Two guesses who they were talking about.

"You need the money," Malachi countered. I peeked from my hiding spot. The two of them lingered near the work desk, blocking out the light with their bodies and leaving me in nearly complete darkness. They would have to be looking for me to notice me.

"He doesn't deserve my help," Wes complained, scribbling furiously into the booth log.

"True. Jake is an asshole, but he has the cash to spare. Take him for every penny you can get out of him," Malachi advised.

"That's all he's good for," Wes grunted.

The Grady Twins shuffled off toward the exit as someone called over the radio that the print had arrived. I let out a long low whistle, gulping a stale breath to recenter myself.

22

YULE LOG

That was a close one, I thought, wiggling out from under the coffee table. Chasing after them was unlikely to result in being seen, but it could be. The exit by theater three faced the manager's plate window. If Bette or anyone else was in there, they'd have questions for me.

I decided to head back the way I came and risk being spotted by theater six. At least then I could claim a smoke break or garbage run. I'd made it half a dozen steps when I experienced an epiphany.

The booth log.

The book was where the daily hiccups and successes were recorded by booth operators. The record for all the names of people who worked in the booth regularly. I didn't need to question anyone. It was just there for the reading. I quickly retraced my steps.

The well-worn red leather journal lay on the desk in the dim light of a lamp. Someone had written "Captain's Log" in black sharpie over the cracked face. I thumbed through the pages, noticing about five different signatures and handwriting. Two of them were difficult to read and might have been the same person. I flipped to the most recent entry and recognized Halia's flowery script immediately.

"We had a lovely day. The gears on thirteen are sticky, but otherwise a smooth shift. No word when the print will arrive. I guess Wes will have to assemble tomorrow." Halia was always the glass half-full girl.

"Still no print. These MF are going to wait to the last GD minute. Will have to assemble and run sans screen test. Projector five is off its axis. Again. Will check with Gene about parts. Unclear what dislodged it this time."

It was the entry from this morning… Before the meeting. Malachi, it seemed, had strong feelings regarding the studios distribution methods. I grinned, thrilled by the little crack in his polished demeanor.

I tore out a blank sheet of paper from the back to write down the obvious names, Malachi, Halia, and Wes. The other two were so close to chicken scratch I couldn't make it out. I made a bold underline with a question mark, absently thumbing back to see if any entries could help clarify my thoughts. Then, I noticed I was not the only one who had torn out pages.

Once a week or so, someone had carefully torn out a page on perforated edges, leaving small gaps as the spine tried to sandwich together missing pages.

"Interesting," I said quietly.

The most recent missing entry proceeded Halia's flowery sunshine and rainbows day. Malachi's bold hand growled through paper and ink after. It could just be a coincidence. Maybe.

I skipped back about six months' worth of entries to when Malachi first transferred and when the new watermarks became a part of *Key$troker's* signature.

"Guess who's back? Back again! I estimate another fruitful summer of

blockbusters. New parts arrived for five. Installed them myself."

It looked masculine to me. Both in tone and in the angle of the pen. I wished the signature looked less like a doctor's prescription and more like a name. In contrast, Malachi's handwriting was bold and easily legible. Still, it could have been him. It was possible. The page directly after the entry was gone, so there was no way to identify the response. I flipped back to the most recent week. Surprise, surprise. It was missing a page.

The page that *was* there was cheerful and clearly addressed to Malachi. *"Merry Christmas to me! Three new assemblies. I got two of them done before I had to pack it in. You're up, Dark Lord."*

The suspicious sinking feeling twisted in my gut. Someone was talking to Malachi. And the responses were being ripped out. But who was ripping it out? Who was talking to him in the first place?

"Who are you?" I asked the dark room.

23

POLAR EXPRESS

I'd replaced the booth log exactly where I'd found it. I folded the sheet of paper, tucking my list of suspects into my back pocket before heading down to the lobby. My final hours, I was to be locked in the fishbowl, also known as the box office. I sighed and took over my till, sending an all but giddy Lyssa on her dinner break.

The seven o'clock block was always the busiest hour on any day of the week. The line began to build in anticipation, overzealous customers showing up at 6:15. By 6:45, the line was down the hall and out the doors. Christmas tempers were starting to show.

Even my carefully curated calm had started to fray. Customer after customer it was always the same. Greet them. Ask them what they would like to see. Explain the prices of a ticket and card them if it was rated R. Hand off their admission tickets. Tell them to enjoy the show. Rinse. Repeat.

You see why my days felt like déjà vu even before we got here?

Lyssa returned just before 7:00, a naughty smile and husky glow to her cheeks. *Where have you been?* I wondered. It didn't matter. She logged on quickly, and we began hacking away at the never ending line of customers waiting for tickets.

In some more modern theaters, corporate had opted for self-serve computer stations. The customer was entirely responsible for their tickets and show times. They even got to pick their preferred seats. Not us. Cascade 14 was still a stone aged, analogue customer service driven establishment. We had to people with people. It's not as much fun as it sounds.

Forty-five minutes, and you're a free woman, I reminded myself. My double would be over by 8:00 p.m. I could go drink myself into oblivion at the Gatsby House party. Flirt recklessly with Malachi and pretend I'd make it to tomorrow.

"Hi, welcome to Cascade 14—"

"Four tickets."

The moment I saw her, I just knew she was going to be a pain in the ass. Her obnoxious chunky-bleached blonde bob cut in a futile attempt to make her look young. The overdone Sephora contour because she *wanted* you to know she shopped luxury lines.

Three bored-out-of-their-minds preteens were nose deep in their phones, ignoring everyone around them. The tiny carbon copies of mom and dad were probably strategizing their plan to sneak into something rated R. Mommy dearest had been periodically stepping out of line *just* far enough to stare at me. For her, the line in front of her was her life's biggest inconvenience.

"Sure. For which film?"   I asked sweetly. I was personally ruining her day.

"Why do you need to know?" she barked in a shrill breathy voice.

She's joking, right? I blinked several times, an effort to conceal my incredulity. I guess it made me appear slow because she followed up.

"Did you hear me? Why. Do. You. Need. To. Know?"

Okay. Don't reach across the counter and slap her. That would just be bad manners. It might as well only be one of us that's an asshole today. The pulse in my throat was beating fast, a spike of adrenaline commingling with my own simmering rage. She could not possibly be *that* stupid. I opted for the rational approach first.

"Ma'am, this cineplex has fourteen screens and eleven different movies. I just—"

"It is *not* a ridiculous question," she squawked. Her arms were crossed, her DKNY shirt pulling tight at the elbows. This entitled suburban HOA secretary was done with Christmas shopping and was ready for a 'family' movie.

And completely enraged by having to wait in line.

Fuck it.

"All right. Four tickets to *Alien Resurrection*." The film wasn't even in theaters, but that wasn't the point, was it? You could not explain stupid to some people. Some people had to burn their hand to learn manners. I tapped random keys as though I were finalizing her purchase.

"You think you're funny?" she snapped.

I continued punching buttons. My screen jumped back and forth and did absolutely nothing.

"On occasion," I said mildly.

The children with her snorted. She silenced them with a vicious glare before turning on me. The woman's toxic sludge pink lips pulled back into a sickening smile. If Delores Umbridge had an uglier sister… The woman adjusted her knock off Versace purse strap, and jut a hip out so far I feared she may have dislocated it.

"I would like to speak to your manager," she smirked, triumphantly. This was the moment she lived for—putting people like me in my place.

I considered quitting on the spot. No one needed to take this woman's abuse. But, if I quit, I failed my mission. "Oh, of course."

I turned my attention to the manager's office. Bette had her head bent over some project. She was barely visible through the window. I dialed up the internal extension on the phone. Bette didn't stand to look down at the lobby. Just reached out reluctantly and tapped the speaker.

"Bette?"

"Yeah?" Her typical honeyed voice was heavy, as though I'd awoken her up from a deep sleep.

"There is a very nice lady down here who would like to speak with you," I said sweetly.

The woman thrust her chin higher in the air, victorious. She was completely oblivious to the increasingly agitated people behind her. Or the disdain and sarcasm in my voice. She would be victorious in her quest to crush me under her polished heel.

"I'll be right down," Bette sighed.

24

JACK FROST

A good five minutes went by. The customers in line were edging toward tearing the woman apart with their bare hands to bathe in her blood. Not really. Maybe. I mean…

It was opening weekend of some good shows on Christmas Eve. We'd reached the point where nobody cared about the holiday anymore. Everyone was itching for a fight. I'd have happily served the woman a slice of Minny Jackson's famous 'chocolate' pie.

I leaned on the box door, watching for Bette. When she rounded the corner of the lobby, I cringed. Her softly polished exterior had frayed at the edges. She was a step shy of a full blown meltdown. She looked like she could use a stiff drink or a good night's sleep. Probably both. If I didn't know better, I'd say Bette was sick. Really sick. I opened my mouth to ask if she was okay when the Karen cut in.

"Are you the manager?" she demanded before Bette had finished closing the box door behind her.

"Yes, I'm the manager," Bette said with perfect gentleness. The world did not deserve Bette. Certainly not Banana Girl. "How can I be of assistance?"

Cascade Karen recoiled from the register as though one of us might be contagious. Our privileged C-you-next-Tuesday was expecting someone who looked like my white middle-aged father, not the black goddess who came to earth in the human form that is Bethany Monroe. I wanted to throw my shoe at Cascade Karen.

"This obnoxious girl thinks she's funny. She tried to sell me tickets to a horror film."

"I'm sorry, I don't understand. We don't have any horror films at this time," Bette began. She glanced my way with a *'what did you do?'* look. I shrugged my shoulders. Cascade Karen was bonkers. It wasn't my fault the woman didn't read.

"I asked for four tickets. When I didn't want to say for which film, she gave me four tickets to that silly alien movie."

"She didn't want to say," I repeated.

Lyssa let out a huff of frustrated air, flipping her blonde hair over her shoulder with a manicured hand. She narrowed a death glare at the woman before thrusting tickets at her customer and beckoning the next person forward. The customer stepped up with a healthy dose of side-eye for Cascade Karen before they turned and smiled sympathetically at Lyssa.

"What exactly do you intend to do about it?" Cascade Karen demanded haughtily.

There it is. It all became so irritatingly clear. The calculated hip jut, the arms crossed, the air of expectation and privilege, followed by the demand to speak to an authority higher than minimum wage. The goal of most customers throwing a temper tantrum like this clown shoes—give me free shit.

Get out of here with your bullshit, Karen.

"I'm so sorry there was a miscommunication between you and my staff," Bette apologized, another long cautionary glance warning me to keep my mouth shut. "I hope these will help."

Out of her pocket, Bette pulled a pad of coupons. Each coupon entitled the bearer to one small soda and one child-size popcorn. It cost the theater nothing to give these away. Bette tore off five coupons.

"That's it?" Cascade Karen crossed her arms, contempt and righteousness all over her face. Of course it wasn't about the movie, or the tickets, or the questions. She wanted something *significant* for free. She *deserved* something for free. And by God, she would tantrum until she got it.

"Ma'am, if you don't want to see your movie, you don't have to." Bette's lips curled at the corners, morphing her smile into a venomous warning for the woman. Cascade Karen had entered the danger zone. She didn't seem to notice.

In a weird instant replay some part of me knew what was going to happen as I watched. A Christmas miracle and an agonizing moment later, the stubborn woman snatched the coupons, clutching them in her plump manicured hand.

"Four tickets to *Toy Planet*," she barked.

Please would have been a step too far. I entered her transaction mechanically. Bette was trembling by the time the woman finally walked away.

"That was fun," I said.

"You and I have different definitions of fun, Zuzu," Bette sighed, sounding resigned. "Malachi will be down in ten to close you out. Stay out of trouble for five minutes, will you?"

"Always," I quipped with a grin. But my jaw hit the floor when the next guest stepped into view. "Mary?"

Mary Christmas was in my line.

25

O CHRISTMAS TREE

"Hello, Zoë, fancy seeing you here." Mary was stunningly beautiful for any age. She was dressed exactly as she had been the day I first laid eyes on her. Fancy red cocktail dress, knee-high black boots, murderously gorgeous green coat that could only be the product of Keebler elves. Her perfectly coiffed snow white hair drifted lazily down her back. She looked like Christmas incarnate.

"Apparently I live here now," I snarled. It took me a hot minute to get over the rage before my brain connected to facts. That night. This woman. Lousy tequila. I was so livid I could barely see straight. "You did this to me. *You* are the reason I'm here!"

"My dear girl, you did this to yourself," she clucked, withdrawing a coin purse from her pocket and sliding her currency across the counter toward me. "One for Titanic, senior pricing please."

I punched in her order, violently jamming her payment into my till and slamming the drawer shut. "How do I get out of here? How do I get back to normal?"

"What is normal anyway? And why would you want to go back?

Were things so wonderful?"

"I happened to like my life," I replied, tartly. Her ticket finished printing. I tore it off and thrust it at her.

"Really?" She smiled broadly. That smile would have lit up the night sky. "The last time I saw you, you started the day drunk under a table, and ended up drunk at a bar. You had just been fired from your 'fake job,' which was going to get you fired from your real job. You asked for a do-over. As far as I can tell, I've done you a favor."

"You call this a favor? This is a nightmare!"

"Well, perhaps you haven't discovered what you need to learn yet." She flounced away from my register, almost bouncing as she handed her ticket to Thor for tearing.

"What was that about?" Malachi appeared above my shoulder.

"What?" I was rage watching Mary, and it took more effort than was rational to return my attention to the handsome man beside me. He gestured for me to step back again. I took a breath and moved aside.

"That bit about firing you from your fake job so you can do your real job?" He began methodically counting cash and coin, half focused on the work, half focused on me.

I was at a complete loss. I mean, at this point, honesty was probably best. *Tempting*... But what would it really serve? I'd already tried honesty with Halia and got exactly nowhere. Malachi wouldn't believe me, either. Even if I started at the beginning.

"You ever experienced déjà vu?" I finally asked.

"I work at a movie theater. Every day is déjà vu. She can help you at the next register." He waved aside a customer, hooking me with a boyish grin as he did. "The variety is the people, not the day."

That was the most thought-provoking shit I'd heard. Ever. It could work. Couldn't it? Focus on the people and not myself? I mean, what would Bill Murray do?

No. Do not drag anyone else into this suck fest. That only worked in movies. I needed to clean up my own mess. Solve my case, and get my ass gone.

I centered myself and truly looked at Malachi. His smile was radiant. I couldn't help but beam back at him. "I guess this means you're sending me home?"

"Yep. I figured you've been held captive long enough," he joked.

"Ain't that the truth."

Before I could stop myself, I gave him a hug and a kiss on his cheek. He seemed both startled and delighted. I flashed him my most enticing and naughty grin.

He smiled. It was the kind of smile you might see on a favorite friend or star-crossed lover. It was warm, and jolly, and kind. It was more than a little mischievous in its own right. Malachi's smile was enough to make any Grinch heart melt. Mine certainly did. I turned to leave, a new bounce in my step.

"Zoë, why is there a leaf in your drawer? And two acorns?" He held up an oak leaf the color of spring's first green.

I was bewildered. "What the Halo?"

He twirled the leaf in his fingers. As he did, hand to heaven, it looked like a five-dollar bill. I tipped my head to one side dumbstruck.

Then I heard a laugh like the tinkle of a brass tea bell rising over the symphony of people in the lobby. *Mary Christmas.* It had to have been Mary. I was so mad at her I hand't even noticed what sort of nonsense she'd handed me to pay for her ticket.

I spun around and spotted her. That damned green coat and silky white hair. She had a popcorn bag tucked under one arm, soda in her free hand as she collected paper napkins. She grinned when she saw me, winking an arctic blue eye before flouncing out of sight.

"Mary Christmas," I muttered, as I hustled down the far hall after her.

26

MARY CHRISTMAS

Mary sat dead center, white hair shimmering like stardust in the low glow of track lighting. The auditorium could easily seat 200 people. With crowds the way they had been, it should have been bursting at the seams. But the theater gaped empty. I'd bet all the gummy bears in my pocket it was Mary's doing.

Her black boots were propped on the seat in front of her, lacy red dress slipping to mid-thigh, exposing a scandalous amount of flesh and fishnet stockings. She munched lazily on popcorn, pleasantly content with herself.

I glared at her, steeling my emotions and calming my heartbeat with slow breaths and every ounce of my willpower. No point in losing it now. No matter how much I wanted to throw this strange sex-kitten granny into a vat of hot popcorn oil, she was my ticket out of this mess.

I claimed the empty seat beside her and waited. In a game of poker, sometimes it's important to let the other person blink first. See what cards they're holding. I didn't have any, so I waited, patiently counting in my head to keep my blood steady. By the time I got to 182, I was ready to scream.

"I'm sure your mother told you to never to take candy from strangers, but just this once," Mary extended a tin of Christmas cookies toward me.

My eyes went wide. "What was in that cookie?" I breathed, struggling to control my temper.

"Magic," Mary said, matter of fact, popping one in her mouth and extending the tin to me again.

"Magic," I echoed flatly, as if repeating it would somehow make it go away.

"The Magic of Christmas, if you like. But, magic all the same." She was enjoying herself thoroughly. Rage surged through my veins in a fiery torrent. I sat on my hands to keep from choking her.

Then, something occurred to me. If this was not a dream, and she was indeed able to keep me trapped here, then Mary Christmas was not entirely… human. "You're Mrs. Claus, aren't you?"

"Heavens, no one has called me that in forever," she scoffed. "But yes, that is one of my many names."

"I don't understand."

"You wanted a second chance, I have given it to you."

"I didn't ask to be trapped in a waking nightmare."

"It's only a nightmare because you want it to be. Christmas is not so vile, as you make it. Magic is not a force for good or evil. It's a tool. Like a hammer. Or a rolling pin. I simply used it to open your eyes."

"Why?" I repeated, my voice thin as I struggled to control my temper.

"Why, what?"

"Why me? Why this?" I waved my hand around my head, gesturing to the theater.

She slurped at her beverage, the liquid gurgling through the straw. Most people did this unintentionally, usually during that one critically quiet scene, thus ruining the movie for the rest of us. Mary was doing it unapologetically on purpose.

"Who are you, really?" I asked quietly.

She looked at me for a long moment, the mischief in her eyes dimming as she considered how to answer me. I realized I was holding my breath and released it slowly. She must have taken it as a signal that I was prepared because she parted her pretty red Channel lips into a warm smile.

"I am the Lady of Winter," she said, as if that should mean anything to me. "I am your fairy godmother, for lack of a better term. Surely, your mother mentioned me at least once."

And time stopped dead. I mean, I guess it was already dead. Or at least very, very broken. How else was I still in this shit show? But my mother... Why did Mary Christmas know my mother? My heart nearly broke my ribs it was beating so fast.

"What did you say?"

"She wanted you to have a life, and you've had it. But you are miserable, child. It is time to let it all go. This life is the last thing your mother would have wanted for you."

"How do you know my mother?"

"I am your *godmother*. Gracious, people say I'm stubborn and hard of hearing."

My head was buzzing, making it troublesome to focus. The dizziness threatened to make me pass out, which I absolutely could not do. Not unless I wanted to start this whole nightmare of a Netflix marathon again. I wrestled my fear into submission, forcing down my roaring emotions with nothing more than my own will. I focused on the only coherent thing my brain could remember.

"You are Mrs. Claus?"

"Yes."

"The Lady of Winter?"

"Yes."

"My fairy godmother?"

"I would think that much is obvious by now, goodness me."

"Lady, what in seven hells are you talking about?" I managed to ask.

Mary sighed in irritation, dusting popcorn salt from her fingers on a paper napkin before discarding it on the floor. "How else do you think the reindeer fly? How do toys get delivered, if not by magic?"

"Magic isn't—"

"Ah, ah, ah!" Mary pressed a fingertip to my mouth, effectively silencing me. "We must never say, I don't believe…" She dropped her voice conspiratorially low, looking all around and taking a deep pause. Her voice was a breath above a whisper. "In fairies."

Suddenly, Mary gasped, clutching at her chest. Her left arm flailed at her side as she flopped back into her chair. I was on my feet in a breath, attempting to maneuver her for CPR.

"Mary? Mary, can you hear me?" I pressed my ear to her chest, but I couldn't hear her heart beating as her breath stalled in her lungs. I moved to angle her head back when she coughed in a fit of giggles.

"What. In. The. Actual. FUCK. Is wrong with you?" I seethed.

"Oh, when did you stop having any fun?!" she demanded, as if she hadn't just given me a heart attack… while pretending to have a heart attack.

"I don't find any of this fun!" I snapped, turning to storm away from her. Away from the nonsense. There was a perfectly good party where I could drink myself into oblivion. I'd start this shit show again tomorrow, sure. But anything was better than staying here.

27

THANK GOD IT'S CHRISTMAS

Mary Christmas' voice chased me up the auditorium stairs. "Wait, wait. Just wait, my dear girl."

I ignored her, running for the door and barreling out of the theater. A storm of thoughts swirled as I burst into the hallway. I collided with a poorly dressed Santa toting a sad looking loot bag.

"Ho, ho, ho!" he squeaked in a false bravado. "Where are you off to, little girl?"

Pecks. *It's like he took lessons in succubus.* Gross. I hurried by him, aiming for the stairs. My only goal was to get out as fast as humanly possible. I marched into the women's locker room, popping open the flimsy steel to my locker with a metallic thunk.

"Going somewhere?" Mary Christmas crooned, popping out of thin air and leaning against the wall, arms crossing her chest.

"Jesus! How did you get here so fast?"

"Magic, child." She spread her fingers in a fan and waved them Fosse style in front of her face. "Magic."

"Yeah, well, I'm done with your magic," I shot back.

Mary sighed. "If only it were so simple."

I slammed my locker. Instead of latching, the flimsy steel bounced back into my hand with a twangy whine. Mary's lips twitched in a smirk, sinking into the folding chair beside the lockers with great delicacy.

"What do you want from me?" I demanded, fingers gripping my locker door for balance. "I'm not a Cinderella princess who hasn't made it to the ball. I don't want to be."

"Don't you?"

"What?"

"Isn't there a fancy party you've been invited to? Where all the fairest in the land will dance to win the hand of the handsome prince?" Mary purred, her voice was silk and honey. And not in a good way.

"I haven't made it to the Gatsby house party and that's why I'm stuck?!" I was incredulous. I shut my locker firmly, making certain that it latched this time, turning on Mary with a scowl.

"Perhaps," Mary smiled. "Perhaps, you just haven't found what you are looking for."

"I didn't solve my case in the first twelve hours, so you trapped me in a time-loop? Just break the spell," I demanded.

"Oh, no, you must break the spell on your own."

"How the hell do I do that?"

"By not shouting at your elders, for starters," Mary huffed indigently, rising to her feet, nose in the air as she marched out the door.

"Please," I said more softly. "I have to know how to get out of here."

"You were the one that wanted in!" Mary snapped over her shoulder. "In, out. In, out. Goodness! Young people just can't make up a mind."

"Wait, please!" I ran after her.

I'll tell you one thing, Mary Christmas was *fast*. She was halfway into the mall before I made it to the landing. I was nearly breathless when I caught her on the grand concourse beneath the massive Christmas tree.

"Please. Just tell me what to do," I begged.

Mary looked up at the glittering decorations with a wistful smile. I followed her example and looked up at the mall's Christmas tree. It was the size of a small house, baubles the size of basketballs glittering in the tungsten lights. It was pretty. Just like every other mall Christmas tree in the world. I sighed and waited for Mary to speak.

"When did you stop believing in magic?" she finally asked. Her tone was perfectly neutral, but the question was so loaded I took a full minute to myself.

"Eight. I was eight years old."

I could picture it like yesterday. It wasn't a bad Christmas. But it was the year I stopped being a little girl and started being a grown up. My mom had been sick. Really sick. Dad had to take care of her. He couldn't work as an ironworker anymore, which often took him to construction sites far, far away. Mom had been the rock, the whole reason to believe in magic. And like most homes, my mom was where the magic of Christmas lived. Even in her sickness that year, she managed to get gifts for us.

I remembered tenderly turning over a box with Santa's name on it. I intended to save the wrapping paper in case we needed it later. You did that when you didn't have much. Saved every scrap of tissue paper for next time. I'd thumbed open the tape as gently as I could manage, careful not to tear the wrapping.

Written on the box inside were the words: *Girl, ages 8-10.*

I couldn't remember if I wanted anything in particular that year. I didn't even remember what was inside the wrapping. But I remembered the box. The box sharply reminded me my family was too poor for presents. The box told me that Santa—and by extension, Christmas—wasn't real.

Mom got better. She did her best to keep our traditions alive. But I never had high expectations for the holiday again. I expected to be disappointed. That way I would never get hurt.

Less than ten years later, she got sick again. Then a terrible car accident took her from us forever on Christmas Eve. I tried not to blame Halia as the thought skidded across my brain. I'll never know if mom would have beat her disease a second time or not. She never got the chance.

Christmas felt darker now. Though, I supposed I hadn't let it truly shine since I was a child. The magic was gone. I didn't think it would ever come back. I didn't think I would ever experience Christmas the way the rest of the world did.

That's when it dawned on me.

"You have got to be kidding me," I shouted. "I don't believe in the magic of Christmas. That's what this is about?"

Mary was delighted by my sudden understanding, clapping her hands with glee.

I'd been holding out hope that somehow I could get out of this mess in a logical, old fashioned way. Whatever that might look like. True, one could argue magic was the original old fashioned way. But I am stubborn and was raised in a STEM obsessed world. I couldn't exactly process what I was hearing.

"It's not about believing, my dear girl. Magic is real whether you believe it or not. It's a little like truth. You don't have to believe it for it to be real. Truth is truth," she explained.

"Okay, so the magic of Christmas is real. What exactly do you want me to do about it?"

"Believe," she said simply. Mary reached out to touch my cheek. Her skin was soft, her eyes sorrowful.

An announcement trickled through the air. It drew my attention to the skylight, where the message sounded from invisible speakers. The mall was closing and guests were encouraged to complete their Christmas shopping.

When I turned back, Mary Christmas was gone.

28

PUMPKIN SPICE

Mary Christmas had left in a poof of nothing. There one minute, gone the next. As if I'd dreamed the whole thing. As if everything had been a dream since I woke up under that god forsaken table.

I wandered through the mall, wondering how exactly one was supposed to "believe" in Christmas when you *knew* for a fact there was a wicked fairy queen hell bent on ruining your life.

This was some Constantine *level injustice of believing versus knowing.*

I sat at a crumb covered table in the food court to people watch and think. Believe in Christmas? I did. I do. So, why was I still stuck in this ferris wheel of space-time? Angry with the white witch of the north. I sighed and felt the weight of exhaustion creep over me twelve minutes to midnight.

Then… Nothing.

A heartbeat later, I gained consciousness… Once again stuffed under a coffee table in the dark.

"This is not my idea of Christmas!" I screamed into the void.

My voice echoed back at me until it was swallowed by the noise dampening walls. I sighed and crawled out from under the table rushing through the usual motions of my morning at breakneck speeds to avoid any of the usual interactions with people.

I was peopled out.

Coffee and donuts in hand, I marched along, intent on disappearing down the hall by theater six. The door banged open just as I stuffed half of a maple bar in my mouth. Malachi shouted in alarm when he careened into me. His paperwork went flying, donuts flipping into the air, coffee arched in an umber shower. I landed firmly on my ass.

Luckily, this time, I did *not* hit my head. Instead, I rolled to my knees, sputtering and coughing.

Malachi recovered quickly and went to his knees, bending to rub my back. "I am so sorry! I didn't see you."

It took an effort of will not to bite his hand. Mania was threatening to turn me into a wild monster. I kept my head down, pulling deep breaths through my teeth. If I were a werewolf, people would be dead.

"Why... does this... keep happening!" I roared in exasperation when I'd finally caught a breath.

"Zoë!" Halia shrieked. Her footsteps pattered on the carpet as she rushed to my side. "Are you okay?"

"Peachy," I growled.

"I see you've met the new manager, Malachi," Halia said, unaware of the imminent volcanic eruption that was my temper. I took her offered hand and struggled to my feet. Over Halia's shoulder, the supervisors counted merchandise, staffers verified their starting cash.

"I really am sorry. I wasn't expecting a person to be there," Malachi apologized.

"It's fine," I said grumpily. "I look good in coffee."

I stormed away from both of them. What was the point of courtesy today? I mean, yeah, *they* didn't know it was the same conversation, different day. But I did. I had no intention of talking about gummy bears or coffee preferences with either of them.

I disappeared into theater nine with a refill on coffee and a fresh donut. I wasn't letting anyone get in my way of coffee and nutrition today. Staff meeting be damned.

I reemerged just as the meeting wrapped up. As punishment, Bette put me in concessions, dead center where the lines were the longest. I laughed. She had no way of knowing it would be easy peasy because I'd served every one of the customers at least three times now. I knew exactly what was going to happen next.

"Zoë? Zoë Bly?"

Fuck. Forgot about him. "Hi, Jake," I managed peaceably.

"Holy shit!" he exclaimed, unhooking his arms from the girls with him and leaning against the counter. "It's me! Jake, Jake Landen."

"Wow," I replied dryly.

"You look exactly the same. How long has it been, three years?"

"Ten. Almost ten years, Jake. I know you can count." He could not be this stupid. I wondered if he knew. Like he saw me when he was choosing a line and picked mine on purpose. It could have been chance.

Unlikely.

"Man, just like yesterday!"

"Exactly like yesterday," I retorted sourly. *And the day before that.*

Jake laughed and slapped the counter in excitement, elbowing one of his dates. "We were high school sweethearts! What a life, right?"

"Your name is Zoë? That's little girl's name, isn't it?"

I leveled her with a look to melt iron. She had sense enough to backdown when facing a dragon. Good.

"Hey, we should get coffee or—"

"Jake, I'm working," I cut him off. "Order something, or go away."

He straightened up, a look of bewilderment on his face.

"Well, that was rude," the other girl pouted. She'd obviously missed the dragon memo.

"You should see me on a bad day," I retorted.

Jake grinned as if this was the most fun he'd had in ages. "We'll take that combo thing. Coke and butter." He leaned across the counter conspiratorially. "Do you still like gummy bears?"

"Jesus, Jake. It's Christmas Eve. I'm working, and you're on a double predatory date. Do you have to be so scum-suckingly disgusting? Just get out of my life!" I yelled, punching his candy order into the computer with such vehemence I'm amazed the screen didn't crack.

His cheeks flushed red, and his lips thinned to a grimace for a fraction of a moment before morphing back into false confidence. I'd been loud enough that several nearby customers balked at my outburst.

"What are you looking at?" I demanded. They looked away. I slammed my register drawer closed and turned to run. Time-loop or no, I was getting out of here.

"What can we do for you, Mr. Landen?" Malachi had slipped behind me unnoticed, again.

It all happened so fast I barely registered what our bodies were doing. My forehead bumped into his chest. He set two firm hands on my shoulders, his fingers strong and supportive. His thumb absently massaged the tense muscle in my left shoulder. I steadied myself with my hands on his hips, fingers instinctively linking into his belt.

Bad idea, Zoë. I reminded myself. *Do not get too close to this trickery.*

My insides roiled, conflicted about all the things. I did not deserve his kindness, not after how rude I'd been this morning. Disturbingly, I wanted nothing more than for Malachi to wrap his arms around me and take me up to the projection booth. Plenty of dark corners, if you understand me.

"Seeing double-oh-seven," Jake said tersely. "Ladies dig an action flick."

Nope. Not necessary to hear the remainder of this conversation.

I escaped from Malachi's hold and bolted. Halia tried to catch my arm, but I shook her off. I needed to get out. *How do I get out?*

"Perhaps you should get to your theater, instead of holding up my lines," Malachi advised Jake just before I disappeared behind the bar.

I ran for the walk-in refrigerator, tugging open the heavy steal door and diving inside. The icy air did nothing to calm my ever-growing frustration. I started counting, bracing myself for what I knew was next. Halia would open the door any moment.

Man, I *wanted* the fight. I wanted to yell at her, however unjustified. I just wanted to scream at somebody.

But, as the minutes ticked by, my frustration was replaced by a sinking feeling. What if she didn't come? What if I was wrong?

Of course I wasn't wrong. I knew what was going to happen next. Why else would I be trapped in this nightmare? I had to learn what happened every day, thus making it easier to solve my case. *Not to believe in Christmas, you rotten faery.* I had a job to do!

The door cracked. I turned, ready to tell Halia just where she could shove her self-righteous Sprite and judgment. I gasped in surprise.

Malachi, in all of his tall-dark-and-brooding glory, stood there with sympathy in his eyes. I wasn't sure if I was confused or relieved. He joined me inside, allowing the door to snick shut behind him.

"Are you okay?"

I had not been expecting Malachi. I was not prepared for Malachi. I stared at him for several heartbeats before I remembered he'd asked me a question.

"I'm… having a very strange day," I mumbled. That was putting it mildly at best.

"I guess that's why you decided to take your break in the fridge," Malachi said, a quirk at his mouth belied the seriousness of his face.

"What?"

"It was getting a little heated out there." He laughed nervously. "I'm sorry that was terrible."

"I like dad jokes," I admitted.

Malachi's smile widened, a boyish grin that softened his features. "That's good to know. May I ask why you're in here?"

I slowly raised my eyes to his. "The winter bite calms me down. I love winter. The snow, the frost, the pumpkin spices—"

He was laughing at me.

"Don't judge! Cinnamon, ginger, and nutmeg are known to ward off evil. So, if you don't like pumpkin spice, you go ahead and ask yourself why!" I told him with a passion that surprised even me.

Why I ever went to school in sunny California would be a thorough conversation with a therapist at some point in my future. After, of course, we unpacked this time-loop business. Priorities are very important.

"Easy, girl. I like pumpkin spice. Ginger is one of my favorites," he replied, a soft smile on his lips.

I took a hard look at Malachi. He leaned against the cool wall, the picture of a winter prince. He was the most beautiful human I had ever seen up close. His eyes held a gentle light, and I wondered if I could be honest with him. What could it hurt?

"Do you ever feel like you are repeating the same day over and over again?" I asked tentatively.

"All the time," he answered with a laugh, tracing his finger over the frosted steal, drawing swirls. "We work at a movie theater. The day to day is always going to be a bit repetitive. The good days are when you have an obnoxious guest to gossip about with your friends behind the bar."

It was difficult to gauge if he was being nice or honest. He didn't seem the type to gossip about anyone. He adjusted a box that wasn't quite squared on the shelf, fussing with it until it rested more perfectly. No, definitely not the gossiping type.

"I like the cold," I announced. "It's why I take my tens in here. Usually, it's just me. My fortress of solitude. Most people avoid it."

"I like the cold too. A nice escape from the noise and burnt popcorn. If you ignore the freon, it almost smells like fresh air."

He turned to face me, completely at peace in casual conversation in what was an abnormally cold space. I could see his breath in the frigid air. The warm mist hovered between us before dissolving into the nothing.

He was near enough I could feel the heat from his body, which instantly made me shiver. On instinct, Malachi inched closer and rubbed my bare arms to warm them. *Kind sir, I am not shivering from the cold.*

I took my own deep breath, and exhaled slowly. Repeat day or not, there was no denying the magnetic pull I felt for this interesting man. He must have felt it too because he raised a hand, tucking a strand of hair behind my ear. I inched forward, resting my fingers on his abdomen, ready for just about anything. Wanting just about anything to happen.

The crack of the fridge door sent both of us leaping apart as if we had been caught doing something far more nefarious than gazing stupidly at one another. Bette stood there, hands on her hips. Her raven hair was haloed by the tungsten bay lighting. A playful smile tugged at her lips, which she quickly schooled into a frown. As the GM, she couldn't exactly endorse this sort of behavior. If the theater had an HR department, I'd bet we had violated some policy or other.

Malachi's face bloomed crimson, embarrassed to be caught in a compromising position with a staffer. He couldn't quite find his tongue. He shoved his hands into his pockets and looked at the floor.

"Are you two done?" Bette demanded. "Garbage needs to be taken out and Thor needs a break. He's been at the door stand all day."

"Yes, my time is up," I said, slipping by Bette and stepping into the warm air of the back room. Burnt popcorn, crippling heat, and the sticky-sweet smell of the garbage assaulted my senses. Trivial sensations compared to the icy-fire I felt a moment before. I really needed to get my head in the game.

Like, yesterday.

29

NAUGHTY OR NICE

I decided a quick jaunt outside to the dumpsters was better than being trapped at the door stand. Thor wouldn't honestly notice and maybe someone else would give him his break. I muscled the wheelbarrows outside and started chucking garbage bags and empty soda boxes into the gaping maw of the putrid steel trash compactor.

I exhaled and tried not to breathe too deep while my brain rattled on. It had been a weird day. Okay, it'd been a weird week. By my calculations, I was on day four. Unless you counted the magic cookie day. Then this was day five. The fifth day of Christmas. I wanted my gold rings.

But, nooooo! I had to figure out how to 'believe' in Christmas.

"I don't understand why you're making it such a big deal," Jakes voice was sullen. Two sets of feet made loud crunching sounds on the packed snow.

"I have never liked you and I'm not about to start now," Wes said, just as sullen. How these two had ever stayed in the same place long enough to exchange words let alone a proper business transaction was beyond me.

I tossed the last bag in the compactor and pressed the large red button. The mechanism screamed in a whining whir of metal and pressure. The sound of foot falls stopped as I hefted the wheel barrow from behind the gate and shoved into view. Wes went pale. Jake lit up like Christmas.

"Fancy seeing you here," Jake said. I rolled my eyes, shoving past the both of them. "Need any help?"

"You don't work here," I reminded him and whistled badly as I made my way back inside.

Thor was still at the door stand looking forlorn and bored when I returned the wheelbarrows to their hiding spot behind the concessions. I washed my hands thoroughly before hustling into the lobby to save the Lord of Thunder.

There wasn't another movie starting for nearly forty-five minutes. The lobby was deserted while I stood at the door stand giving me plenty of time to brainstorm my churning thought onto the back of my exit sheet.

"Excuse me, when does this movie start?" A white haired woman with bulging bottle glasses and a billowing green puff coat thrust a ticket forward.

"Uh, on your ticket, ma'am, it has the time and the theater." I pointed as politely as I could manage, tearing her perforated paper rectangle in half. "Theater nine, at 2:30."

"Thank you, dear. And where is that?"

I pointed to the obnoxiously large red and yellow sign across the lobby, resting under a spotlight, *Theaters 6-14* scrawled in a bold font. She smiled and trotted toward her theater. She was fifteen minutes late, but it didn't seem to bother her. I shook my head as she trotted off.

"Who's Mike Cassidy?" Malachi asked, just over my shoulder, looking at my timeline I'd been doodling. I flinched in alarm snatching the paper and shoving it in my pocket. With people breezing by me at regular intervals my threat radar was offline. I hadn't noticed his approach, again. He smiled broadly.

"I'm sorry. I didn't mean to startle you," he said, a gleam of mischief in his eyes.

"You didn't. I was just..." *trapped in a vicious cycle of toxic dumpster fire thoughts. How's your day?* But that would be a strange thing to say out loud. I finally settled enough to collect myself. "I was just thinking," I mumbled.

"Ah, well, that can be dangerous," he quipped. "I was just curious if you had seen our courier?"

"Oh. Not yet," I replied mechanically.

"Wishful thinking then." Malachi sighed in frustration, pulling his own folded sheet of paper out of his pocket, focusing on it intently. His head was angled away from me, I could just see a tattoo peeking out of his shirt collar. Probably his dragon scales. He braced his elbows on the podium, stretching his back. My eyes automatically swept over his muscled back and long legs.

God, he's inhumanly handsome. I mean, what? Who said that? I wasn't being weird. I was just calculating the risk. Of falling completely head over heels for a suspect. *What is wrong with me?*

Intent on his task, Malachi thankfully didn't notice me watching him. He was striking lines through staff names. He'd squared everyone into sections that made sense to him, and only him. When he came to my name, he traced the Christmas star he had etched. He'd done this enough times the pen was beginning to tear through the paper. A wicked thought bloomed in my brain.

"He's makin' a list, checkin' it twice," I sang.

"Gonna find out who's naughty or nice," he purred like a warm bass drum.

"Definitely naughty, haven't been on the good list for years," I grinned. An excited energy pulsed through my veins when he looked up, long lashes fluttering as he blinked in shock and amusement.

He repressed laughter, an enchanting smile lighting up his face. He shook his head stubbornly and went back to checking his list. I was keenly aware of his mouth and absently wondered what it might taste like. Hopefully, the spiced orange and cinnamon that filled my senses whenever he was near.

"I suppose that's what makes Santa so jolly," I teased before I could register the words coming out of my mouth.

"Why's that?"

"He knows where all the naughty girls live," I said sweetly.

Malachi had the decency to turn red, and we both started laughing.

"I am so sorry. That was—"

"Wildly inappropriate, stunningly insubordinate, and magically perfect," he laughed in delight, pocketing his list, turning his full attention on me. The smile was so warm I feared I might dissolve into a puddle right there.

"Yeah… yes. I mean… but… you're the boss," I stammered, desperately trying to recall how words worked. *Tongue. Cheek. Teeth. Speak clearly, you donut!*

"You're gonna have to try a lot harder than that to offend me," he said. The laughter gave way to a thrumming tension. It was increasingly difficult to breathe the longer I looked into his amber eyes.

"Is it time for ushering, Mr. Malachi sir?" Thor asked, his voice sounding like he'd smoked a full dime bag of weed before returning. A glance at the clock told me it had been much longer than the thirty-minute lunch allowed. Stoners, man.

"I think staying at the door stand would be more advisable, Thor" Malachi said dryly, the corners of his eyes crinkled in amusement.

With a flourishing bow, Thor resumed his post and Malachi ushered me aside.

"At least he came back this time," Malachi chuckled. "There is always the possibility he completely loses track of time and just goes home."

I laughed.

"Wait a moment, she's right here." Bette held out the receiver as we breezed by the managers station. "Zoë, phone."

I froze. The only person who could possibly be calling me here would be my boss at the FBI. I'd skipped our morning check-in, counting on the fact he wouldn't be dumb enough to come to the theater and blow my cover.

"He says it's an emergency," Bette said softly, patiently holding out the receiver. "You got a boyfriend we should be worried about?"

Malachi stiffened beside me and I cringed. "No. No one should be calling me. I'm sure it's a wrong number," I said, rounding the desk to accept the phone.

"Good. Tell whoever it is they can't call you here at work unless it is a real emergency, you hear me?"

"Yes, ma'am," I said solemnly, waiting for her to wander off before I cradled the phone to my ear.

"Hello?"

"What the fuck, Zoë?" Mike Cassidy growled. "You were supposed to check-in hours ago. Where are you?" Mike demanded. Mikes voice was loud enough I was pretty sure Malachi could hear him. His lips thinned into a frown as he pretended not to notice, focusing on his staff list glancing at me from the corner of his eye. I turned my back, attempting to shield the conversation.

"Oh, hi… *Dad*. I'm at work. Where did you think I'd be?" I tried to sound nonchalant, hoping Mike would get the hint there were people present.

"You think you can just disappear without a word, without answering the goddamned phone?"

"I was gonna call you–"

"I don't want to hear it. There are rules, Zoë. I expect them to be obeyed."

"Sure, *Dad*. Whatever you say."

"Don't be cute with me. I'm sticking my neck on the line for you, and I won't tolerate any more of your shit."

I laughed bitterly, bristling with rage so hot it made my eyes water. It was my neck, my personal relationships on the line. Meanwhile, Mike got to call the shots from his couch on Christmas Eve. So, Cassidy could kindly fuck right off.

"Hang up, Zoë," Malachi said softly near my ear.

"I'll call you later," I said with false pleasantness, slamming the phone down harder than was strictly necessary. The cradle chimed with a phantom ring, the force convincing the circuits of an incoming call. I sighed and glared at the phone, hoping Mike could feel my venom from a distance.

"That sounded… intense. Are you alright?" Malachi set his hands on my shoulders, a touch I was starting to crave. Which was about as useful as screen door on a submarine.

"I'm fine. I promise." I pivoted around to face him, a smile a mile wide just for him. "Just one of those days."

"Okay. Maybe ask your dad not to call here," he suggested.

"Yes, sir," I saluted.

"Sir?" He made a disturbed face, crinkling his nose. "I don't like the sound of that. How about just Malachi?"

"Okay," I agreed. How was he doing that to my insides? I shivered. I needed to break this spell before I drowned in it.

Malachi rubbed my arms again. His hands had slipped to my low back as he held my eyes for an endless moment. Maybe I could just… stay a while. There was nothing wrong with drowning if it was in his smoldering gaze.

"Do you have plans for lunch?" he asked, startling me into blinking more times than was necessary.

"I… what?"

He must have realized our proximity and position was bordering on inappropriate for staff and took a big step back. He rubbed the back of his neck sheepishly, a blush blooming on his cheeks as he hurriedly glanced around. Malachi was a professional and a gentleman. We were at work. In his mind, I was his employee. His *new* employee. And the propriety of it all must be protected. No one seemed to notice, though.

"Lunch. Your break is coming up, and I was wondering if I could take you. Maybe for sushi—" I scrunched my nose. "Or teriyaki, if you prefer," he quickly countered.

"Teriyaki. I can do teriyaki," I confirmed.

"Wonderful. I just have to run a deposit up to the drop," he said, snagging a stack of blue leather pouches from the desk and tucking them under his arm. "Care to join me?" I nodded and followed him into the concessions stand.

The tidal wave of customers had dulled into lapping ripples. Malachi stood beside each register, counting out cash from their drops before tucking it inside the corresponding leather pouch. I lingered near the end of the bar, trying to melt into obscurity before anyone could ask me to do anything.

"There you are," Halia exclaimed, twisting her hair off her neck and into a messy bun. "Wes said you were out at the dumpsters with Jake." She gave me a reproving side eye.

"I was not at the dumpsters with Jake," I hissed.

"Good, because dumpster diving is beneath you," Halia said primly, serving herself a scoop of popcorn. "You can't come to my party if you do." Her threat was hallow, but it made me laugh just the same.

"Actually, I have a date," I told her. I nodded toward Malachi. His fingers tapped a screen, and he stuffed a rubber banded wad of cash into a pouch. Halia's eyes went wide, and a grin spread across her beautiful honey-brown face.

"Well then!" She bumped me with a hip. "He better not keep you from the party tonight, or I'll put toothpaste in his bed." Halia was super grown up sometimes. We laughed in spite of ourselves as Malachi returned, his arms overloaded with cash heavy blue leather pouches.

"Ready?" I nodded with a grin and trailed him up the stairs. He struggled to balance the lopsided bags of various sizes and weights.

When he reached the landing, he fumbled for the keys in his pocket and the pouches tumbled in a pile out of his arms. "Shit."

I knelt to rescue bags for him, rapping my knuckles against the muted red steel door. A moment later, Bette opened the door. She stuffed down the laugh that leaped to her lips at the sight of Malachi's dismay. She schooled her face into a stern manager mask before he noticed.

"Hey, B," I said.

"It was a busy run," Malachi explained. "Zoë's helping me."

Bette nodded, a knowing smile twinkling at the corners of her brown eyes. She reached out and collected the bags with a grace that would put a ballerina to shame. She waved a hand dismissively at the two of us.

"Go on, take your breaks," she said.

She knew. I almost stayed to argue with her, but instead, I allowed Malachi to escort me into the Christmas chaos.

30

THE HOLIDATE

The aroma of spices, melted cheese, and fried things drifted through the air. My stomach rumbled, reminding me I hadn't had anything but sugar, and more sugar, since I woke up. Food. I needed real food. Fast.

I spotted the sushi place tucked at the far end of the court. It boasted an array of rolls and other food items. I crinkled my nose in distaste. Mall fish sounded about as appetizing as a chum bucket. But a plate of sticky rice and some teriyaki chicken sounded delightful. Which was decidedly a Japanese dish. And also 100% not fish.

Which was good since I *hated* fish.

We weaved through the crowd, Malachi blocking a path for me without realizing he was doing it. Or maybe he did. We placed our order at the sushi counter. The girl lit up when she saw Malachi. She was easily fifteen years younger than him, but that did not seem to bother her in the least. I didn't think Malachi even noticed the hero worship.

"The usual, Mal?" she asked in a cheerful and clear voice.

"Yes, please." He smiled warmly at her. "And one order of chicken teriyaki too." Her bright face fell when she noticed me. She caught herself barely and shouted something over her shoulder in Japanese. From the way Malachi's shoulders stiffened, he had understood her, and it had not been kind.

"Thank you, Kaiya," he said gently, as he paid.

She scowled as she scooped rice and chicken into a container, drizzling a dark brown sauce over the top from a squeeze bottle. She was careless, slopping the teriyaki into the pitiful clump of iceberg lettuce before she doused it in a mayo of some kind. Contrastingly, she was meticulous and careful with how she prepared two fresh sushi rolls and an order of dumplings into a box for Malachi.

We collected our food, and he directed me back into people traffic, looking for an open table. He was a good head taller than the crowd. A useful advantage when you needed to survey and conquer.

"There!" He pointed and marched forward without waiting. *He's certainly proactive.* A couple had just finished putting on their coats when he arrived. "Excuse me, are these seats taken?"

"We just finished. All yours."

Malachi smiled broadly and waved me over. We had sat down before a disgruntled woman with discount-mall boogie clothes could rush between us and the seats. She hovered for a minute, as if we might recognize how we had offended her sense of entitlement.

Malachi turned to look at her, snapping the cheap wooden chopsticks apart, striking them against one another. She thrust her chin in the air and stomped away. *The Dark Lord, indeed,* I thought with a laugh.

"So. How's your first day?" he asked, gracefully selecting a sushi roll and dipping it in a sauce before eating it. I crossed my arms and frowned, chewing on a tender bite of teriyaki and rice.

"Yeah. I mean, a staff meeting. Exactly how every girl dreams of spending Christmas."

"That was *not* my idea, just to be clear." He shook his head, looking down at his hands. They trembled nervously, and he dropped a piece of sushi into his dip with a splash. He fumbled and got the rolled rice back between his chopsticks and chanced a look at me. The way he looked at me sent shivers down my spine.

"I'm not great at small talk," I admitted quietly.

"Not my favorite thing," he agreed. "But, how else does someone get to know you?"

I had to think. I hadn't gone on a proper date in a long while. After Jake, I was determined not to get distracted, or heartbroken again. The FBI lent itself well to living in isolation. I'd never truly connected with anyone outside the office. Living behind my computer added more layers. I was quickly becoming a stinky onion, ripe for peeling. And not everyone enjoys a ripe onion. Consequentially, not a lot of people knew me anymore. I sighed. I needed to try and let someone in.

"I... I grew up here. I left for college, in L.A."

"What made you pick L.A.?" he asked.

"They picked me. I went to USC..." I just barely cut myself off before spouting off my real major and subsequent recruitment into the FBI.

Malachi was pensive, like he knew I was only giving him the cliff notes of the story. He nodded. "I guess we had similar trajectories, then. I grew up here, left when I was recruited to the Marines."

"You're a jarhead?"

"Isn't it obvious?" he asked with a laugh, gesturing to his tailored black clothes.

"Uh, yeah. No. It's not at all. You, sir, have far too much hair for a Marine."

"I guess so," he said and ran a self-conscious hand through his wavy night dark hair. We both laughed.

"What brought you back here?" I asked. "You could go anywhere after the Marines."

"My aunt got sick. She never had any kids. So, no one to take care of her. When a position opened up, I took it."

Of course he's here to take care of his sick aunt, you judgmental ginger! I scolded myself. He's not pirating movies. That would be completely out of character for him. *Because he is a genuinely nice guy.*

"You're a good man," I said as neutrally as I could manage. Considering all the feelings I felt at that exact moment, I was proud of myself for not vowing oaths of fidelity and childbearing right then and there. Manners, you know?

"What makes you say that?" he asked.

"No one came to help when my mom died." I looked down at my plate of teriyaki, not really seeing it. "I mean, some did, for like five minutes. Then, they just sort of stopped asking if we needed anything after a while. Long before we were actually okay."

"I'm so sorry." Malachi reached out and took my hand. His eyes held such a deep sorrow, as though it pained him to know I had been abandoned. I wondered what he would think of me if he knew I had abandoned my family too as soon as I was old enough.

It made me think of my dad. I felt ashamed. I hadn't even called him to tell him I was in town. I couldn't tell you why. Maybe I was embarrassed. I shook my head.

"It's okay. I left too, as soon as I graduated. I haven't been back in years," I said. "I miss my dad."

"Didn't you just talk to him?" *Shit.* I forgot about that.

"Yeah that… wasn't my real dad. Just…" Lying was harder when you knew people. After I collected myself, I continued. "Mike… kind of took on that role of authority figure."

"After your mom died?"

"Yes," I said.

His expression was riddled with questions. But he was polite and didn't push harder. "Is your real dad still… alive?"

"Yes." *When in doubt, be vague.* "I need to call him. I haven't been a great daughter since… my European tour."

"European tour?"

This is why you don't do undercover with people you know, I grumbled internally. "Yeah. I took off with a punk band for a hot minute to Germany and the Netherlands. We did not go very far. Obviously."

Malachi remained unconvinced. "Is that what brought you back here?"

"Sort of." Another white lie. I hated lying to Malachi. I considered just telling him the truth for half a second. What's the worst that could happen? *Plenty*, I reminded myself and schooled my features into a pleasant neutrality.

"I needed a fresh start, I suppose. Where better to have a fresh start than at home?" I finally admitted, in full honesty.

"I couldn't agree more. That's another reason I came back. Fresh start." He smiled, warm and full and just for me. My heart fluttered until he looked away to glance at his watch.

"Damn. We need to wrap up. Manager I may be, but thirty minutes is thirty minutes," he sighed.

"Food service is borderline cruel and unusual," I agreed, closing my half-full Styrofoam container, shoving it back in the plastic bag. "Especially when it takes twenty minutes just to get food."

"I'll make it up to you," he said, throwing away his empty sushi plate. "Come with me to the Christmas party tonight."

"At the Gatsby house?" I asked. As long as I had known her, Halia had a tendency to name her residence. She had dubbed this rental "the Gatsby House" because she loved to host parties. *Themed* parties. It was not uncommon for staff to stagger in the following day still drunk. Let's be clear. Not hungover. Still drunk.

I wrinkled my nose.

"It does have a reputation." He grinned, and seemed years younger. I loved when he smiled. "It's actually closer to the Goonies than Gatsby. A hodgepodge of people and tastes. Wes, Me, and Halia are the mainstays. We try to keep the young ones in line at the parties so there are no regrets the next day. Well, I do at least."

"So no gin-rickeys, then?" I teased. "Got it."

"Gin-rickeys can be arranged." His eyes snapped with whiskey fire and mischief. I nearly hit system overload melted right then and there. Grounding my teeth to steel my nerves, I stood tall and offered him my elbow.

"Shall we?" I asked.

"M'lady," he said with a dramatic bow, hooking his arm through mine.

31

HOLIDAY HEIST

Bette was waiting as we walked back up the steps. She had a grim look on her face as she swept her eyes over the two of us. I felt Malachi tense at the same moment I did. When you knew a person, you knew when they were mad. Mama B had turned into Bette the Manager. She was very still, very calm.

And very, very angry.

We instinctively unlinked arms and cautiously mounted the three short steps that lead from the mall to the theater lobby. Silver stanchions were linked by nylon rope to direct people toward the box office first. Bette was on the inside of the ropes.

"Come with me," she commanded, snapping one of the retractable rope clips free with a whiz pop. Malachi sucked in a breath, waiting for me to pass before he carefully stretched the rope, hooking it back into the stanchion. We reluctantly began to follow Bette.

"Not you, Zoë," she said firmly. The shock must have been significant on my face because she quickly transformed her voice into the Mama B I knew and loved. She squeezed my shoulder once and then nodded over my shoulder towards the far hall in the opposite direction. "You can go clean theaters. Thank you."

The predictability of ushering on the floor forced me back into a sense of my earlier déjà vu. I hated how I kept feeling like I'd done all of this before. Which of course I had, but hadn't. Lunch was new, sort of. I had teriyaki instead of never quite getting to my pizza. Malachi sat through a meal with me. Things were different and yet the same.

How many different ways could you live one day?

I was so caught in my own thoughts I couldn't honestly recall how I'd found Jake on the floor or if he found me. He was in the plain clothes he'd been in earlier, but he didn't seem to notice or care. Just picked up a broom and started cleaning with me. Which was weird, because I knew he didn't actually work here. If my brain recalled anything at all, he was actually an undercover cop. So, what the hell was he doing?

"What are you doing here, Jake?" I finally asked when my brain caught up with me.

"What's it look like?" He held up his broom and dustpan as if it were obvious.

"You're not staff."

"A guy can't help a girl who needs it?" The sort of help Jake had to offer was not anything I wanted. I was still bitter about being arrested four days ago. Still angry about his behavior earlier today.

"Aren't you a cop?"

Jake froze in his tracks. His face hardened as a muscle twitched in his jaw. "Did the Dark Lord tell you that?"

"Maybe," I said noncommittal. What Jake didn't know wouldn't kill him.

"He shouldn't have said anything," he said venomously.

"Why? Are you undercover or something?" I asked innocently. Jake flinched and nearly dropped his broom. "Relax, Jake. I don't care."

Jake hesitated for a long moment before uneasily returning to cleaning. "It's good to see you again," he said. What did he want me to say to that? I kept my head down, eyes focused on picking up garbage. "Remember the summer I shut down the shop so we could go to the Coliseum and see Britney Spears?" He asked quietly.

Ok. I know I do not *look* like a Britney fan, now or then. Let's be honest. Everyone was a Britney fan that year. Just admit it. You're a Britney fan too.

Jake's family ran one of the largest tulip farms in the county, if not the state of Washington. Maybe even in the entire country. The point is, they have a HUGE tulip farm. Miles of multicolored flowers.

In middle school, someone had nicknamed him the *"prince of flowers"* for obvious reasons. In high school, he wore his tulip crown like a badge of honor. His family made a fortune off the tourism that accompanied their happy little flower farm.

Jake had shut down the gift shop to take me to the Britney concert. Being young and dumb, we were convinced no one would notice. Apparently, tourists *really* loved fake windmills and imported Dutch cheese. Not to mention tulips. It had taken exactly thirty minutes for some well-meaning neighbor to check in with Jake's dad, Richard, to see if there had been a death in the family.

There very nearly had been.

I couldn't help but giggle, my traitorous lizard brain lighting up with the pleasant memory.

"Don't laugh! It was your fault. Ten years later, he still doesn't trust me with his precious tulips any further than he can throw me."

Jake had worked every summer in the gift shop until his own father had fired him. Which was why he'd applied to work at the theater with me. And here we are.

"*I* trust you about as far as I can throw you," I laughed harder.

"It's good to hear you laugh," he beamed with a devilish charm. Chatting with Jake *did* make the work go faster. And there was nothing to prove. I could allow him to be a new person. I didn't need to be mean to set boundaries.

I sighed. We tag-teamed the next two theaters. By the third, we'd fallen into a competitive banter. I was laughing out loud when we rolled the overflowing garbage cans back to the concessions to toss the contents in the wheelbarrows.

Halia was changing out soda boxes when we got there, one wheelbarrow completely overflowing in cardboard and plastic syrup bags. Her body was tense, an unusual air of worry hovering about her. The look she shot over my shoulder at Jake would have blasted a crater into Mars it was so furious.

"Halia, how are you?" Jake asked in an over exaggerated tone of disdain. The exchange was frigid and sucked the laughter right out of the room.

"The garbage needs to be taken out if you're so interested in working here, Jake," she snarled, tossing her last cardboard box on top of our garbage bags.

"Sounds fun," Jake said with a grin, slipping out of the room and letting the door swing shut. *Thanks a lot,* I thought in irritation as he made a quick exit.

"What are you doing?" Halia demanded, dragging me further into the room and away from the door. I had the distinct impression she was making sure Jake couldn't hear her. "You said he wouldn't be a problem."

I immediately felt my face flush. This escalated to a mountain from a molehill a lot faster than it should have. What was I supposed to do, be a raging bitch because we used to have a thing? I'd already done that with exactly subzero effect on the golden boy. "He isn't."

"What about Malachi?" she snapped.

"I was just talking to him, Halia. He helped me clean theaters," I defended myself, alarmed by her vehemence. We'd been through this already…Several times.

Unable to speak, Halia threw up her hands and spun around to storm away. I grabbed her by the arm to stop her. Tears welled in her eyes.

"For real now, this is me talking to you. What is going on?"

"Bette fired Malachi," she wailed.

"What? Why?" I must have heard her incorrectly.

"The deposit he brought to her just before you two went on your lunch date," she hiccuped a sob, taking a breath to steady herself enough to speak. "He was short."

"That's enough to be fired these days?" I was incredulous. "Didn't you almost kill someone with orange popcorn salt out of spite once?"

"Yeah," she laughed, a harsh bitter sound. "But that was a long time ago. I was a stupid kid. Malachi is a grown up. He's a manager."

"How much was missing?"

"Almost $2,000," she sniffed.

"Holy shit!"

"Bette and Rosemary were doing the verification count, and it was off. They thought maybe he'd left a bag downstairs or missed a till, but he didn't. All the registers and drops matched. It was only the cash run where it went missing."

I couldn't figure out where Malachi could have possibly pocketed any cash. I'd been with him from the moment he left the concessions until he handed it off to Bette. Besides, it felt really out of character for him. True, I'd only known him for a day. Ok, four days. And I'd spent most of those days panting after him like a dog in heat. But it just didn't feel right. This was *Malachi*.

"But... but he was with me. The whole time," I stammered.

"Don't tell Bette or you're gone too," she hissed in warning.

"I was right there when he dropped the bags. The money probably fell out when we picked them up." Some jerk customer probably snagged it and didn't bother knocking to see if we were missing it. As we have established, customers are assholes.

"Bette knows he probably didn't do it. He's family!" Halia's voice had gotten shrill in her panic. "But she has to take action. $2,000 is not a 'whoops I shorted my till by twenty bucks.' It's serious."

The back door opened, and Bette gave us one of her tight lipped smiles. We were whispering furiously, more than obviously talking about what was happening in the manager's office. Any normal person would feel angry. Bette just sighed.

"Zuzu, I gotta ask you to come with me," she said.

Fantastic.

32

STRANGER THINGS

Bette led us up the stairs quickly, holding the office door for me to pass. It latched shut behind us with an ominous clunk. I was surprised to find Malachi in the managers' office. The look he gave me would have been appropriate if he had indigestion.

"You're still here?" I asked before my brain could stop me. I should *not* know he'd been fired. Halia absolutely should *not* have told me.

Bette lumbered over to her chair. I recognized it was hers from the swirling purple glitter on the back I'd noticed last time. She melted into the seat with a weary grunt and spun to look at me. *She could use a good night's rest,* I thought. She sighed as if in agreement and gestured for me to take the open chair beside her.

"Zoë, do you know why I called you upstairs?"

"Yes, and I just want to say he didn't do it." Bette and Malachi both blinked, a heavy look passing between them.

"What do you mean?" Bette asked, cautiously.

"I was right there with Malachi and there is no way he could have stolen anything," I said confidently.

"Thank you," Malachi said, a quirk of his lips that was almost a smile. "But we know I didn't steal anything."

"Okay…" Then it dawned on me. "You think I took the money?" I looked between them, and they both looked as though they had swallowed something foul.

I was getting fired. Again. What the hell?

"I was really hoping it wouldn't come to this," Bette murmured.

"But then I found this." Malachi lowered himself into a third chair beside me. He flipped over a DVD copy of *Titanic*. The one I'd put in my locker every day after theater checks for the last week. It was so routine at this point I'd completely forgotten the damn thing until this very moment.

Play dumb. That was the only way out of this. "I don't understand, you have a dvd?"

"Zoë, if it had been just one thing it would only be a write up and we'd go on with our day," Bette said, rubbing her temples as if she had a migraine that just wouldn't quit. "I'm sorry, Zuzu, but I have to fire you."

"But, but… I've been such a stellar citizen today," I whined. Bette almost laughed but schooled herself and squared her shoulders. She had a job to do.

"Malachi will walk you to your locker, then escort you to the door." Bette wiped her eyes, swiveling away in her chair so she wouldn't have to watch us go.

At least I'm not getting arrested today, was all I could think.

The walk of shame after you've been fired was 1000 times more embarrassing than the walk of shame after a one night stand. Every face you recognized felt like judgment and no one would look you in the eye. A manager had to watch me, a farce to make sure I didn't steal or destroy anything on my way out the door.

I could just leave. It wouldn't change anything. This was my second time being fired in this ridiculous charade. What did I care? We'd be back to square one by midnight.

But Malachi... I was really starting to have feelings for the man. I cared what he thought, even if none of this would be the same in the morning. Unless, of course, I was supposed to get fired. This whole rouse was for nothing. I really was getting tired of fate.

Where was that damned faery when I needed her? I laughed bitterly, struggling to get the combo on my locker right. It refused to comply. I tried to force the lock in frustration. Malachi's gentle hand settled over mine.

"Seven, twenty-six, three," I said, but he was already spinning the dial. *Of course he knows my combination.* I felt like crying. Maybe I should.

"I'll step outside for you to change," he said.

Of all things, the stupid uniform?

I stumbled through the process, throwing the garments angrily to the floor before changing into my jeans and Christmas Things t-shirt. I collected my dirty clothes from whatever nightmare got me here in the first place and opened the locker room door.

Malachi raised his gaze to mine, back straight, one foot hitched against the grey drywall. His arms were crossed, his chestnut eyes solemn with doubt. He gave me a sad soft smile before he gestured for me to follow.

We walked in silence to the glass exit doors at the back of the hall, past closing staff and straggling late night customers. On any other day, for any other reason, it would just be a gentleman walking a lady to her car. No one even noticed.

I dug in my bag and found keys for the borrowed Buick waiting in the first spot. It was draped by growing drifts of snow. I still couldn't quite recall parking it, and barely remembered driving it here in the first place. But I did remember the lingering cigarette smell. It reminded me of the casinos my mom worked at when I was little. When mom was still alive. Before…

I shivered and brushed past Malachi. He reached out to stop me before I could open the glass door.

"You didn't steal anything, did you?" he asked, tentatively.

"Does it matter? I'm already fired."

"It matters to me," he said, a firm hand holding my arm.

I searched his face for a long moment. His eyes sparked, deep honeyed pools of a firestorm, just like this morning. My insides ached to tell him everything. Who I was. What I was here for.

"No. I did not steal anything," I sighed. I just didn't have it in me. He wouldn't remember tomorrow anyway.

Malachi nodded crisply. "I didn't think so. You haven't been here long enough to…" he trailed off, a quick shake of his head. Creases at the corners of his smoky eyes were bare shadows of his thoughts, smoldering just before the fire winked out. He didn't want to do this any more than I did.

This has been a very strange day.

Considering all the strange days I'd had up until this point… I really needed to go home, curl up in my bed, and start over tomorrow. I'd bet money my dad would have a zillion questions if I showed up on Christmas Eve looking like I'd been run over by a reindeer. But honestly, would it matter tomorrow? Maybe I should just sleep in the car.

"Zoë, I'm sorry. For all of it," Malachi said, cutting into my thoughts.

"Not nearly as sorry as I am," I replied, slipping outside before he could say more.

33

MEAN GIRLS

There was a huge gap in my memory between the minute I walked out the glass doors into the storm and waking up under the coffee table in the booth the next day. Seriously, how many times can that happen before it's all just a blur? Don't answer that. I don't honestly want to know.

I whipped through the usual routine on a low boil, snapping and popping attitude anytime anyone got too close. Bette sent me to clean theaters hours before the time-loop usually did and I didn't argue. Avoid people at all cost. That was my M.O. today.

I watched Jake and his arm candy from across the lobby as I finished exit greeting theater two. There was a small joy in avoiding that particular conflict, even if it did mean that I didn't get a one-on-one with Malachi. I didn't bother cleaning anything. What were they going to do, fire me? Instead, I ducked down the hall connecting the two wings behind concessions to avoid Jake entirely.

"Thank you for coming to Cascade 14." Malachi's velvety baritone surprised me. He was exit greeting customers on their way out of *Toy*

Planet by theater thirteen. Moms in their thirties perked up when they noticed him, their postures changing from tired and grumpy to shoulders back, smiles on.

"What are you doing here?" I snarled territorially, which surprised the blonde mom of three. She dropped her gaze and hurried her children away.

"Thank you for coming to Cascade 14," he repeated with a tight smile, as another customer exited.

Being fired yesterday had set my teeth on edge. I was pretty sure Malachi hadn't stolen anything. I was pretty certain it had been a customer. But, with my luck, well I'd just avoided him all day to be safe. Apparently he'd noticed and had decided to come rescue me. I nearly snarled again.

"You look like you could use some help. Maybe a friend," Malachi said mildly with a sincere smile.

I completely deflated and crossed my arms sullenly, turning my attention back to the exiting customers. "I suppose."

Remember the long game, Zoë, I reminded myself. Getting close to get all the facts was a better plan than throwing a temper tantrum and alienating him. I took a deep, calming breath. "You didn't have to do this."

Malachi shrugged, happy to wait in companionable silence until the last customer left the theater. He ducked through the doors just to confirm it was empty, then handed me a broom. Without another word, we began to clean.

Malachi snaked through the isles collecting trash and depositing it in bins as quickly as his long limbs carried him. He left me the easy job of sweeping spilled popcorn and discarded napkins to the end of isles with the push broom. I swept each pile into a dustpan while Malachi grabbed the remaining super sized sodas and full popcorn bags. I will never understand paying more than minimum wage for popped air and then leaving it behind.

I watched Malachi finish the last run of garbage in sullen silence. He was so attentive to the people around him. He truly seemed to care about each person. He was even polite to the people he clearly didn't care for, like Jake. I'd been a brat most of the day, and none of the staff deserved it. Malachi and his damned instincts robbed me of my rage and replaced it with embarrassment.

"Thanks," I finally said quietly.

"Of course," he snagged the kitchen broom, the dustpan, and the push broom from my hands, gesturing for me to roll the garbage can out of the theater.

"There you are!" Halia called out. She was about half way down the hall. She narrowed her eyes as she approached. Malachi was holding all the cleaning supplies, two brooms masterfully balanced in one hand while the free arm guided the garbage roller. To Halia's perspective, I was avoiding work.

We hadn't had a fight about Jake or my mom. No Sprite in the face was a win in my book. But I had barely said a dozen words to her today. She knew something was wrong.

"Bette would like you to check the restroom," Halia said.

"Sounds like a plan," Malachi chimed in, nervously passing me back the brooms. "I got some manager things to do myself."

"Thanks," I said dryly, leaving it purposefully ambiguous if I was talking to him or Halia. Could be both. They'd never know.

Malachi nodded, whistling a Christmas tune as he strode down the hall.

I hate today.

"Bette would like *me* to clean the restroom?" I repeated to Halia with a smirk.

She pursed her lips with a hair toss, hands resting on her hips. "Fine. I want you to clean the restroom. It needs attention. Badly."

"Are you mad at me?" I asked.

"If there's anything you don't want to handle, just lock the stall," she said in an exasperated tone. "Everyone has to clean the bathrooms, Zoë."

Definitely mad at me. "He offered to help, Halia. I wasn't just goofing off."

"Whatever," she said dismissively, turning to stalk away.

"Halia!" I snapped, grabbing her arm and yanking her to a stop. "What's the matter with you?"

"What's wrong with me? What's wrong with *you*? You stomp and storm around the place all day like a tantruming toddler, but I can't?" Halia shot back.

"Are you two about done?" Bette demanded. "Because I am just about done with the two of you."

She was standing about a dozen paces away. She was wearing her purple winter coat, her purse slung over her shoulder. She was coming back into the theater from wherever she had disappeared for the mid-morning rush. Halia and I snapped our mouths shut. The tension ratcheted up a thousand degrees. When Mama B was mad, it was best to give the proper respect and hold your tongue. It was hard to keep reminding myself this was day one for them.

"Sorry, Mama B," I said, mostly keeping the edge out of my voice.

Bette waddled toward us with some effort. She was tired and it showed in the slump of her shoulders and the struggle of her gait. She eyed the two of us with the look only a mother could perfect, despite never having children of her own. She thumped one fist on a hip and stared us down until our eyes fell to the floor with some Jedi mind trickery.

"You two are best friends. You haven't seen one another in long enough that a reasonable person would recognize some unresolved baggage. But if you keep running it around my theater, you can both find yourselves somewhere else to be, you got me? Clean it up."

"Yes, ma'am," we said in unison.

Bette shuffled past us, muttering about young women squandering their friendships and something about the evils of the U.S. medical system. I had to agree with her on both points and sighed.

"I'm sorry, Halia. I really am. It's just… This is not what I expected the dark side of twenty to look like, you know?"

"You left, Zoë," she said softly. She hadn't quite lifted her eyes to mine. She dug a toe into the carpet. "You just left and never came back."

My fists were still clenched by my sides, nails digging into my palms. Not because she was wrong, but because everything she said was true. Getting out was so important to me, I never stopped to look at what I had left behind. I consciously relaxed and took a deliberate step toward her. Halia flinched.

"May I touch you?"

After a long moment, she nodded, sniffing and wiping away tears with her palms. I wrapped my arms around her and pulled her into a warm hug. She snaked her arms around me in a crushing embrace until we both were laughing and crying. "I was never running from you, Halia. You're my family."

"I'm glad you're back. I missed you," she said. I nuzzled my head onto her neck, kissing the top of her shoulder.

"I know," I replied. "I missed you too."

"You were never meant for this. You were always going to see the world." The disappointment in her voice made my heart ache. She pulled back enough to look me in the eye. "Did you?"

"Did I what?"

"Get to see the world?"

"Yeah."

"I'm glad," she sniffed, her lips curling into a heartbreakingly beautiful smile. Halia had always been happy right here. I had asked her once, begged her to come with me. I knew she wished I had stayed.

"Thank you," I said, hugging her tight and then releasing her.

"Man, we need a do over so we can get this reunion right. I know a good spot for Rein-beer games," Halia said, shaking her hands as if shaking off the emotionally sticky weighted blanket we'd wrapped ourselves in over the last five minutes.

"Rein-beer games? That sounds like a felony in the making." Halia grinned, her breathtaking smile unspooling the last of the wet blanket strung between us.

"People working a Christmas double deserve a Christmas hangover," she declared confidently. "Besides, you owe me after bailing last night."

It was possible that I never actually made it to the Night Before Christmas party. That was what she meant when she said I bailed.

I remembered flying. I remembered landing at the airport. Then what? Then nothing. Nothing but a disjointed fracture of memories that overlapped and looped until I was starting to go bug nuts.

What day was it even? Five? Six? I had no idea who *Key$troker* might be, and I was quickly becoming compromised in my own investigation. I was falling head over heels for Malachi, despite the fact that he'd fired me. Twice. And let's not forget that I'd been sleeping in the theater, rolling around in the evidence like a dog leaving their scent. The defense attorney was going to have a field day.

"What, you don't remember bailing on me?" Halia laughed and tossed her long ombre hair over her shoulder. We linked arms as we headed back to work. "It's fine. Malachi will be there. He's actually a roommate. Did I mention he's single?"

I rolled my eyes. This girl was going to be the death of me if I let her. "You're rotten, you know that?"

"To the core," she agreed.

I skipped the bathroom check because… would you honestly do it if you were in a time-loop? So, I just went straight to lunch. After lunch, it was suddenly the last hour of my double shift. Some sort of tunnel vision left me where I didn't remember *anything* about the middle of the day.

I decided the lapse was the part of my brain trying to quantify five days of memories that were all the same but different. No point in dwelling. Drama free. Almost there. Maybe I could get to know the real Malachi tonight if I made it that far.

"Hey there." Malachi's velvety voice caught my attention as I washed up in the back of concessions. I knew he couldn't read my thoughts, but it felt like he could. My shoulders tensed as if I'd been caught thinking out loud. My body did weird things whenever he was nearby.

"Hi," I replied tonelessly, keeping my attention on switching out garbage bags.

His smile faltered. "Can you break box? I know you're almost out of here, but we don't have anyone else," he continued.

I shrugged, as nonchalant as I could manage. "Sure."

"Right. It's been that kind of day." Malachi said, a deep soul searching look in my eyes. It sent butterflies darting about my belly, and I struggled to remain cool. Don't ask. Bodies are weird and we only have so much control, alright.

Lyssa sighed in relief when I told her it was time for her lunch break. She practically skipped away as I settled in at my register.

I was bored to tears in five minutes flat. I helped exactly one customer. And that was to sell a $5 gift card. I puffed out a breath in exasperation, mindlessly helping customers starting to drizzle in after 6:15 as my brain hamster ran fruitless laps. The lines grew longer and I had to start concentrating on what I was doing.

Lyssa returned to the box office just before 7:00. The beacons had been lit. Gondor called for aide. Alas, everyone was sleeping off a hangover in Rohan. There was no way I was getting out of working down these lines until they were gone.

I groaned and motioned forward the next customer. "Hi, welcome to Cascade 14—"

"Four tickets."

Damn. I completely forgot about you. Cascade Karen. "Sure. For which film?"

"Why do you need to know?" Her voice grated, a whiny giant mosquito. I prepared to respond when she cut me short.

"Did you hear me? Why. Do. You. Need. To. Know?"

I exhaled in frustration, no longer able to restrain my contempt. "Ma'am, this cineplex has fourteen screens and eleven different movies. I just—"

"It is *not* a ridiculous question," she snapped. She assumed her power pose: arms crossed, chin out, legs apart. Everything was so tight, I thought she might pop.

I smiled broadly, schooling my features into a passive aggressive professional mask. I had been waiting all my life for this perfect moment. A no consequence moment where I knew the outcome and I was okay with it. I smiled sweetly, maliciously.

Patience, I told myself.

"All right. Four tickets to *Hell Raiser 5.*"

I didn't even know if that was a movie. Didn't matter. We're making a point here. Keeping the poker face was going to be the key. *Wait, for the opportune moment,* I reminded myself. I gleefully tapped at my screen.

"You think you're funny?" she demanded.

I paused long enough to look her dead in the eye and grin. "Yes."

Her teenagers choked on their laughter. She'd have burned them alive if looks could kill. Then, she turned her murderous gaze on me. The Ghostbusters pink goo lipstick stretched into a repulsive smile. "I would like to speak to your manager."

A satisfied thrum of excitement pulsed in my veins. "Oh, of course."

I reached for the walkie-talkie to my right. I know what you're thinking. If I had remembered to use the walkie day one, I would have saved myself a whole lot of trouble. I forgot it was here, okay?

The walkie-talkie to my right had two channels—one reserved for managers and one that sent out a theater-wide call. I could have made the moment private, just us girls. Or… *Or* I could make it public. Broadcast it so we could all share in the joy.

I pressed the second button.

"Bette?" I called gleefully.

"Yeah?" Bette replied in a bothered tone.

"There is a very nice lady down here who would like to speak with you."

"We'll just see who's laughing now!" the woman trilled, thrusting her chin in the air higher if that's even possible. I smiled at her, the fakest you-asked-for-this smile I could manage. If the people standing in line behind her were angry before… *Oh, I can't wait.*

I pressed the button on channel two again. The air cracked, echoing throughout the theater. Every radio bounced my voice further. Every customer and every staff member within ear shot would hear.

"Also, I quit."

34

IT'S A WONDERFUL LIFE

The Stepford wife's confidence dropped like a hot potato, her mouth gaping open in shock. I replaced the walkie, taking my time to shut and lock my cash drawer before withdrawing the key ring.

"Have a nice day." I smiled at her one last time.

Lyssa stopped helping the customer in front of her, staring in horror or glowing in wonder. It was difficult to say. I tossed my hair over my shoulder, beaming as I walked out of the box office, slamming the door for good measure.

The customers who heard my announcement turned to see who had caused the drama. I waved at them and bowed.

Above on the balcony, Malachi emerged from the booth. There was surprise on his face, but he gave a small nod of admiration as I walked away.

I made it halfway up the stairs before Bette emerged from the manager's office. Her eyes were red as if she'd been crying, though I didn't see any lingering tears. I had a fleeting moment of regret before I shook it off. Tomorrow she wouldn't remember a thing. Today, I needed this moment. I met her at the landing.

"You couldn't wait until the end of your shift?" she asked, as I pressed the key ring into her hand. I checked my Ms. Pacman watch.

"It is the end of my shift." I gave her a hug and a kiss on her cheek before I flounced toward the break room.

"Hey, on a scale of one to ten, how crazy is she?" Bette asked.

"Easily a twelve," I replied lightly, pulling open the staff door. As it closed behind me, I heard Bette holler at Malachi. He'd been lingering on the balcony as if he were waiting for someone. Bette would make him deal with Cascade Karen. I chuckled and opened my locker.

With nowhere important to be, I took my time changing, happily content to strip out of the popcorn saturated uniform and slip into my Christmas Things t-shirt. 'Tis the season, after all. I pulled on jeans, thankful they were cool after running around all day. I borrowed a dab of lotion from Halia to freshen up.

Maybe I'd make it to the party for once. See what happened. Maybe I'd make it to tomorrow. I felt really good about the possibility.

I shouldered my computer bag and stepped into the hall. Soft cries whimpered from the break room. Abandoning my mission to party, I found Bette, leaning on the wall for support. Her shoulders were slumped and trembling. Her neck was bent as though her head was too heavy to hold. She was softly murmuring encouragement to herself.

"Bette?"

In her hand, she held a wig, a perfectly groomed secret. Stubborn strands of translucent hair clung to her bald scalp. Her makeup was flawless, hiding her dry, patchy brown skin. The precious caramel color of her eyes was muted, her inner light diluted and tired.

"Evening, Zoë," she said, chin lifted ever so slightly as she turned to face me.

Bette has cancer. The thought burrowed into my mind without a shadow of a doubt. *How have I not noticed before?* She replaced the wig on her head, a slight tug to secure it behind her ears. She waited patiently, giving me time to process.

I couldn't breathe. My vision blurred. Memories paraded across my mind, cinch marks scratched across faded super 16mm film.

There was nothing jolly about the house. The tree leaned in a corner, naked of decorations. It was starting to drip pine needles onto the carpet. Boxes of ornaments were stacked haphazardly nearby, unopened. There were no presents anywhere, not a single bow of holly to be seen. Decorating had taken an abrupt back seat.

No one was home. The windows were dark, the curtains were drawn, the kitchen dull and lifeless. There would be no family meal full of laughter and songs. If this was Christmas, it was the most depressing sight you could imagine.

We'd been at the hospital all day, Mom resting in her bed. A brutal needle was buried in the crook of her right elbow. Plastic tubes ran into her nose, every breath calculated by the rhythm of a noisy machine.

Bandages tinged with red splotches peaked out beneath the green silk scarf covering her bald head. Mom's luminous pale skin had become a dull waxy yellow. A stark contrast with the crisp white sheets and blooming purple bruises. One eye was swollen shut completely.

Dad's brown eyes were wet with tears. He sat at the bedside holding mom's limp hand. His sharp jaw was tight, an unreadable emotion locked under the tension.

I sat across from my father. My fire red hair an unwelcome beacon of color in the stone cold room with its blue paint and ultraviolet lights.

Mom had asked us to watch "It's a Wonderful Life" on tv. It was a family tradition for her since she was a girl that we had continued. My dad spent twenty-five minutes flipping channels before I shouted, "Fuck it," and found a bootleg copy online.

Mom scolded me for my use of language, but not for the illegal copy of her favorite holiday film. I hooked up my laptop, a Christmas present from my mom that year, to the ancient tv mounted on the wall and pressed the spacebar to let George Bailey tell us how precious a life was.

Mom died before Zuzu's bell could ring, but an angel still got her wings. There would be no Christmas. Not then. Not again. Not ever.

"Zoë?" Bette said my name as if I'd gone somewhere far away. My eyes refocused. Bette's hand settled on my shoulder. The flood of emotions and memories was too much to bear. My heart dropped through the floor. Bette smiled softly and folded me into her arms. We held each other, me sobbing, Bette soothing.

"It's all right, Zoë. Everything's gonna be all right." My work-mom cradled me as if I were her own child. Trapped in my own trauma, I remembered how my mother had often comforted other people during her first round of treatments. "Just let it out, baby girl. Let it all go."

She stroked my hair, and I bawled harder. She hadn't called me baby girl since I was seventeen. Right after my own mother died from the car accident. *I can't loose her too.*

"Why didn't you say anything?" I sobbed into her arms. "I would have—"

"What would you do, hmm? What can Zoë Bly do that the good Lord and my cancer doctors aren't already doing?"

"I don't know, *something*." What does a person do when someone they love was diagnosed with cancer? I felt as useless as I had when I was a child.

We stayed there for an everlasting moment, lending each other strength as we allowed all of our grief to flow out of us. Letting go of my fear, letting go of her pain. The unspoken truth weaving around us, *I am here for you.*

Which meant it was time, past time, to tell her my truth. Why I was here. What I was doing. Maybe even tell her about where it all went wrong. I withdrew just far enough to look her in the eye, my arms still clasped around her waist.

"Mama B, there's something I need to tell you."

"I already know, Zuzu," she chided.

"What?"

"I know you didn't just come back to this place because your band broke up, or whatever other nonsense you were spewing. I know there's more going on than you told me."

"You do?" I sniffed, and she wiped my mascara leaky eyes with a tissue.

"Mmmhmm. 'Course I do. You never fool me, Zuzu."

The door swung open with exuberant force. The fakest Santa I had ever seen kicked through the door. He was hefting a large red bag draped listlessly over one shoulder. He stopped dead in his tracks when he spotted Bette and me. The staff room door banged shut behind him.

"Ho, ho, ho! I wasn't expecting to find you good girls here!" That infuriatingly high-pitched voice. Pecks.

"What are you doing here, Greg? I thought you went home hours ago." Bette let me go, straightening her shirt and self-consciously touching her hair one more time to make sure it was in place.

"I forgot stuff in my locker," he said sheepishly, swinging open the door for the mens locker room. "Doing a white elephant tonight at the party." Pecks saluted us and disappeared behind the door.

"You going to that tonight?" Bette asked, gesturing for me to follow her out of the staff room.

"Halia wants me to," I said, wiping away tears. I just knew my makeup would be a hot mess again. "I haven't made it yet. I'm not sure it's a great idea. But at the moment, my whole evening is up for grabs." *As long as I don't fall asleep or get hit by a bus, maybe I can make it to tomorrow.* I didn't add that last part out loud.

"Alright. If you do, just be sure you and Halia don't get any bright ideas. The Gatsby house has a reputation." She smiled, but it didn't quite reach her eyes.

"Nothing I can't write home about, I promise."

"You know you still have a job, right? If you want it?" Bette sighed, collecting herself with a last touch to her wig.

"I know. Thanks, Mama B."

"Good night, Zoë," she said, giving me a fierce hug before sending me on my way.

35

JINGLE AND MINGLE

The Gatsby house… looked nothing like a Gatsby house.

The craftsman build was painted such a dark shade of green it nearly looked black. The trim was a rich shade of purple. Large casement windows spilled warm orange light onto the icy porch. Someone had stuffed an oversize Christmas tree into the center window alcove and decorated it with a hodge-podge of ornaments. Multicolored strings blinked invitingly.

It was more Brothers Grimm than F. Scott Fitzgerald. Either way, it was most definitely a party house. The house was rented to Wes, Malachi, and Halia. It was an odd pairing. Halia and the Grady Twins. It sounded like a rom-com or Nancy Drew mystery.

I exhaled slowly then took a deep breath. I'd driven around for hours, avoiding the party in a listless attempt to figure out what to do next. After I'd circled onto the freeway and back twice, I decided maybe it was time to try something truly new and ended up at the Gatsby house.

I hadn't made it to this party. Not once. I had no earthly idea what to expect. And, if I was being perfectly honest with myself, that made me a little scared.

No turning back now.

I made my way to knock, but Halia was already waiting, drink in hand and wearing a Nutcracker print onesie that left very little to the imagination. A flap over her butt read *"Let's Get Cracking"* in bold letters.

"You could be more garish, but you would have to try," I laughed. "Always the life of the party."

"Go big, or go home!" She saluted me with her red solo cup, holding the door open for me.

Inside, the Gatsby house was filled with joyous noise. Nearly everyone who had worked Christmas Eve was huddled in groups, chatting or playing games. Competitive Beer Pong had been set up just outside the sliding doors on a covered patio. Inside, people helped themselves to pizza and drinks laid out in the open dining room to the left. Christmas music spilled from an unseen sound system, elevating everything to a discord of party sounds.

"Who's ready to party?" Halia trilled, as she raised my contributions of beer and snacks above her head in victory. A cheer erupted, and she steered toward the kitchen with my loot. I deposited my coat onto a pile near the door before I trailed after her.

The open kitchen shined in polished tones of white and bronze. A large island counter with white marble tops was covered with food trays, and bottles of alcohol. There was a bathtub posing as a punch bowl. Malachi was filling a Solo cup with the mixed potion sloshing in the glass basin.

Wes opened the fridge door for Halia. She stuffed the beer I brought into any available space she could find. She offered Wes a can with a smile. He shook his head and raised a brown bottle of his own brew. He tipped it to her in solemn salute.

"Hey, it's the new girl!" Pecks blurted, his high pitched voice grating like nails on a chalkboard. He wore the same fake Santa suit I'd seen him in earlier. I noticed the pants were actually his college sweats, an angry red bird aggressively stamped on the left hip. Maybe a Cardinal? The felt of his Santa coat was pilled, as if it had seen ten too many Christmases. I cringed, warding him off with both hands raised as he tried to claim a hug.

"Hands off, Pecks!" Halia scolded, munching on a carrot she'd dipped in ranch from the snack tray.

"Lost your Santa hat and bag, I see," I commented as I side stepped. Drunk bros were the worst.

"Yeah, gotta keep it a surprise for the kiddos," Pecks slurred, a finger to his lips as he shushed me with a lopsided grin. By the look on his face, he'd had more than his share already. He turned his attention to Malachi, who had somehow managed to put his body between me and Pecks, forcing Pecks to retreat an unsteady step.

"Gregory," Malachi said, a tone of warning.

"Hey, congrats man on the promotion!" He fist-bumped Malachi in the shoulder as if they were best buds. If Malachi's face was any indication, it wouldn't be long before he throat punched him. I hid a smile.

"Thanks," Malachi drawled.

"Yeah, I put in for it. But then I thought to myself, I'm going to make movies. I don't want to be a manager. I'd hate my life."

"Right," Malachi said. Pecks snagged the drink Malachi had in his hand, drinking deeply before sauntering away with zero awareness.

"I'm certain that's the only reason Bette didn't promote him," Halia chided shaking her head.

"Do you think he knows I can kill him with my pinky?" Malachi quipped.

My ears perked up. That was a bootcamp line. One even I picked up during my time at the FBI academy. Typical posturing of anyone who'd been through the rigorous military style training.

Wes shook his head, cracking the fridge open. He judgmentally glared at the beer I brought before snagging two of his own AFK brews.

"I could do it, you know. No one would know," Malachi continued. Wes handed him a brown bottle. "I know. Who would I give shit-detail tomorrow?" The idea seemed to please Wes. They clinked bottles with a crystalline ring.

I allowed myself a laugh. Halia hopped off the counter and took me by the elbow as she dragged me back into the party. "Come on, I want to introduce you to people."

The thought had me cringing. Most of the staffers were barely out of high school. At least Malachi was in my age bracket. We'd find something more interesting than work to talk about. Like how did Malachi know how to kill a man with his pinky? That was the interesting conversation.

"You were in a band?" a young man around eighteen with shaggy green hair and an afternoon stubble asked as I took a seat. He extended his hand for a handshake. "Jerry Garcia."

"Your name is Jerry Garcia?" *No, it is not!*

"Just like the rockstar," he beamed. I resisted the urge to dump punch on him because he looked *exactly* like the bad Nirvana impression from day one. I knew he wasn't Kevin because of the green hair dye. But still. Hard not to dislike him on sight.

"I'm in a band. We should jam sometime," Jerry Garcia offered.

"Nice," I said, turning my attention elsewhere. I tried to disconnect from the moment and listen to the conversations around me.

Pecks was flirting with Lyssa. I cringed. That was not a voice I wanted to hear. Thor had struck up a conversation with Jerry Garcia. The two of them crooned about *Pineapple Express* and their other favorite movies.

I sighed and looked around. Malachi and Silent Bob were still standing guard in the kitchen. It was really hard to ignore them.

"Did you talk to Zoë?" Malachi asked.

Wes shrugged.

"I've talked to her, a bit."

Wes shrugged again, lifting his beer and drinking.

"Dude, say something!" Malachi apparently reached his tipping point.

"Why? I don't talk to girls," Wes said. "Especially that girl."

"You can't blame her for Jake." Malachi shook his head.

Wes grunted.

I just managed not to flinch. I had forgotten how cruel Jake was to people he thought were not in the cool crowd. Wes had never been apologetic about his nerdom. He'd proudly touted Magic cards around the lunch room or wore obscure comic t-shirts completely lost on most of the high school crowd before Disney bought Marvel and made it a thing. Jake did not like nerds. Wes was their champion. In some ways, he was also my champion because it had taken a long time to get right with who I was after high school.

"In all the theaters in all the world…"

"For fuck sake, Mal. Just tell her you're impotent. She will spend the rest of the night trying to prove you wrong," Wes damned near shouted.

I choked on my drink as I tried to stifle my laughter. *That's my cue. Time to leave.* Especially when I was so close to making it to Christmas Morning. If I could just make it to midnight, I might be okay. I set down my red solo cup and made for the door.

Halia headed me off. "Where do you think you're going?"

"I… probably should just go."

"You just got here! Come on. Have some fun," Halia raised her eyebrows at me. When I made no move to come back, she pouted, taking both hands and stomping her foot. "You remember fun, don't you?"

"You are incorrigible. A terrible friend," I shot back as she pulled me back into the party.

"I know." Halia slapped me on the ass and shoved me toward the kitchen. "Get a drink, bitch!"

I had forgotten how stubborn and bossy she could be. Especially when it came to getting me into trouble. I turned around and ran smack into Malachi. Two red Solo cups splashed their magic potion all over me from head to toe. A whoop of cries filled the air, some cheering and some alarmed.

"This is why I don't talk to women," Wes muttered, a smirk of pleasure on his lips. Probably because of my sopping t-shirt. *Glad I could entertain*, I thought sourly.

"I am so sorry. I… oh wow," Malachi stammered, as he rushed to grab something, anything, to help me dry off.

"It's fine. I'm washable," I tried to reassure him. The faster he stopped trying to fix it, the faster I could leave. He'd just done me a huge favor.

"I did not mean to—"

"It's okay. Really." I sniffed my sopping shirt. "Oh, god. It smells like college."

The comment seemed to have thrown him for a loop. He choked down a nervous laugh and stopped babbling long enough to look at me. His eyes were incredibly warm and kind. Something cracked like lighting, a spark leaping from his eyes and ensnaring me in his fire.

I felt lightheaded. It's *gotta be the punch,* I assured myself. Definitely not the way Malachi looked like a dragon who'd found a new piece of gold. It was absolutely the punch. Which I'd absorbed through osmosis. *Riiiiight.*

"Can I get you a change of clothes at least?" he offered. I felt the room's eyes on us, excitedly anticipating the drama. I knew it would be better to leave. For unknown reasons, my head nodded.

"Finally!" Halia saluted with her Solo cup in the air. A mock cheer went up from the cheap seats. I flushed as red as her cup and trailed after Malachi up the stairs.

His room might have been the master suite for as large as it was, though I didn't notice a bathroom. Maybe it was just that it the space surprisingly clean for a single man. There was absolutely nothing out of place or on the floor. A queen sized bed braced against the wall, the stylish grey comforter with red piping crisply made with the edges firmly tucked beneath the mattress. A backless bench held up the foot of the bed with a red cable knit blanket.

Framed pictures perched on his desk and walls. Close friends and family from the looks of them. His bookshelves were bursting with a carefully curated mixture of comics and literature. A jade carving of a happy little elephant tooted its trunk beside his laptop computer. The screen was on. Flashing images swirled in a glow of blue light.

"Here," he said, shutting his closet door and distracting me before I could get too close to his desk. He set an offering of a navy blue sweatshirt with red USMC lettering and matching sweatpants on his bed.

Well, that explains a lot.

"I don't exactly have girl clothes, but these ought to at least keep you warm."

"You were a Marine?" I asked. I knew that. I did. This many days of memories and they were starting to bleed into one another.

"Still am. Reservist now," he said. "Bette said you did a tour in Europe?"

I started laughing.

"What's so funny?" His expression had gone from curious to wounded.

It made me laugh harder. I wiped tears from my eyes. I couldn't help it. "I was in a punk band for 2.5 seconds," I explained through my mirth. "We hit some low level clubs on the Eur-Asia circuit. Nothing to write home about," I continued, simmering down where I could offer Malachi a sincere smile.

It was mostly true. The band I had picked up with in Amsterdam did shuttle jumps on the weekends. It was a great cover story and got us into some of the more interesting places Americans were not typically allowed to go on several continents. But it was short lived, and it was for work. I was never the romantic jetsetter the phrase "European Tour" conjured. But I let him think it anyways.

"Well… that was not what I was expecting," he said. We stood in a sort of awkward pause, unsure what to do next. A palpable tension stretched between us. I met his eyes, steady for the first time.

The door to his room suddenly burst open. A drunk Pecks stumbled through the door with Lyssa, giggling like teenagers. I reminded myself they *were* teenagers, or at least barely twenty-somethings.

"Oh! Looks like this room is taken," Lyssa demurred, twisting her fingers around to take Pecks by the hand.

"Malachi, my man!" Pecks shouted, as Lyssa dragged him from the room, closing the door behind them.

I reached for the dry clothes at the exact moment Malachi did, and our hands clasped. It was difficult to say which of us was more embarrassed at the static charge that zapped between our fingers.

"I'm sorry," he said, withdrawing his hand.

I let go of the clothes. "No, I am. I should just go," I argued.

"You don't have to."

"That way no one gets any wrong ideas tomorrow." I turned to leave but he caught me by the hand.

"Stay." The sincerity in his eyes was pleading. I hadn't ever met a man so genuine before. It was unsettling as it was captivating. "Please, stay. I'll go. You change. I'll wait outside. Don't worry about Greg. He's an idiot anyway." Malachi didn't wait for a reply, exiting into the hall. The door latched quietly behind him.

I peeled off my top and looked for a place to set it where it wouldn't ruin his meticulously well-groomed room. The computer chair was the obvious choice.

I draped my shirt and began to shimmy out of my jeans, which were spared the brunt of the rum-punch but were starting to look like I was on my period. I stopped short, the belt undone and lip of my jeans just barely over my hips.

The dark glow of ones and zeros on Malachi's computer attracted me like a moth to a flame. *I know this code.* One box in the upper left corner ran a program. Every ten seconds or so, it filtered and reset itself. A search tree with boxes and arrows meticulously color coded peaked from behind the first box. The third window tucked in the lower right corner scanned a video scene of some kind.

I was so enchanted by the orderly data it took me several moments to connect dots. Malachi was a programmer. His little command tree was artfully separating files and running code, the viewer window showed off a soaring cinematic... On his personal computer.

"Two plus two equals four, Zuzu," I scolded myself.

Knock-knock. Malachi slipped in the room with a towel to find me leaning over the chair, half naked, and reaching for the mouse, my body bathed into the blue glow of his monitor.

"I thought you might need—"

"Oh!" I exclaimed, snatching my shirt to my chest as I spun around. My cheeks burned with embarrassment. Luckily, he seemed more distracted by the bare skin and didn't notice I'd been snooping.

"Towel..." he extended his hand, offering the plush waffle weave bath towel.

"Thank you," I said.

Malachi inched closer, eyes on the floor desperately trying not to look. I could see flecks of green in his tiger eyes when he glanced up and met my stare. My mind raced. I needed to know more, but I wasn't going to find my answers here. Not tonight.

"I have to go," I decided suddenly, yanking my sopping shirt back over my shoulders, buttoning my jeans and making for the door.

"Wait, you don't have to. I'm sorry I burst in like that."

"It's okay. I really need to go," I repeated, hustling down the stairs and whipping my coat around my shoulders before anyone could stop me.

The icy air of Christmas blasted my face and woke my senses right up. I heard Halia ask Malachi what happened through the door as I made for my car at the end of the drive. I didn't pause to hear the answer.

36

GHOSTS OF CHRISTMAS

Outside, it was uncomfortably cold. The borrowed Buick was swept with piles of snow from the storm that had blown in over the last hour or so. It had positively *dumped* snow. A foot at least. And I needed to get out of there as fast as possible.

I started scraping snow away from windows with my bare hands, wearing nothing but wet jeans, a soaked t-shirt, and a sticky leather coat for warmth. I had at least trampled enough snow around the vehicle while scraping the windows to clear a path.

It was an awkward fight, racing to get inside before falling snow thwarted my progress of clearing the vehicle. I fumbled in my bag, fishing out the keys and making a shivering attempt to get them in the door.

I sank into the carpeted bucket seat and yanked the door closed behind me, jamming keys into the ignition. Thankfully, the poor little engine that could turned over on the first try.

I set the defrosters to full blast and waited. A lingering scent of clove cigarettes and Old Spice body wash assaulted me. The FBI could be real cheap when they wanted to be. If I had to guess, this car belonged to Mike Cassidy.

The smell of burnt dust blasted into the car as the heater finally began to kick in. I couldn't drive until I could see through the windows, so I waited. No point driving anywhere until I got my head on straight anyway.

The melting snow and frost sent icy rivulets of water trickling down the windows. The temperature inside the Buick began to gradually increase, warmed by blanketing snow. The blasting rush of air whispered like the whir of the projection booth. It was soothing, like a droning white-noise machine. I sighed and closed my eyes.

"Well, now we're getting somewhere," Mary Christmas said with delight.

I screamed and flailed.

She was just there. The door never opened or closed. She was just suddenly sitting in the front passenger seat beside me.

"Jesus! Where the hell did you come from?"

"The North Pole, obviously," Mary tsked, as if I'd said the silliest thing she'd ever heard. "Hot chocolate?"

She offered me a paper cup with a plastic lid. She held one in each hand. When I didn't immediately take her offering, Mary rolled her eyes and set one cup on my dashboard within easy reach.

"How did you get in my car?"

"Magic," she said with a flourish to her free hand, a wicked grin on her pretty lacquered lips. She sipped her cocoa.

I scowled at her. "What do you want?"

"Same thing I've always wanted, dear." She checked her makeup in the flip-visor mirror. "To help you." Mary turned to me with a wicked smile.

My scowl deepened. "Help me out of this nightmare, then. Send me home."

"Oh, I wish I could. But that's not how wishes work, is it?"

"You mean curses, don't you?"

"Curse, wish. They're not entirely different if you're not very careful. Magic is fickle that way. Especially Christmas magic." She wiggled around in her seat until she was facing me, one knee tucked primly underneath her bottom, both hands cupping her cocoa.

"You said I had to believe. But you can't make someone believe in something."

"True. Believing has very little to do with logic, now does it?"

"Then, what am I doing wrong?"

"Oh, absolutely nothing, dear." Mary smiled, sipping her cocoa and sighing in sounds that were a little inappropriate for molten chocolate. She snuggled into her seat as if it were the most comfy chair she'd ever settled in. She looked at me expectantly.

"I could just go around telling everyone what I'm up to and ask them point blank if they know anything," I said sullenly.

"True," Mary agreed with a long suffering sigh as she sipped more of her beverage. It could be cocoa. It could be gin. There was absolutely no way to know with Mary. "Though I'm certain that would land you right back where you started. Get yourself fired, then end up drinking tequila and eating nachos with a beautiful and mysterious stranger."

"So what then? What am I supposed to do?" I whined.

Mary seemed to be considering her options. After a moment, she nodded. "Yes, that just might work." She snapped her fingers.

I blinked, and we were no longer in my loaner vehicle. We were in a dark room, clean, and cold. It smelled faintly of caramel coffee and lemon cleaner. Wall to wall beige carpet and white walls bounced back the exterior lighting in a wash of dull sheen. A touch of frost had gathered on the balcony windows that overlooked the Washington Memorial.

My apartment.

The furniture was neutral grey and pinewood. Functional was the word that came to mind. Nothing too comfortable, nothing too fancy. No personality in any of it. Nothing like me. Nothing like my childhood.

"Well, if this doesn't look like you assembled a life out of an Ikea catalogue." Mary shivered, and not from the cold. As far as I could tell, cold didn't bother her one bit.

"Just a place I hang my hat at night before I go back to work in the morning," I said.

"How inspiring," she replied dryly.

"What's your point?"

"This is your Christmas?" she asked in distaste. Mary swept her gaze around the tiny living room and balcony. "If you had not been called home for a case, you would have had no Christmas at all. No friends, nothing?"

"So?"

I didn't do Christmas anymore. It wasn't that I didn't like Christmas, I did. I used to. I called my dad at least. But leftovers and a Netflix marathon were my go to these days. I just didn't have anyone that made the effort feel worthwhile. What was there to celebrate?

"Well, it's worse than I thought," Mary said. "Thank goodness you have me." She snapped her fingers again.

We were inside a cozy, warm, love filled home. It was an old house. A Victorian style craftsman built sometime before World War II. It had been lovingly updated for functionality and modern conveniences. Warm buttercream walls complimented vaulted ceilings trimmed in white crown molding. Real hardwood floors were so polished they shined. The air was warm from a brick fireplace, still smoldering not far from a tall tree decorated for Christmas in a mismatch of family ornaments.

A garland of dried orange slices, cinnamon sticks, and clusters of bright red holly berries stretched around the room, pinned with gold stars at regular intervals. A wreath of mistletoe with pearls of white berries and round green leaves centered the garland above the walkway. No presents were under the tree, twinkling in front of the large plate glass window. But a tray of cookies and a half consumed glass of milk were balanced on the mantle of the brick fireplace.

The living room opened onto a pleasant dinning nook with more of the same. A large wrought iron and cherrywood banquet table with matching benches was trimmed with a Christmas tartan and opened wine bottles. An empty cup of hot cocoa rested beside the half-full wine goblets.

My parents were likely tucking little me into bed.

"Why did you bring me here?" I demanded, unable to mask the hurt with rage.

"You are an obstinate girl, aren't you?" Mary huffed. "I thought you might appreciate a vision of what was."

I was about to argue with her when my father, dressed in an ornate Santa suit, sauntered into the room with a large velvet bag. My mother made his ensemble by hand sometime before I'd been old enough to crawl. Crafted of a rich luscious red velvet, she had trimmed it in black fur. A black silk sash belted the coat around his ribs. Silver buttons she'd ordered from an artist on Etsy, etched with three horses twined like a whirling wind, trailed down the double breasted duster. The boots were polished leather, silver buckles cinching them to a snug fit. He had grown his beard, as he always did in winter, and dusted it to look white.

A moment later, my mother entered, wearing a dress of forest green velvet, trimmed in silver fur. It cut into her waist trimly, then cascaded to the ground where it swept around her bare feet. Her fiery curls were pinned back, sweeping down past her shoulders. She wrapped her arms around my father as he set down his gift bag to kiss her.

They looked as if they had stepped off the set of *Lord of the Rings* directly into our living room. I watched in breathless wonder as they crouched to begin stuffing exquisitely wrapped gifts under the tree.

"Mom," I finally sobbed, reaching out to touch her. She didn't even notice, just hummed happily along to a holiday song as she worked. "She can't see me?"

"Or hear you," Mary agreed. "Though, I think she can feel you."

My mom stopped, as if she could indeed sense me. She looked around the room, her eyes settling on me. Behind me, the stairs lead up where little me, presumably, was sleeping snug in my bed.

"What is it?" my father asked. "Is she awake?"

My mother shook her head, reluctantly turning back to look at him. "It's nothing. Just a feeling. Let's hurry up before she really does wake up." She kissed him softly and they continued to dress the tree.

"Is this just a memory?" I asked. I was inches from my mother but couldn't touch her, couldn't hold her, couldn't tell her how much I needed her. She was just as gone as she had been for a very long time.

"Heavens no, at least not yours. You were always a good girl when it came to Christmas. Never looked for presents before Christmas morning,"

"Then why? How is this supposed to help me?" I slumped miserably onto the floor, wishing desperately to hold my mother.

"Every mother is a Christmas, every father is a Kringle," Mary cooed softly. My parents finished their holiday magic and were slow dancing to a song only they could hear in the firelight. They looked truly happy.

"I miss them," I admitted with longing.

"I wanted to show you a few things. Perhaps, they might help you rediscover your why."

"Why what?"

"If I knew that, if you knew that, we wouldn't be here, would we?" Mary tsked. "Come along, it's late, and we have more to see."

"I don't want to see any more," I said.

Mary snapped her fingers and dropped us right in the middle of a raucous party.

At first, I thought we were back at the Gatsby House, with the red Solo cups and beer pong happening in the living room. Holiday music blared from some distant speakers, and everyone was in their version of an ugly sweater or other holiday themed outfit. Wes sulked against a wall, a black *Nightmare Before Christmas* t-shirt paired with an all black ensemble in defiance of the red and green pandemonium around him.

After another glance around, I could see I knew all of these teenagers far better than I knew my new coworkers. There were football players, theater kids, cheerleaders, and even the robotics club.

It was the last high school party I ever attended.

"Come on, Zoë. You've had enough," Halia scolded. I turned my head to see my seventeen-year-old self stumbling away from my seventeen-year-old best friend. We were wearing matching v-cut ugly green sweaters and red miniskirts. We'd made them ourselves, complete with sparkling silver garland snaking around the torso and red and gold baubles sewn at irregular intervals. My mom had helped us make them.

"You're not my mom!" my younger self shouted. Or tried. It came out, *'Ear no' m' mim.'* I'd clearly had way, way too much to drink. I didn't remember drinking that much. Though, I didn't remember a lot from that night.

"Take it easy, H. We're just having fun," Jake said, as he slipped an arm around my shoulder, a red cup in hand. He wore an equally bright red shirt with white lettering asking, *'Where my Ho's at?'*

Me, my adult self, I cringed. "I don't remember any of this," I told Mary.

She nodded, gesturing with a polished finger. "Watch."

Jake steered my younger self away from my best friend, a firm grip on my elbow as we made it to the snack and beverage table. There was enough alcohol to sink a ship. Jake grabbed various bottles and mixed a White Russian with practiced ease.

Halia had trailed after us. "Stop it, Jake."

"Stop what?"

"Stop making her drink. She can barely hold herself up anymore," Halia snarled. My younger self had my arms folded across my stomach, a vacant expression on my face as I held up the wall by leaning on it. I didn't think she could hear or see anything that was happening right in front of her.

"I didn't see you complaining when I mixed your drinks," Jake shot back. Halia's face flushed. Jake fumbled in his pocket for a minute. Lighting fast, he grabbed the cups, dropping a white tab the size of an aspirin into one cup before swirling.

Jake put an arm around my waist, offering the spiked drink to me. My hand automatically grabbed for the drink without really comprehending what it was.

"I'm calling your mom, Zoë," Halia warned, her eyes on Jake.

"You better not!" My younger self stumbled forward, almost clear enough to be understood. Halia swatted the drink out of my hand, its vodka-coffee contents splattered all over Jake's mother's white carpet. It would never wash out.

"She just saved your life," Mary whispered.

"What?" I'd been so trapped in what I was witnessing I had nearly forgotten about her.

"Your friend. She saved you. Whatever that tosser put in your cup, you'd have overdosed. You were too far gone already."

I thought back to the fight I'd had with Halia in the freezer. How angry I had been she had called my mom. Blaming her and holding her, at least in part, responsible for my mom's death. And in reality, if anyone was at fault, it was me. For ignoring good sense, even when she threw Sprite in my face.

I turned back to watch another fight, the only part of the party I vaguely remembered. Halia demanded my keys. I told her to leave. In tears, Halia stormed out of the party.

My younger self managed to stumble and trip her way to a large leather couch against the wall. I slumped into it and was instantly unconscious. Jake started toward me but someone blocked his path. With their back to me, I couldn't tell who it might be. The confrontation lasted a tense moment before Jake stomped back to his party.

My mysterious guardian wore a heavy navy blue peacoat that he shuffled off his shoulders and dropped over my sleeping form.

"I still have that coat," I said absently. My mysterious guardian perched on the arm of the couch protectively.

"Yes, yes. A very nice coat," Mary teased, a wicked glint of her pearly white teeth. "I'm afraid that's all the time we have."

"Wait, who is the—"

She clapped her hands, and we were gone before I finished my sentence.

We were back in my parents' home. The fire was growing dim. It felt empty, quiet. A small tree no taller than my shoulder was draped in ropes of light by the front window. The signs of Christmas were not as vibrant, but they lingered. As if no one could quite scrub it clean of the space. Christmas was determined to hang on.

"I haven't been here in a long time," I said softly.

My father entered, wearing his Santa coat with pajamas and fuzzy slippers. He had a glass of brown liquid in a cut rocks glass. It sparkled in the fading firelight. He tucked a dozen identical presents under the tree, small boxes wrapped in a brown paper and tied up with string.

"I'll be home for Christmas..." my dad began to hum, lightly waltzing around in a square with an invisible partner. The four steps twirled him by me, and I felt the air move in his wake.

"Dad," I said softly. He stopped turning, looking around the room as if he could hear me. "Dad," I said a little louder.

He sighed and made his way to the fire, using an iron poker to stir the embers to an orange glow. "If only in my dreams."

He finished stirring the embers, standing to stretch his back. He touched a silver frame on the mantle lightly with his fingers. The serene photo held time frozen for eternity.

My mother snuggled newborn me in the large picture window. Spring blossomed in blurred colors behind us. My dad dipped his head forward to kiss the glass before he sank into the big green leather chair beside the fire and kicked up his feet.

"Merry Christmas, my loves." He raised his glass to the heavens, sipping at his nightcap before closing his eyes with a contented sigh.

"He seems lonely," I whispered.

"Yes," Mary agreed. "But he doesn't let that stop him from living. Tomorrow, this home will be filled with love and laughter, as it always is."

"What?" I was perplexed. And, if I was being honest, a little jealous. I didn't know my dad still had Christmas. Without me.

"He hosts a holiday for people who don't have anywhere to go. Maybe their family abandoned them, maybe they have to work late and can't make it home," Mary explained, fondness in her voice as she watched my father sleep.

I looked around, finally noticing our family banquet table was set for a holiday meal. My mother's Blackwatch tartan runner and mismatched china sets collected from thrift stores over a number of years were artfully placed down the length of the table.

"He makes sure there is food, drink, and a holiday for many people," Mary said. "Several nurses and paramedics working doubles at the hospital will stop in for cider and pie."

And I was missing it. She didn't have to say it. It was loud enough to hang in the air without words.

I blinked, and we were back in my freezing, borrowed Buick. The windshield had finally melted enough to see through it, but the air was still chilled. I turned to Mary. "You showed me the Christmas past and present. What about the future?"

Mary lifted a delicate shoulder. "I gave you twelve days. Personally, I think you are wasting the time you have already."

"What happens after twelve days?" I asked.

"Child," Mary said in a huff of exasperation. "Your future is up to you."

37

BAH HUMBUG

On the eleventh day of Christmas, I burned the pear tree to ashes.

The storm coursing through my veins was adrenaline laced rage, threatening to destroy anything it touched. Waking up after a visit from the ghosts of Christmas past was the last straw.

I was no longer in denial. I had no more bargains to make. I was just plain angry. Angry at the darkness. Angry at the godforsaken ghost light. Angry at the hangover I couldn't kick, despite never drinking.

I was angry at Halia for lying to me, pretending she didn't know what happened to my mom before she died. I was angry at Malachi for being a nice guy when in fact he was a computer hacking liar-liar face. I was angry at Mary Christmas for being a time succubus of the first degree.

And fuck that garland of gnomes. Who hangs Christmas decorations that low?!

I had officially gone rogue.

Burnt popcorn already saturated the air when I stepped into the lobby. I swiped two donuts and a black-like-my-soul coffee. My decadent milkshake posing as a caffeine was not an option for the foul disposition I was in.

I avoided the stairwell and snapped at the other staff until they steered clear, plunking my rear down at the manager's station to think. This whole thing was rooted in some sort of curse. A magic curse. Any good fantasy reader would tell you, in magic there was power in circles, stars, and salt.

A movie theater has lots of salt.

Last night's popcorn was typically stored in giant yellow bags, waiting in the back room to be dumped into warmers the next morning. If you were ever suspicious your popcorn was stale first thing in the morning, you would be correct.

Seeing as I was completely over it, I marched across the lobby, collecting supplies—a super bucket full of stale popcorn, a metal box of orange salt, and several bags of Reese's.

"Hey, you can't just grab whatever you want!" The morning supervisor, Rosemary, protested. I growled at her and gnashed my teeth. It was too easy to stare her down. I was no longer in my right mind.

I made my way to the center of the lobby and carefully crafted a super sized circle of popcorn and candy. Next, I set to work on a star inside the ring from the orange salt, careful to contain the star within my popcorn circle. For added flair, I accented each point of the star with chocolate and peanut butter candy.

Satisfied with my creation, I stepped into the center and sat cross legged, resting my hands lightly on my knees. The smell of salt and sugar swelled in my nose as if by a subtle wind. I wasn't really sure what I was doing. But I had to try something, anything, to get out of this nightmare.

I read somewhere you needed to infuse a magic circle with an effort of will, then offer it blood. My solution was to chew on a hang nail until it gave me the painful drop of sacrifice I needed. I let a single bead fall onto a kernel of popped corn.

I closed my eyes and tried to focus my will, focus my desperate desire to get the hell out of this place. Electronics and machines quietly hummed. The small arcade chimed as game cabinets warmed up. I used the rhythmic beeping and buzzing to calm my mind, zoning out to the white noise of capitalism.

"Breathe in, breathe in…"

Gobsmack's song *Voodoo* just sort of spilled out of my mouth in a chant before I registered what I was saying. I was about to repeat the verse when a broom and dustpan broke my circle.

"The ratio of people to popcorn is too big," Thor's stoner warble shattered the last of my calm.

"Hey, man! You ruined my circle!" I shouted in protest. Thor, Knight of the Socially Awkward, methodically swept salt and candy into his dustpan. I lay myself out like a Vitruvian drawing, stretching my feet and hands to block his process. "I'm trying to go home, Thor!"

Thor continued to scoop Reese's and popcorn, grumbling about the wasted orange salt I was laying on. I actually had to bark at him, literally bark like a dog, before he stopped and stepped away. He hovered nearby, waiting impatiently for me to move. He has a thing about spilled food on the floor.

By now, more staffers had begun to notice me. Rosemary was pointing and whispering to Malachi. He didn't seem alarmed so much as amused. It wasn't the weirdest thing anyone had done in this place.

Not by a long shot. I glared at him.

This is your fault, I thought sourly.

My attempt at magic foiled, I sat up and grabbed what was left of my bucket of popcorn, orange salt clinging to my hair and clothes. I shoved popcorn into my mouth. Probably a better breakfast than donuts and coffee anyway. Maybe.

I sighed, considering my options when Halia bounced her way into the lobby looking like perfection. She could easily be a Bratz or LOL Surprise doll in her purple sweater with golden snowflakes. She was that well put together for a goddamned staff meeting. She hadn't made it all the way up the front steps before she stopped and stared.

"Zoë? What are you doing?"

"Summoning circle," I said.

"I see that. What's it for?" Halia asked.

"An exorcism," I said.

"I'm sorry, did you say an exorcism?" she asked, glancing cautiously from me to Malachi, Thor, and Rosemary, then back again. Malachi shrugged, gesturing her forward. "An exorcism for who?"

"For me." I shoved another fistful of popcorn into my mouth, scooping Reese's off the floor and eating those too.

"So, you thought you'd summon a demon?" Halia asked, incredulous.

"Faery," I corrected. *I'm trapped in a nightmare. I want to go home. A wicked faery Queen got me in here. She can get me out.*

Halia pursed her lips, sighing through her nose, a frustrated sound of disapproval. Surprisingly, she didn't judge me, just sat beside me and dug into the bucket.

"Did it work?" she asked through bites of candied popcorn.

"Nope." I stuffed another bite of popcorn in my mouth and munched. "Worth a shot."

"Do you think maybe it's because you can't do magic?"

"I think it's because the Lord of Thunder over there broke my popcorn circle and ruined my magic," I pouted, shooting Thor a look to melt glaciers. He had the decency to hide behind Malachi, who stifled a laugh. I growled at them both.

"Zoë, you do realize you are at work… don't you?" Halia asked.

She was always looking out for me, even when I forgot to look out for myself. I'd spent more time at her house than my own after my mom died. I'd even lived with her for a month until I abandoned ship for college.

Suddenly, I was sobbing.

"Hey. Hey, what's wrong?" She searched my face, brushing away tears. "What happened?"

Halia slipped her arms around me, squeezing me just like she used to when I had nightmares. I cried harder, my shoulders shaking and my breath hitching in my lungs. I didn't feel worthy of her love. I didn't feel worthy of Halia's kindness. Fear and confusion swam through my body until I'd cried my last tear.

"Better?" Halia asked softly.

I wiped my eyes with my sleeve, futile with a leather jacket. Halia offered me a napkin she produced from nowhere. I wiped my nose. I laughed as I cleaned up the hot mess I'd made of myself again.

"I haven't cried like that since…" I couldn't finish. Halia knew. Tears beaded and threatened to escape again. She didn't allow it, pulling me back into a hug. I was lucky to have Halia.

"Better out than in," Halia said. I nodded absently, nuzzling into her embrace like a kitten trying to get cozy.

"Can I ask you a question?" I managed to ask through hiccuped breathing.

"Shoot."

"If you were trapped in a time loop, what would you do?"

"Anything I want," Halia said decisively.

Lightning struck my brain. *I'm in a time-loop. I can do anything. Go anywhere.* Why hadn't I tried something really new, something really different? Why was I repeating the same thing and expecting different results? Wasn't that the textbook definition on insanity? I jumped to my feet.

"Come on. We're goin' on an adventure," I declared loud enough for everyone to hear. If you were going to cut class, you might as well let everyone know.

"We have a staff meeting," she reminded me, gracefully standing to her feet and dusting her pants free of orange salt.

"*You* have a staff meeting, I haven't even started working yet. Come on, we're having a girl's day." I turned to go but she didn't follow. "They're not going to fire you, Halia. You're sunshine and rainbows."

"They might. It's Christmas."

"They didn't fire you for the orange salt incident. They won't fire you for this. Bette will only write you up. You are her golden child. Tomorrow, you'll be right back where you started today."

In more ways than one, I thought but quickly squashed the panic that surged. Today, I was trying something different. Today, I was going to rekindle my friendship with my best friend.

"Come on, Hali. For old times' sake." I offered Halia my hand.

38

SECRETS UNDERGROUND

Seattle was just over an hour south… without traffic. There was always traffic. Luckily, we made it in just under an hour and a half. Our first order of business was breakfast at Roxy's in Fremont, the self-proclaimed Center of the Universe. Who knows, maybe it is. Certainly the best breakfast in town.

Halia ordered challah French toast. I had latkes and eggs with a side of bacon. We drank Ladro coffee and talked for hours, catching up on all the things we'd missed.

Being in the center of the universe led us to a run of all the classic tourist destinations. Just under Highway 99, we climbed the Fremont Troll, made globally famous by *10 Things I Hate About You*. A nice elderly woman from a tour bus took pictures of us standing with the Volkswagen clutched in the trolls concrete fist. A grumpy looking man photo bombed us, peeking out from behind the trolls ear. He looked like a startled troll himself. We kept the photo.

Next, we swept in to Pike's Market for an original Starbucks coffee. The line twisted out the door, and there was no where to sit. Halia ordered Christmas in a Cup off the secret menu. In defiance of a faery queen, I ordered a Cinderella latte. The drinks were exorbitantly sweet but warmed our cold fingers. Neither of us had exactly planned on an urban outing at Christmas.

Thank the stars, the first stall in the market was the Seam Ripper, a disturbing scythe and thread black signboard swinging above their door. Three sisters ran the shop, fussing over us as we tried on vintage coats lined with faux fur. Halia picked a red one threaded with gold roses for herself and a forest green one trimmed with silver leaves and stars for me.

Around the corner, the urban legend that is the Gum Wall was crawling with tourists. We chewed the bazooka gum we'd picked up at the Moon Dragon novelties shop and added our sticky confection to the Christmas tree someone had made out of gum.

We split a hazelnut and cream Piroshki while I convinced Halia to catch a fish. *If you know, you know.*

"It won't come off!" she whined, sniffing her fingers. "I smell terrible."

"You smell like a Victoria's Secret model," I countered, as we took the stairs into Seattle underground and knocked "Shave and a Hair Cut" on the door of the Can Can Culinary Cabaret.

"I smell like a wet seal," she complained.

"I thought you liked that store."

"When I was twelve," Halia protested.

A beautiful woman with neon blue hair and charcoal around her eyes opened the door to the Seattle Underground. She wore a hook-eye red corset and green bowler hat that would not be out of place in a Sherlock Holmes novel. With a beckoning wave, she invited us in, sweeping us into her wake as she led us to a stageside table.

"Coats," she said, taking our new purchases from our shoulders before we could protest. "Lunch will be served after curtain." She disappeared into the shadows.

It was lunchtime at the cabaret, packed as full as any evening show. The Can Can dancers were the best in town. Halia had talked about the troupe for years but never made it to a show. That was about to change.

"Thank you, Zoë."

"For what?"

"For coming home. For including me in your life," she fiddled with her napkin, folding the white linen into origami. "Why didn't you come back?"

Because I joined a clandestine group of miscreants and having a personal life isn't easy.

No. That wasn't the truth. That was the lie I wrapped myself in, pretending no one wanted to hear from me. The truth was it was an excuse to hide.

Our eyes met in the dim candlelight of our table. Shadows danced across her face as though sadness was trying to swallow her. I couldn't see my own face, but my heart cracked into pieces.

"I kept meaning to call. But then... I didn't know what to say. So, I'd wait for a good time and then..."

"And then it was ten years. I used to write to you," Halia said.

"I know. I have a shoebox full of your letters. I kept them all."

"You did?" She was shocked.

"Of course. Halia, you're family," I said, squeezing her hand for emphasis.

"What about your dad?"

"It's different," I shrugged. "I knew you would always be there for me. But with my dad…"

After my mom died, my dad had no idea how to be a dad. He focused on work and when he came home, it was constant projects. The house never knew so many renovations. He tore down old rooms and rebuilt them as if he tore away just enough rot, renewed just enough life, maybe she'd come back.

"He loves you, you know. Calls me once in a while to see if I've heard from you," Halia said quietly.

"I'm a mess. I don't know why I run away."

"It's easier than being hurt."

For a minute, I was back in the icy refrigerator, Sprite dripping down my neck. I was trapped in a swirl of rage at the remembering and sadness at the knowing. *It isn't her fault.*

Halia blinked, the muscle in her jaw feathering. She knew something had crossed my mind that I was unwilling to say. She didn't remember the Frost Sprite incident. Was it even fair to say anything to her? I didn't want to ruin the day. But Halia always did see right through me.

"Zoë," she said softly. "You know you can tell me anything. I'm right here. I've always been right here."

Halia studied me as music swelled with horns and drums. Leggy dancers in fishnets, pasties, and feathers began their show. I did my best to make my face neutral, but this was why I never played poker. I had very little game face when people knew me. Heaven only knew how I ended up in undercover work.

Halia reached across the table, squeezing my hand. "But I guess that isn't always true, is it?" she asked, her gaze fixed on our hands as if she were afraid I'd take my hand back. Suddenly, it was hot and I wanted to snatch my hand free very much. I just managed to stop myself, returning the pressure to assure her I was okay.

I was decidedly not okay.

"What do you mean?" I asked.

"I... I'm the one who called your mom to the party. I'm the reason she was on the bridge." Halia sighed, her eyes glittering in the stage lighting with the possibility of tears. "And when I left the party... I was the reason she had an accident. I'm the reason she—"

"Stop," I commanded, withdrawing my hand. She flinched as though I'd slapped her. I sucked in a deep breath. It smelled of old leather and, faintly, of Halia's mango lotion. For some reason, the scent settled my temper, which had shot off like a rocket.

"I know," I finally managed to say. Halia was shell shocked. She sat back in her seat with an audible smack as her spine met the crisp leather backing, her antique seat groaning in protest. The hostess with the blue hair shot us a warning look. We were disrupting the show.

"How?" Halia asked, dropping her voice to just above a whisper.

"It's a long story, but I know," I whispered back. Halia squirmed in her seat uncomfortably. I realized suddenly how unfair it was to be so mad at her. When I was really mad at myself.

"I'm sorry," Halia said softly.

"Me too," I agreed. Tears threatened to ruin my face again. I wiped them away before they could. Halia slipped her arms around me. We stayed that way, heads bent and arms encircled around one another as we watched the show.

39

FIGGY PUDDING

When we finally stepped out into the evening air, a light snow had started to fall. We pulled our new coats tight around ourselves. The sightseeing and burlesque cabaret would have been more than enough fun for one day, but Halia wouldn't hear of it.

"Figgy Pudding!" she trilled.

"Is disgusting and should be illegal," I replied flatly.

"No, you goober. The caroling competition. It's tonight. I was super pissed about working because of it. Bette had already given Rosemary the night off and said I had to work." She blinked as it suddenly occurred to her what she'd done. "I am so getting fired."

"The cabaret would hire you," I suggested. Halia had that spark, that mysterious beauty. An *it* factor you just couldn't teach. She would have no problem getting another job, if only she had the courage.

"Well, if I'm getting fired, we're going out with a bang! We're going to Figgy Pudding. Come on!"

The Westlake shopping center had been turned into a Christmas bonanza. There was a giant tree nearly as tall as the building outside.

There was a matching tree inside the mall. There was even a carousel and a tiny bazaar of circus games whirling in Christmas cacophony on the cobblestone plaza.

In the middle of it all, Westlake Boulevard was shut down for a square mile with dozens of caroling groups and thousands of spectators.

It was absolute chaos.

The first group we came upon was the Silver Belles, a group of thirteen women over sixty who were in their church choir. Only, they were all dressed in wild, psychedelic holiday dresses. Neon poly fibers spiraled around their soft bodies. Beehive wigs perched on their heads a mile high in shades of pink, purple, or blue. They were the happiest most energetic geriatrics I had ever seen, even the one with tennis balls on her walker.

"We wish you a Merry Christmas…" the women sang and twirled and danced. Soft soled rubber shoes thumped in perfect time against the salted asphalt. Halia and I paused to watch their set.

"Good tidings we bring, to you and your friend…" One old lady grabbed my hand, twirling me into the center. A second granny grabbed Halia and did the same. "Good tidings for Christmas and a Happy New Year!"

Halia and I were passed gracefully from grandmother to crone and back as if we had been part of the act the whole time. We spun and clasped hands, twirled and danced. The song was a raucous mashup of several songs, starting and ending with "We Wish you a Merry Christmas."

I was laughing and out of breath by the time they twirled Halia and me back together. Several women on the outside circle grabbed giant silver bells they were using to mark off their dance space. They lifted them over their beehive wigged heads and rang the bells vigorously in a grand finale.

Cheers and whistles erupted from all around. The pure joy was contagious. We bowed dramatically as whistles increased. An old woman with startling blue eyes hooked her elbows to mine and Halia's. White curls peeked out from under her pink wig as she walked us forward.

"Beautiful dancers both of you!" she announced in delight. With a graceful twirl, she spun us out of the Silver Belles circle.

The crowd folded us into its chaotic embrace before the applause could fade. We continued to drift through the sea of spectators and performers, arms linked, both of us reveling in the spirit of Christmas. I couldn't remember enjoying Christmas in so long, it was embarrassing.

"Hungry?" Halia asked.

"We just ate!" I laughed.

"Yeah, but we just danced it all off. We need sweets!"

The smell of spiced cider and warm baked goods intermingled with the scent of fresh snow. We paid cash for fresh churros and hot chocolate at a street vendor. I sighed in pleasure at the first taste of crispy fried dough doused in cinnamon and sugar.

Halia laughed, guiding me toward the next act, a group of kids with a glittery sign declaring them *Chillin' with my Gnomies*. The kids wore polished boots with metal plates on their soles and heels. They tapped on a portable floor like Lords of the River Dance to a Christmas song I did not know. They tapped so fast and with such reckless abandon I thought they might crack their floor. But it held firm.

"How are children this talented?" I demanded with a laugh. "There is no justice in the world."

"Kids these days," Halia agreed, sipping on her cocoa. "What about those grandmas! Have you ever seen an old lady move like that?"

"Life goals, right there." I smiled back at her. Then, my mind felt like someone had zapped me with a stun gun.

I know those blue eyes.

"Mary Christmas!" I shouted in a panic. "Mary Christmas!!"

"Merry Christmas!" a chorus of voices chimed in from every direction. Halia squeezed my waist in a sisterly hug.

I tried to turn. Tried to find the Silver Belles. But the crowd had swallowed them completely. We were more than a block away. I couldn't see a pink wig in sight.

"The woman back there, the Silver Belle... Her name was Mary Christmas."

"That's just lucky, I guess," Halia said, poking me in the ribs as she bounced with the beat. "Sing with me, Zoë!"

"No, you don't understand," I protested. "Mary Christmas is what got me into this mess in the first place."

"What?" Halia was still wrapped in the Christmas spirit and could barely hear above the rat-a-tat-tat being drummed out by the children. I dragged her to the side, away from the noise until we found a quieter spot.

"Have I ever lied to you?" I asked. She gave me a dubious look and sipped her cocoa. "I mean when it's important!"

"No, okay. Zoë, what's gotten into you?"

How did you explain to your best friend, who you had not seen in ten years, that you were both an FBI agent and trapped in a Christmas time-loop?

So… the truth.

"I'm an undercover FBI agent, Hali. Someone in your theater is burning copies from the projectors. That's why I was sent back. Not because I flamed out from a punk band. Not because I'm broke and living in my dad's basement. I'm here to investigate the theater and the staff."

I let it sink in for a moment, then pressed on. "I am also 100% sure I am trapped in a time-loop."

"What, like Palm Springs?" she asked, skipping right over the *I'm an FBI agent* portion of my monologue.

I rolled my eyes and sucked in a breath. "I'm going to assume that's a time-loop movie?" I asked.

"Yep," she confirmed.

"Sure. Something like that," I agreed.

"Are you sure you didn't just stay up all night hacking or whatever? Maybe you had a weird dream," Halia suggested.

"No, Jesus, Halia!"

"I had to ask. Everything about today has been…" She paused, looking to the sky as if maybe the right words might fall like snow. "Magical. I've loved every minute. But none of it is normal. It's super out of character for me."

"When you first saw me today, I was attempting to exorcise my way out of this nightmare. You trusted me enough to come with me today," I argued.

"You clearly needed a friend."

"Of course I do!" I snapped. "I've been stuck in Christmas Eve for over a week!"

Halia crossed her arms. I hated taking the wind out of her sails, but I had to find a way to get out. Today was magical, but tomorrow… who knew what might happen. I needed tomorrow to be possible. I closed my eyes and took a slow breath before speaking again.

"I need you to believe me, Halia."

"Alright," Halia finally said. "Tell me something only I would know that happened between us."

"The first day, you threw Sprite at me because you didn't want me to get back together with Jake."

"Are you getting back together with Jake?" she hissed.

"Of course not," I shot back. "I just didn't get any warning from you people that he's an undercover cop who works at the theater from time-to-time. You or Bette should have told me."

Halia blanched, her arms dropped to her side, and she took a step back.

"You're really in a time-loop?" Halia said. "There's no way you would know that. Unless you've been secretly talking to Jake all this time instead of me."

"Absolutely not. I abandoned that clown shoes ten years ago. Never you."

"But you kind of did," Halia said. "You did abandon me when you left for L.A. Then you never came back. Like you blamed me."

"I asked you to come." With the adrenaline racing through my veins, I was shaking.

"What was I going to do in L.A.?" she snapped.

Startled, I took a deep breath and took a good look at her. The hurt was still buried, lurking behind her eyes. Despite the fun we had today, she was in pain. And I was the root cause of it.

I closed the space between us, wrapping my arms around her. It took Halia a long time to relax her arms and return my hug. When she did, we just stood there, remembering what it was like to have a friend, what it was like to have someone who truly knew you.

"Listen to me very carefully, Halia Kai." I leaned back, taking her face in my hands. "You *always* have me. You are more to me than any idiot guy could ever be. I will *always* love you."

"Stop, you're going to make me cry and ruin my makeup," she sniffed. I didn't care. I hugged her again, firmer this time. Tears welled in both of our eyes. It felt good to cry.

"So, what do we do?" Halia asked when we broke apart. The temperature was dropping, and we weaved back into the crowd. It was thinning as snow began to fall heavier.

"Mary Christmas said I need to believe."

"Who's Mary Christmas?"

"The wicked faery queen who trapped me in this damned time-loop."

"And she wants you to believe in what?"

"The magic of Christmas, I think."

"This doesn't count?" She gestured to the cacophony of carols surrounding us.

"I guess not," I said disappointed. I'd done a bang up job of being festive today. We did touristy things, joined a caroling competition. If that wasn't Christmas, I didn't know what was.

"What happens if you don't make it to tomorrow?"

"I'll wake up under the coffee table in the booth and start it all over again."

"And you've done that for a week?"

"At least."

"Maybe it's not that. Maybe it's your case," Halia suggested thoughtfully. We had weaved our way past the grandstand toward Pike's market where we'd left the car.

"Maybe," I agreed. "I have a lead. You're not going to like it."

I told her about Malachi and how I'd come to the party only to get doused in rum punch. How I'd gone to his room for a change of clothes and discovered his computer running suspicious software. How I went from no suspects to considering Malachi my number one.

Halia said nothing as we got in the car. She was quiet as we buckled in and waited for the windows to defrost. She blew on her hands, then rubbed them on her legs, hoping friction might stave off the chill.

"I know he's your roommate, but I have to know. I... liked him. Like, really liked him before I found out," I said.

"Well, then. We only have one option," Halia said, putting the car into gear. "We have to go snoop around in his room."

40

CHRISTMAS OFFICE PARTY

I startled awake when Halia's door closed. I hadn't realized I'd zoned out. Not actually sleeping for a week, just blacking out and waking up to start again would do that to a person. I shook my head and got out of the car, thankful I'd made it back without resetting.

"What's the plan?" Halia asked, locking her car. She gave a rueful look at all the vehicles on the street nestled between snowbanks left by the plows. If the plows came by again, she'd be buried in. If I made it to tomorrow, I'd cheerfully shovel snow to get her out.

"Uh, this was your idea," I said.

"Yes, but you're the one who suspects him. How do you want to play it?"

"Well…" I had to think for a minute, facing the quaint house with its cheerful holiday decorations. "If the party is going full swing, we just pretend everything is normal."

"I can distract him while you pretend to use the bathroom and go snoop," she suggested.

"Will he fall for that?"

"Maybe. He likes you, so I don't know how charming my wiles will be."

"What did you just say?"

"You didn't know?" Halia laughed at my expression.

I did know, but only because I'd spent eleven days flirting. How would he like me before I'd said a word to him? His only impression of me *today* was a crazy girl constructing a magic circle out of popcorn and candy before running off for the day like a mad woman. What was there to like about me?

"He went to school with us, remember? He's Wes's big brother. He confessed he had a crush on you in high school but was too chicken to say so because you were with Jake. He'd given up. Then I told him you were coming back. He fell all over himself trying to figure out how to say hello."

Well, damn. I really hated it when I fell for the bad guy. I grumbled. "Okay."

Halia grinned and flung open the door. "Who's ready to party?" she trilled. Shouts of exuberance echoed back to her from every room. The party was in full swing.

We closed the door and shuffled out of our new coats, tossing them on the pile. People were largely where they had been the last time I'd done this dog and pony show. Thor and Jerry Garcia were on the couch chatting. Pecks, still in his god awful Santa sweats and pilled felt coat, heckling Malachi. They were in the kitchen as Malachi attempted to fill a drink. Wes lingered nearby, sipping from a craft brew bottle and glowering at everyone.

"Hey, it's the new girl!" Pecks lumbered into the living room, slurring with every step. He had claimed the drink Malachi had been making. Staggering forward, he hooked his free arm around my neck. "Do you girls want to tell Santa what you want for Christmas?" he squeaked, suggestively gesturing between the two of us with the red cup. The drink sloshed over the sides and down my front.

"Seriously?" I protested. *How did it happen every time?*

"Pecks, go crawl up another tree, will you?" Halia scolded, peeling off his arm and redirecting him toward the couch with a shove. To me, she leaned in to whisper in my ear, "This is perfect. You pretend to go get cleaned up. I'll distract Malachi."

I nodded, gesturing at my ruined top with exaggerated frustration. Halia pointed towards the second floor.

"Second floor, second door. Take whatever you like," she said.

Halia could give lessons in misdirection to anyone at the bureau. The second door on the right was indeed Halia's room. The second *door*, as in the second one you come to, was Malachi's. She winked at me as I disappeared up the stairs.

I slipped into her room first, discarding my sopping shirt with a wet squelch. I snagged the first clean shirt I came to. A passing glance in the mirror told me it was her favorite purple shirt with blocky white letters that read *'Rebel Girl'* next to a blaster armed silhouette of Princess Leia. I smiled.

Malachi's room was next. I shut the door firmly behind me. It was so tidy. I didn't know why I didn't think that wasn't suspicious before. Only sociopaths kept their rooms this tidy all the time. *Ask me how I know.*

I pulled out his rolling chair, envying the craftsmanship in his fancy SecretLab Titan Eco chair. "Probably can afford it cause of all the pirating," I griped. The chair retailed at over $500.

I sat down and basked in the luminous glow of the monitor, my fingers resting lightly over the mouse as I drew myself closer to the desk. His adorable little jade elephant watched me suspiciously beside the computer. I turned it around.

I tabbed though his screens. They were as neat and organized as his room, each labeled with a number code that I was sure made sense to Malachi. Nothing popped immediately to my eyes as nefarious.

The final screen, though, the one that was actually running the code, was linked to a pop-up window that played through video. Perhaps copying files? I scowled and opened the video.

A swash buckling cinematic of a woman fighting off a contingent of scorpion like ninja warriors on deck of monstrous skiff made out of whale bones. The gruesome skiff floated over lava, and it appeared the woman had to battle the arachnids and steer the skiff at the same time. She successfully maneuvered the skiff only to be taken unaware from behind, where the POV faded to black.

I laughed.

Just to confirm, I toggled to the first screen, pressing the commanded keys instructing the program to run. The window expanded and the cinematic scene repeated.

"It's a game!" I laughed again, minimizing the window and tabbing through the windows once more.

The third page was a blue command tree of action on a white background. Each branch was a choice a player could make and how that choice would affect the character. It branched in dozens of directions in cerulean fractal tendrils of possibilities.

It was beautiful.

A wave of relief rushed through me. Malachi wasn't my guy. I mean, he wasn't my bad guy. He was a kind, generous, *adorakable* nerd, working on a game in his free time. A good game, judging by the cinematic promise. I sighed in relief, returning his settings to where they had been and set the screen to sleep.

The door flung open a moment later. My heart lurched right into my ears. I whirled in a dead panic, readying to face Malachi. For some reason, it was Lyssa and Pecks who had burst into the room, twittering like toddlers. They hardly noticed me until Lyssa stumbled into me in a drunken shuffle.

"Oh!" Lyssa cried in surprise, then giggled hopelessly as she realized who I was. "Ooh, you do move fast. Looks like this room is taken!" She smiled slyly at me, turning on heel and pressing her hands to Pecks's chest.

"Hey! New girl!" he slurred, saluting me with his cup. Lyssa dragged him from the room, the door snicking shut behind them. Pecks shouted loud enough I could hear him over the party and through the door. "Malachi, my man! Way to go new girl!"

My heart froze. That idiot was going to get me caught. I cracked the door and watched as they stumbled away toward another room. With a little luck, it was Wes's room. I waited for another breath before I slipped out and shut the door. I turned to find Malachi blocking my path.

"Hi," I breathed in surprise.

He blinked a few times, then smiled. "Hi," he said. "Did I hear Gregory shout my name?"

"Oh…" *Think, Zoë, think.* "He thought the bathroom was a bedroom. He had Lyssa with him." Malachi's eyes narrowed to slits. He tilted his head as if considering more than just the noise of the party.

"I redirected him, but I'm not sure where they stumbled off to," I said. I really hoped my explanation was enough to distract him from the fact I just left his room, not Halia's.

"Just my luck," Malachi sighed.

"At least they're both over twenty one," I offered.

"That's true," he said. "I don't have to be their manager tonight if they're adults, legally speaking." He gestured toward the stairs and allowed me to descend first. He stuck his head through his door, but when nothing leaped out at him, he followed me to the party.

Halia raised an eyebrow, regarding me with curious brown eyes. I shook my head and gestured behind myself. Malachi stood over my shoulder.

"You good?" Halia finally asked.

I nodded. "Great. Just a long day. Driving really takes it out of me," I sighed. Malachi wasn't *Key$troker*. It shouldn't have relieved me as much as it did, but I felt relaxed for the first time in days.

"Yes, how was your little outing? Thanks for that, by the way," Malachi scolded us both. "Bette was in a mood all day. And, I might add, I had to work until just before closing."

Halia grinned, draping an arm over my shoulder and squeezing. "A girl's got to do, what a girl's got to do."

"Even when her lunatic friend tries a summoning circle in the middle of the lobby?" Wes muttered into his beer.

Halia blanched, unsure if she should defend me or agree with the roommate she was crushing on.

"I never really had any talent for magic myself," Malachi interjected smoothly. He shot Wes a warning look.

"Come on, Zoë," Halia said, plastering a smile on her face. "Let's party like we're still in high school."

She guided me away by hands on my shoulders, directing a murderous glare toward Wes. He relented and threw up his palms in defeat. I laughed as she dance-walked me into the chaos of the living room. Cheers erupted from coworkers. Halia snagged an iPod connected to a Bluetooth speaker with a tripping-hazard of a cable, thumbing through song choices in a circular whir of clicks.

"You still have an iPod?" I asked, incredulous.

She beamed at me. "Goonies never say die," she smirked.

"Got any eight tracks? Maybe some beta tape?" I teased.

She bumped me with a hip as she settled on a song. She dragged me to the middle of the floor where the two of us began shaking our hips and bouncing to the beat. Periodically, our hands holding beverages lifted in tribute to the gods of song. It didn't take long for everyone to join us, belting out lyrics when we knew them and shimmying when we didn't. Malachi and Wes were the final hold outs.

"The Grady twins don't dance?" I asked with a nod of my head in their direction. Halia beckoned for them to join us, scooping air toward herself with a free hand as she swayed to the rhythm. Wes shook his head emphatically. Malachi reluctantly peeled himself away from the wall and joined the frivolity.

"May I have this dance?" Malachi asked, one hand folded behind his back, the other extended toward me. He took my hands and shocked everyone, myself included, when he proved to be an *excellent* dancer. He spun me effortlessly away, then tucked me back in close. His free hand slipped neatly onto the small of my back, guiding me with a light touch of his fingers or a firm press of his palm.

Malachi could *move*.

We danced for the better part of an hour. We Jingle Bell Rocked, Christmas Conga'd, and ran Rudolph ragged until the sudden exhaustion of all the last week caught up with me. I felt it in my feet first, then my limbs. My eyes drooped to a half mast lid just as someone changed the music to Bing Crosby's "I'll Be Home For Christmas," and Malachi pulled me into a slow waltz.

"You're tired," he said.

I laughed in reply. The built in mantle clock on the wall said 11:48 pm. *Twelve minutes. I can make it twelve minutes.* "You're asleep on your feet." Malachi attempted to lead me off the dance floor.

"Just dance with me. Please," I begged, words a mumble of consonants as I tugged him back. I dropped my head against his shoulder, humming along with the music. He clasped my left hand in his right, his free hand holding me close in a slow, swaying motion. I pressed my ear over his heart, enjoying the sweet and spicy scent of him. His warmth wrapped around me like a pleasant blanket.

He started singing softly along with Bing Crosby, his voice a rich timber of baritone. "If only in my dreams," he whispered into my ear.

I closed my eyes, just for a moment.

41

ON THE 12TH DAY OF CHRISTMAS

It was the first morning I did not wake in a panic or a rage. Just quietly opened my eyes, the delicious warmth of Malachi lingering on my skin in the cold darkness of the booth. I sighed and pushed myself out.

Malachi was not *Key$troker*, thank the stars. Just that knowledge alone was going to get me through another day. I mean, we were here again. Time-loop in effect. But the Dark Lord was not my unsub.

But, maybe he could help.

I was waiting for Malachi by the time he burst out of the projection booth, ready to leap down the stairs with his paperwork. He nearly lost it all in the momentary shock of finding himself nose to nose with a person unexpectedly. A smile quirked the corners of my lips, some part of me delighted I was not the one startled into a collision this time.

"Hi," I said flatly. I leaned against the balcony, a foot braced against the balusters, fingers hooked in the empty belt loops of my jeans. I'd decided to skip as many pleasantries of my morning as humanly possible. Today, I was going to get right to it. "Look, this is going to be quite possibly the most bananas thing you hear in your life. I am stuck in a time-loop, and I need your help."

"Okay, shall we start with introductions—"

"My name is Zoë. We went to high school together, but you were a few years ahead of me," I said.

Malachi blinked. His expression impossible to read.

"Bette hired me over the phone last night and informed you shortly after. Your name is Malachi Jones. You were in the Marines. The staffers here call you the Dark Lord. That idiot Pecks thinks you served in Nam." There was a twitch of his lip at that particularly ludicrous idea, but it was in line with what he knew about Pecks. I sighed. "If you can't tell, we have been through this song and dance before."

"Ooooohkaaaay...." Malachi took a deep breath, processing what I just said as swiftly as his brain would allow. "So, what you're saying is—"

"I am stuck in a time-loop, yes. And I need your help."

He looked around, as though he were trying to find answers somewhere. Maybe for a hidden camera. He must have decided I was being truthful because he sighed and gestured for me to walk with him.

"Suppose I believe you. How did you get stuck in a time-loop?"

"I ate a magic cookie given to me by a wicked fairy," Even as I said it, I knew it sounded bonkers. To his credit, Malachi didn't even miss a beat.

"That'll about do it," he agreed.

"You just accept what I said at face value?"

"That story is as old as Genesis. Maybe older. Don't take food from unknown creatures unless you want to suffer a curse." He gestured toward the stairs, and I followed him. We shuffled down the hidden stairwell into the lobby. He held the door for me.

"Besides," he continued. "if I'm taking you at face value that you're stuck in a time-loop, a magic cookie and wicked faery isn't exactly a big leap."

I made an incredulous sound. He had a point.

We made it to the coffee table where he began to fill a cup, for all eyes that cared to look, as though this were just a normal day. I took comfort in the familiarity of his effort, watching him doctor brown liquid with fresh cream and a splash of sugar. He passed me the first cup and began filling a second for himself, ever the gentleman.

Interesting.

"So, how do we get you out of it? And why me?" he asked.

It suddenly occurred to me Malachi did not know me as well as I knew him. He did not know I knew his favorite color was green, his favorite food was sushi, or that he was absolutely terrible at talking to girls he liked. Because in his world, he'd been too shy or gentlemanly to tell me how he felt for a long time.

"You... you've been kind to me. For no reason I can tell, other than you're a genuinely nice guy," I said.

"I'm a nice guy..." His eyes narrowed to dangerous slits. But he couldn't fool me. I've spent too much time with him recently.

"You take care of people who can't take care of themselves," I clarified. "Even on my bad days, and there have been a few, you've just been genuinely kind. I trust you." As if to prove my point, he opened the door for me and ushered me inside where we could continue our strange conversation in private.

The large screen was draped in a crisp white sheet surrounded by the black curtained proscenium. The empty seats waited indifferently.

The bright cleaning lights blazed as annoyingly bright as the ghost light. I shot them a frustrated look as Malachi indicated for me to take a seat with the sweep of a hand. He took the aisle in front of me, leaning against a chair so he could face me.

He raised his cup to his lips and sipped, eyes glinting with curiosity as he studied me over the rim of the cup. "Alright, how do we break your curse, then?"

"I guess the first question is how much do you know about faeries?" I asked. The coffee he'd made was perfection. The exact amount of cream and sugar I would have put in my own cup. *How does he know that?*

"Only what I've read in books," he says thoughtfully. "My understanding is forgiveness, repentance, or death—"

"Let's take death right off the table," I said emphatically.

"Agreed," Malachi laughed. "What did you do to the faery?"

"Mrs. Claus, actually. She goes by Mary Christmas."

"Really?"

"Really. I bought her nachos and tequila, if memory serves," I explained with bitterness.

"Tequila? And nachos?"

"I had just been fired for stealing from the theater." His eyes widened so much I could practically see his brain. "I obviously didn't do it, sir."

"Okay, okay!"

"Anyway, first day. For you, today." I shook my head. This wasn't coming out right. "I'd been fired from here. And I was going to get fired from my real job—"

"What real job?" he asked.

I hesitated. I didn't know why I was still protecting my identity as an agent. Maybe I felt like it made me less trustworthy. Like everything that was coming out of my mouth was bullshit already because I'd been spinning a web of lies to people I cared about. Why should they help me?

"If we're going to do this," Malachi cautioned, "I need the details."

"Fine," I huffed. "Any minute now, Pecks is going to knock his till to the floor and send money flying. Thor is going to make it worse when he tries to help by spilling seed everywhere."

Malachi held up a finger in a *hold-please* motion, marching off with intent down the hall. I knew where he was headed. I followed him, and we watched as did indeed Pecks knock his till down. Cash fluttered every which way, and Thor dropped his popcorn kernel bag.

"That really just happened," Malachi said, incredulous.

I rolled my eyes. "Believe me now?" I asked.

"I believed you before. I'm processing," he said. "You said you were going to get fired from your real job? Can you elaborate?"

Damn. I had hoped he wouldn't notice I had ignored his question. I sighed "Let's just say it is possible that I am here for reasons other than what I told Bette. It is possible that when I got in trouble on my first day, it would have been grounds for termination at my real employment."

"What, do you work for the FBI or something?" he asked with a laugh. I just stared at him. He smiled. "You're fine telling me a wicked faery trapped you in a time-loop with a magic cookie... but your job at the FBI is a bridge too far?".

I glowered at him for a long moment. "Fine. Yes, I am here trying to solve a case."

"And you think that's why this faery trapped you in a time loop?"

"Actually, I don't think that's why I'm here at all."

"Why's that?" Malachi asked.

"Because on the fourth day, Mary Christmas came back and told me I needed to believe."

"In what?"

"In the magic of Christmas," I explained.

"You can't just force someone to believe in Christmas. They either do or they don't," Malachi said.

"Agreed. But I don't do Christmas very well," I admitted.

I could feel him turn his gaze to me. I kept staring at the concessions, watching the chaos clean up. Malachi pointedly ignored them and focused intently on me. It made me shift uncomfortably.

Malachi gave me a sympathetic smile. "Christmas isn't hard," he said softly.

"I'm willing to try," I replied, dropping my gaze to the floor.

"Come on. Let's see how we can save you from your time-loop."

It had taken less time to convince Halia to join our band of misfits. If I hadn't already convinced Malachi, my detailed description of her *Let's Get Cracking* Nutcracker onesie did the trick.

"So…" Halia munched on a donut and sipped coffee, perched on the managers desk beside the box office. Malachi had made it right with Bette and the three of us were pointedly avoiding the staff meeting. "What have you done so far?"

"Every morning, I wake up under the coffee table in the booth. I narrowly avoid Malachi or Bette and get on with the day. The first day, some clown shoes from Suncoast stole a print, and I got arrested for it."

"Why?"

"Because I was trying to be a good Samaritan and give the kid a chance to come clean. I growled at him the next day and he hasn't been a problem since," I said. Malachi laughed at that.

"Third day, I learned my dad is a paramedic now," I told them. "Ask me how I know?"

"How?"

"Because I was knocked unconscious and taken to ER in his ambulance." I sipped my own coffee, expertly prepared by Malachi. "Fourth day, I found Wes's stash of homebrew."

Malachi choked on his coffee. "You know about that?"

"I told you. I know everything."

"Alright," he said. "What else have you tried?"

"I tried a summoning circle with popcorn and Reese's. It did not go well."

"Obviously," Malachi chuckled.

"That same day I made Halia skip work and come to Seattle with me for some Figgy Pudding,"

"Ew," Malachi made a face.

"The caroling competition!" Halia shrieked. "Man, I've always wanted to go. But I always end up working." She sighed. "That would have been fun."

"It was. You had a great time."

I left out the part where I ruined the evening because I needed to find out if Malachi was a suspect or not. And that we had danced until I fell asleep on my feet because it was truly the most amazing thing. I wanted to keep it for myself in case it never happened again.

I sighed. "It was the only night I remember getting almost to midnight."

"And now we're here," Malachi said.

"And now we're here," I agreed. "If you were trapped in a time-loop, what would you do?"

They exchanged a glance, a familiar look between two people who know each other well. Halia tossed her long dark hair over a shoulder with a gentle flip of her hand.

"If it's *Groundhog Day*, then I'd do anything I want," Halia concluded.

"Sure. I'll just rob a bank and fly to Paris," I said.

"Bill Murray never made it out of that town even once," Halia insisted. "You're already doing better than he did since we got to go to Figgy Pudding! Just do what you want."

"Unless it's *A Christmas Carol*," Malachi interjected.

"What?" Halia asked.

"Well." Malachi crossed his arms, leaning against the desk pensively. "Dickens' story inspired *Groundhog Day*. Doing whatever you want was never the point."

"And what is?" Halia demanded. She hated that book in school. Copied all of my homework. Pretty sure she liked the Muppets version, though. Michael Kane played it as serious as a train wreck. Halia found it fantastic.

"Rampant capitalism will be the ruin of us all," I sighed.

Malachi smirked. "Greed is certainly the catalyst for the journey. Money can't buy happiness is the lesson," he agreed. "But forgiveness, family, and responsibility to humanity are the undercurrents." He ticked off points on his long fingers.

"I haven't had enough coffee for this," Halia complained with a shake of her head. "You two finish your Saturday morning book club. I need caffeine. Catch me up when you can. I'll do whatever you need me to. You know I've got your back."

She sauntered away and I watched her in silence for a long moment. My heart ached to tell her everything, not just the time-loop, but everything.

"You know, *It's a Wonderful Life* was also inspired by Dickens," Malachi mused. "It's a time-loop movie too, when you think about it."

"I like when George Bailey gets a chance to see what life could have been like. He gets to see the possibilities. Every choice he made led to a different outcome."

His gaze narrowed as he turned his entire attention on me. The whiskey and lighting practically snapped as they danced in his eyes, the dragon about to pounce on a great treasure.

"So, what choices are you going to make today?" he purred.

42

HOW THE GRINCH STOLE CHRISTMAS

Malachi and Halia followed me around, often making suggestions of different choices I could make. They were both surprised and bewildered when I accurately predicted anything. But at the same time, I wasn't sure either of them were really buying it despite the evidence I'd piled at their feet.

It's much easier to recruit believers in the movies, I thought with a sullen sigh.

Luckily, Bette had agreed I should be on floor and left me to it without much input. I found myself appreciating the quiet work of cleaning theaters on my own. The methodical work allowed my body to do one thing while my mind worked on my problem: *how do I get out of this time-loop?*

"Ho, ho, ho!" Pecks pranced down the roped off line of waiting people at the exact moment I arrived at theater five for my exit greeting. *Huh. That's new.*

The suit was the cheap knockoff he'd been wearing for days, felt instead of velvet, a nasty synthetic beard, and faux leather boots strapped over his sneakers like socks. He still had his stupid sack over one shoulder. And sweatpants. Let's not forget the college athletic pants with the angry looking bird.

"Ho, ho, ho, Merry Christmas!" Pecks lowered his voice and waved in a show of false holiday cheer. Children waiting in line bounced excitedly and grabbed their parents' hands.

"Mommy, look! Santa's here!"

"What do you want for Christmas, little girl?"

He was not addressing the children.

"What are you doing?" I demanded, doing my best to ignore the obvious innuendo.

"Spreading Christmas cheer," Pecks smirked. I rolled my eyes so far back I damn near passed out from sarcasm.

"I'm good, thanks," I replied flatly, furiously studying my exit sheet as if I didn't already have the damned thing memorized.

"You going to the Christmas party tonight?" Pecks asked, sliding up close to me. It took a considerable amount of effort not to trip him in front of the children.

I stepped inside the auditorium rather than answer him. This would be the sixth time today I'd watched old Rose discover the heart of the ocean in her pocket. As the camera swept over photos of her adventures, I felt a familiar pull at my own heart.

The call to do something extraordinary. To experience the world and explore the magic it has to offer. I always felt like this. Like there was always more to do and never enough time. If I could just figure out how to harness time, maybe I could accomplish all the things I wanted to.

Stuck in a loop with infinite time had not changed the longing. Just frustrated and stagnated me in one spot. I wanted something more than this. But first, I had to escape. I wasn't going anywhere if I didn't.

The credits began to roll, and I stepped back out for the exit greeting. Pecks was nowhere to be seen. He had been absolutely useless since he clocked on, just like he had every day this Christmas time-loop. I was pretty sure he'd been sent home, though, so I wasn't entirely surprised he'd wandered off.

I braced myself as 400 people poured out of the theater, meandering their separate ways. Some raced for the bathrooms because they'd been holding their bladder for three and half hours. Others made a straight shot for the glass exit doors to their left. Everyone waiting in line to get inside was shifting anxiously in anticipation.

"Thanks for coming, hope you enjoyed your show." I repeated the phrase to every fifteen or so people. Very few even acknowledged my existence. Well, except the old women who insisted on touching my hair and telling me how much I looked like Rose. Fun fact, I looked nothing like Rose, but I guess all redheads looked alike. Why does everyone want to touch my hair? It's a curly haired girl problem.

When the crowd thinned, I headed back inside the auditorium to see how many stragglers were preventing me from moving forward with the cleaning. There was always at least one group of friends who had no idea their best friends in the entire world were going to the exact same film at the exact same showing. *Isn't that amazing?!*

The friends had to talk to each other at loud volumes, ruining the credits for everyone until even the most stalwart film buff relented and left. Not this group. They were here until the bitter end. I stepped outside and waited impatiently. *Company policy: do not clean in front of customers. It's rude.*

I spotted Malachi heading down the hall toward theater three. I waved at him, and he returned the gesture. We stopped and smiled at one another for an eternal moment before he turned to face theater three as people burst open the doors. The smaller auditorium was also showing *Titanic* mere minutes behind theater five.

Our dearly beloved projection troll, Wes, had figured out an ingenious way to thread one film through two projectors. Annoyingly, that meant we needed additional manpower to exit greet the extra 200 customers leaving at the exact same moment. On occasion, that meant the managers had to exit greet and clean a theater.

Malachi didn't seem to mind. He had a genuine smile for every person, as if he knew them personally. Several stopped to greet him, telling him what they thought of the screening. Another one was blubbering over how handsome he was.

He ran a self-conscious hand over his ink black hair and turned a bashful gaze toward me. When he spotted me still watching, he dropped his gaze to his feet and muttered something to the girl so she'd leave. When he looked up, I waved once more before I returned to my own work with a grin.

The friends that were surprised to find each other (*at the same theater at the same time!*) were finally leaving as I carried the brooms back into the auditorium. The cleaning lights had come up, but it was still murky at best while the credits continued to roll.

Bagpipes and strings sang a heart-wrenching melody as text scrolled over the dark screen into oblivion. I began pushing the large flat broom down each aisle in a rush, sweeping spilled popcorn and discarded napkins under the last seat in the row below. It was too late in the day, and far too long into my time suck, to care about details.

As I methodically ran back and forth down the aisles, my eyes adjusted to the dim lighting. I spotted a red coat and Santa wig crouched at the foot of the steps. Belatedly, I remembered the box of DVDs beneath the curtain. Malachi, Halia, and I had decided to leave them there and see if anyone came to collect them, but no one had.

Or had they?

My gut took an instinctive leap. I dropped the broom and went racing down the steps. By the time I made it to the landing, Pecks was rising to his feet, pulling the drawstrings of his Santa sack closed. The bag was bulging with awkward sharp angles pressing against the cheap fabric. He was startled to see me.

"Jesus, Zoë. You're like a ninja or something," he laughed, hoisting the bag over a shoulder. "I thought you were getting the brooms."

"What's in the bag?"

"Just a little Christmas cheer," Pecks chirped with a mocking smile. He reached a white gloved hand out and tousled my hair. I batted away his hand and trailed after him.

"Greg, stop," I said firmly.

He ignored me as if he couldn't hear over Mariah Carrey blaring the cantankerous loop of *All I Want for Christmas* in the hallway. Pecks threw open the door so hard it crashed into the wall and attached to the magnetic stopper. The customers in line took it as their cue to charge the door. I didn't have time to tell them to stop. Let them sit in filth if they couldn't be patient.

"Greg, I said stop!" I jogged down the hall after him, trying not to look frantic and failing.

"It's Santa, Zoë. Think of the children." His blue eyes twinkled as he gestured to kids darting around the hallway, some tugging on their mothers' arms and pointing at him. He waved at them. "Ho, ho, ho! Merry Christmas!" His voice was gratingly high, nothing like any Santa I'd ever heard.

"Fine, *Santa*. Stop!" I commanded with the authority every drill sergeant and supervising agent had ever used on me. Miraculously, Pecks turned to face me, mouth tight in a grimace as he adjusted the bag. "What's in the bag, Santa?"

"I told you, just some holiday cheer," he said.

"Show me," I told him.

Malachi, in his uncanny ability to manifest exactly where I needed him, emerged from theater three just beyond us. He was pushing a trash can and carrying brooms. He spotted Pecks and I, a pensive expression as he observed the aggressive body language between us. He settled his equipment against the wall and began walking toward us.

"That's not how Christmas works," Pecks laughed nervously. "Only naughty girls ask for presents early. You have to wait for Christmas morning to see what Santa brought you. Ho, ho, ho." Pecks was looking down the hall over my shoulder, distracted and anxious as Malachi approached.

"What's in the bag?" I repeated.

"Just let it be, Zoë," Pecks warned.

"What's in the bag, Gregory?" Malachi growled just over my shoulder as he shifted his position so the two of us had cornered Pecks with his back against the wall.

Pecks face fell as he looked from Malachi to me and back again. Unceremoniously, he dropped the overstuffed bag to the ground with a thump. The drawstrings were weak and pulled open. It was easy to see the DVD boxes. There were more than just copies of *Titanic* in there. There were copies of every movie currently showing in the theater.

"What is this?" Malachi asked, bewildered.

"Would you believe, Christmas presents?" Pecks suggested hopefully.

43

BAD SANTA

Malachi sighed, pinching the bridge of his nose. Even with everything I'd told him today, I was pretty sure pirated copies of films from his theater was not on his weird-shit-staff-and-customers-do Christmas BINGO card. I trailed behind Malachi as he escorted Pecks to the manager's office, hefting the bulky Santa bag over my shoulder.

How does the old man do it? I wondered absently. I mean, it goes without saying, if there was a Winter Queen who also happened to be Mrs. Claus, Santa must be real too. Right? So, how does he carry a planets worth of gifts on a tiny ass sleigh?

Magic, Mary's voice whispered in my ear. I swung around searching for her. The massive felt bag sent me careening into the wall.

"Are you alright, Zoë?" Malachi paused on the steps, one hand firmly on Pecks' arm. "I can come back for those if they're too heavy."

"I'm good," I said, adjusting the bag and shook my head. There were a lot of ways this could go, but I needed to be present to win. I needed to be the one to set this record straight if I had any hope of making it to the end of today. *Please let me make it to tomorrow.* Malachi reluctantly nodded and continued escorting Pecks up the stairs.

He held the door and Pecks sauntered in as though he hadn't a care in the world. Part of me growled as I followed him. The door banged shut behind us, and I had a momentary flash of the time I'd been in here being arrested. *Life is weird, man.*

Bette whirled around in her purple glitter chair to face us. "What's all this?" she asked, adjusting her wig and blotting the sweat away from her brow with a tissue.

"We have a situation," Malachi explained, escorting Pecks to a chair. His voice was dangerously low. "We have a thief in our midsts."

I unceremoniously plopped the overstuffed bag into a corner near the printer, leaning on the wall to observe. Bette hefted herself out of the chair with some effort and made her way to look at what I had in the bag.

"Zuzu?" Bette asked as she looked between the three of us in a panic.

"Wasn't me," I told her.

"It was me," Pecks bragged. He sat and propped his feet casually up on the counter, fingers threaded behind his head. Malachi leveled a stern look at him until he withdrew his feet. A smirk tugged at my right cheek. You gotta enjoy the little things.

"Gregory?" Bette was incredulous. "What did you do?"

"He's been pirating movies," I explained.

"You can go now if you like," Malachi suggested.

It took me a moment to register he was talking to me. I uncrossed my arms and stood up. "I think I'll stay." Malachi pressed his lips together into a thin line.

"Zoë," he began in an exasperated tone. He wasn't angry with me, his attention was largely on Pecks, a dangerous glint in his eyes. He turned toward me and sighed, gentleness returning to his voice. "I think it might be better if you go."

Truth. They deserve the truth, my better angels reminded me.

I reached into my back pocket, pulling out my worn leather badge and ID. After that first day, I carried it with me every day, just in case. I wasn't about to get handcuffed by Jake or anyone else if I could help it.

I handed my badge to Malachi. He flipped the leather open, and his eyes snapped to mine, a fiery burn that sent electricity shooting down my spine. "You were serious?"

"I tried to tell you," I offered gently.

Malachi melted against the wall, a stunned look on his face. Bette stepped forward, taking my wallet from Malachi's grip. She flicked her eyes to me as she ran fingers lightly over the shiny brass badge.

"I guess you should stay," Bette said, handing me back my badge. "Though, I'm gonna have a few questions for you too when we're done here."

"Agreed," I said, gesturing for her to take a seat. She positioned her chair where she could face Pecks, dropping wearily and rubbing a point of tension between her eyes with her thumb and forefinger.

The agony of witnessing her decline in health combined with the stress of dealing with *this* particular clown shoes set my blood on fire. I stepped closer, a gentle hand on Bette's shoulder.

"I can do this," I offered. She rolled aside and allowed me to take point in the interrogation.

Fun fact: the FBI does not need a warrant to ask questions. I mean, there's always some nuance to that, but the gist was I got to ask all the things. All we're doing is asking questions after all.

The deference to my authority seemed to confuse Pecks. His eyes shifted from Malachi to Bette, then back to me. He came to some conclusion because he laughed in contempt.

"Do I get to see what's in your wallet?"

"We'll be asking the questions, Gregory," Malachi growled, joining Bette in a stance of solidarity. He had his arms crossed and his jaw set in a burning determination. He stood behind her, a towering guardian watching over her shoulder. Pecks rolled his eyes, motioning for Malachi to get on with it. I held up a hand for him to wait and stepped in front of both managers.

I hitched my hip on the counter to face him. The irony was not lost on me that I was in the exact same power position Jake had assumed when he was interrogating me. And Pecks was just as indifferent to my authority as I had been of Jake's.

"Hi, Greg. May I call you Greg?" I asked and looked him in the eye. They were watery grey, not blue as I had first thought. It made him look more like a juiced up weasel and less like Clark Kent.

"It's my name, isn't it?" Pecks squawked.

God, I hate his voice. Like nails on a chalkboard.

"I'd like to ask what happened…" I said, gesturing to the stuffed Santa bag. "But I think it's obvious. Is there anything you'd like to tell us?"

Pecks deliberately lifted his feet back up one at a time, a defiant thunk as his ratty Chuck Taylor's came down on the counter. He tipped his head back, a cocky grin on his face. He shrugged.

"I gotta ask. You work alone?" I pressed on.

Another shrug, another smirk.

"How long has this been going on?"

Another shrug, another smirk.

"What made you decide to do this?"

Another shrug, another smirk.

Bette shifted uncomfortably but kept her peace when Malachi settled a hand on her shoulder. Tension clung to the air as Pecks reclined leisurely in his chair, refusing to answer a single question.

It was smart of him, but infuriating to watch. The pure entitlement, because a part of him knew, just knew, that this would all blow over. He fully expected to get away with it. I'd bet dollars to donuts his dad was a judge or senator or something from his attitude.

"How come this new girl is asking all the questions?" Pecks asked with a sneer. "Cat got your tongue, Dark Lord?"

I leaned toward Pecks, smiling sweetly. He grinned back. I reached out and ripped his feet off the counter with a firm yank. It toppled him off balance, and he fell out of his chair with a heavy *whomp* onto the floor. It took a will of effort not to grin in wild satisfaction at the sound.

"What the fuck?" Pecks snarled in his whiny voice. "Who is this girl? I don't have to put up with this!" He clambered to his feet in outrage, his face red and veins bulging in his neck.

Definitely a juicer, I thought absently as he lumbered towards the door.

Malachi put himself in the frame, taking up all the space like a stalwart giant. "I know you weren't thinking about leaving, were you, Gregory?" Malachi's voice was a low earthquake of menace.

Pecks swallowed and stumbled back toward his chair. He dropped into it, visibly shaken. I snagged a chair and lowered myself until we were eye to eye. I smiled. It was not my inviting smile. It was my I've-caught-a-snake smile. If Pecks had been anything close to smart, he'd have seen it for what it was.

I flipped my badge open, holding it out long enough for Pecks to read. His ruddy cheeks drained of color, melting into a sickly ashy green. "Would you like to try this again?"

"I- I- it's just a little here and there. You know?" He stuttered and stumbled. "They weren't going to miss it!"

"Who wasn't going to miss it?" I asked.

"Look, it's not what it looks like, okay?" Pecks cried. "I mean, yeah, we made copies of movies. But only just for fun. It's all just fun." Words tumbled out of him in a torrent. "At least, it started as fun. Copies for ourselves so we could watch our favorites at home. But then people wanted copies of our copies. So, we started selling them to people to pay for college. She said just until we paid off our student loans. No one would be able to track it if we sold online. So, we got ourselves a site instead of ripping hard copies to disks and tape."

"Who is she?" I asked calmly.

Pecks recoiled, realizing what he'd said, practically sobbing. "No, no. That's not... I didn't mean." He shook his head vehemently. "I didn't mean..."

"Greg, I have to be honest," I interrupted him before he could get his metaphorical feet under him. "We've been looking into your operation for a while now." I decided I was only speaking about the investigation, not my downward spiral into madness that was the last twelve days of Christmas. "You're looking at five years and $250,000. Per criminal count. Per. Count. Maybe more."

Pecks swallowed hard. "What do I do?" he asked, resigned.

"The more you cooperate, the more I can tell my boss. The more I can help you," I explained. He nodded in understanding. "Is this all of it?"

He shook his head, entirely defeated. "Theater thirteen. Our second stash is under the screen. We were moving out the rest of the product today because it's my last day before school starts back." He was likely not going back to school. I wasn't sure he knew that.

Malachi let out a low growling breath of anger, shifting his weight to center himself. Bette's chair squeaked, her own voice sighing in reply. This was probably in their top five worst days ever. All this going on right under their noses.

"Does the name *Key$troker* mean anything to you?" I asked.

Greg flinched and nodded. "It's my handle on Twitch," he confessed. "She said if we used my account… it doesn't matter what she said. You're here, and we're caught."

"Who is she?" I asked again.

Greg looked up, a short spark of rebellion flashing across his features. She was important to him, whoever she was. She'd clearly been the brains, and a small part of me felt a little bad for him. A little. About as far as I could throw him because, dude, don't steal shit.

His face returned to chaotic neutral compliance. He shook his head. I nodded, expecting it. We had hard evidence and testimony to start the ball rolling. I had my suspicions, and it wouldn't be too hard to track down whoever "she" was. Especially once we got Pecks into a real interrogation room. He'd tie a bright red bow into knots just to get a lesser sentence. He was that type.

"Bette, I'd say it's time for me to make that phone call," I said.

"Malachi?" Bette asked, leaning back. Malachi stepped forward, tension in every muscle in his body. She sighed, setting a gentle hand on his forearm, soothing him with a touch. "I'd like you to call our undercover. Then Zoë can call her... boss." She said it with a timber of a question. She looked at me, uncertain. I smiled but knew it didn't quite meet my eyes. Malachi nodded and picked up the phone, dialing and speaking quietly into the receiver.

44

ALL I WANT FOR CHRISTMAS

Less than an hour later, Pecks was in handcuffs. Jake had sauntered into the managers offices with exactly the same bravado he had when he arrested me. He'd expressed the same confusion and surprise, ceding to my authority only after careful inspection of my badge and a phone call from his own commanding officer. I felt all kinds of validation.

Mike Cassidy had berated me over the phone for interviewing our suspect without any other officers present. He'd been loud enough that Malachi had drifted closer, as though he could fight Mike on my behalf. I rolled my eyes at the testosterone display, barely listening as Mike threatened retaliation if my meddling fouled up *his* investigation.

I just barely managed not to snap back at him in front of Bette and Malachi, but barely. I had cracked the case. The case we had been working on as a department nationwide for months. In his mind, it had taken me a day. And his small brain couldn't comprehend it. What he didn't know wouldn't kill him.

Pecks's locker had been thoroughly explored, and surprisingly, we had discovered the missing booth log pages with coded notes between himself and Lyssa. We had our suspect for our accomplice. An accomplice who liked to detail her plans in writing and give explicit instructions to her partner. And for some reason, rather than destroy the evidence, Pecks had kept it. Sometimes, criminals really were that dumb. After Christmas, if I made it that far, I'd get a warrant to bring Lyssa in for questioning.

The booth pages were photographed in the manager's office, and the second stash under the screen in thirteen was catalogued as well before being transferred into the trunk of Jake's Crown Vic. Pecks would rot in the county lock up for a day, or several, while our superiors haggled over jurisdiction.

I'd made it halfway to my borrowed car when Malachi joined me at a jog. "I guess this is your first and last day," he teased, as he walked me toward the glass doors at the back of the theater. "If you really are in a time-loop, did you know this was going to happen?"

I sucked in a breath. "No. This would be my first time."

He nodded, relieved. As if I had confirmed something for him. "It's unfortunate. I was really enjoying getting to know you."

"Me too," I agreed.

"Is it inappropriate for you to come to the staff party tonight?" he asked, scuffing a boot into the carpet, his eyes looking anywhere but mine.

"I want to," I said sincerely, stopping to look at him. His gaze was fixed on his boots. By some unfair miracle, he was still as pressed and polished as he had been that morning. Still smelling faintly of orange blossom and cinnamon.

Meanwhile, I reeked of theater body and salt. Even changing into my Christmas Things shirt and dousing myself in the Halia's mango vanilla lotion had done absolutely nothing to get the burnt popcorn smell out of my nose. "But…"

My case was solved. I'd made it to the end of my day. I was about to make it to tomorrow, then I'd be heading home on the first flight. They had all the evidence they needed to arrest Lyssa. It was unlikely I'd have another shift. Again, if I made it to tomorrow.

I was *really* looking forward to tomorrow.

"But…" he trailed, lifting his eyes to meet mine. There was so much hope in them. It made my heart ache. What if, just this once, I truly let go of all the things I was supposed to do and just let things play out.

Believe, a voice whispered in the back of my mind. It sounded a lot like my mother.

"I think I need to go say Merry Christmas to my mom," I hedged.

"Of course," Malachi said, disappointment flashing briefly across his face before he smiled warmly. The understanding in his eyes gutted me. "Family is everything."

"Will you tell Halia where I went so she doesn't worry?" I asked. He nodded crisply.

"Thank you."

45

VIEW FROM THE BRIDGE

It was a little late, and the traffic had all gone home to set out cookies for Santa or get out of the snow. Me? I was the idiot on the bridge.

It wasn't a particularly dangerous bridge. Just a regular old truss bridge sleeping over the dark ribbon of river. But when the winter winds hit it just right, like they were tonight, it was an icy bridge.

I pulled my navy blue peacoat tighter, wondering who gave it to me all those years ago at the party. The party I fought with my best friend at. The party where my mom came to save me from my own ill intentions, only to wreck on this very bridge.

"Hey." Halia's voice carried over the quiet fall of snow. I turned to see her parked, illegally, on the bridge beside me. I doubted anyone would care. Maybe the snowplows if they even came this way.

"Hey," I said. Halia zipped her Columbia coat to her throat and popped her fur lined hood over her hair. Her wipers brushed snowfall away in metronomic consistency on the waiting vehicle.

"Malachi said I might find you here," she began.

"What?"

"He said you were going to wish your mom Merry Christmas," she said. "I figured that meant the bridge."

"I just needed some air," I assured her.

"So, you're not really home," she said sadly. "You're undercover."

"I was. Cover's blown. But that couldn't be helped."

"Bette said you helped catch a pirate."

"Pecks," I told her. "He'd been stealing films and selling copies online to pay for college."

"That tracks." Halia nodded. "He's been super weird about getting shifts on Thursday night assembly for months."

"Sorry, I know you liked him," I said.

Halia made a face. "I'm nice to everyone. You know that."

"I do," I agreed. "Pretty sure Lyssa is his accomplice."

"What makes you say that?"

I could tell her. That I'd seen them together in strange places and the way they behaved at the staff party. The party we were currently missing because, you know, priorities. But everything was nearly done. Two hours, and it would be tomorrow. If I made it, I'd be done. Twelve days. I didn't really want to risk all the good.

"I'm really good at my job," I finally said.

She nodded, pensive, and folded her arms over the railing. She rubbed her arms for warmth with gloved fingers. We stood in silence, snow building a thin blanket over us as we contemplated the blue-black river below.

"I'm sorry about your mom," she finally said. I sucked in a breath. "I shouldn't have called her. Then maybe —"

"Stop," I commanded, turning toward her. "It was the right thing to do. I was out of line. She needed to be called."

Tears frosted on her soft brown cheeks. She started to speak, and I pulled her into an embrace. "It was not your fault, Halia."

"I just wanted you to be safe," she hiccuped, wrapping her arms around me in a deep embrace. "I'm pretty sure Jake spiked your drink. He'd been bragging about how he was going to score on you all day."

"Considering how little I remember of that night, including when my dad came to get me from the party… I'd say you were right."

"He was always a vile waste of carbon," she sniffed.

"Complete waste," I agreed. "I hope you forgive me for abandoning you all this time. I've been a lousy friend."

"Real lousy," she laughed. "But I forgive you. If you forgive me?"

I hugged her tighter, kissing the top of her forehead. "There is nothing to forgive," I insisted. We held our embrace to its natural conclusion, reluctantly pulling apart and returning to our vigil over the river.

"I want to be friends again," I said softly, as the snow drifted in lazy wisps.

"We never stopped being friends," she said, squeezing my hand firmly. "I should probably tell Malachi he can go home. I'll just catch a ride with you if you want to stay out here longer."

I blinked in surprise, turning back to the bridge. Standing next to the SUV, waiting, was the Dark Lord. He had a double breasted navy blue peacoat buttoned up over his broad shoulders. His night dark hair curled ever so slightly as the snow began to dampen it. He offered a reserved smile.

"Oh my god, it was him," I said.

46

LET IT SNOW

"What was him?" Halia asked. I gestured for Malachi to join us. He checked for traffic and then stomped through the snow in three easy strides.

"You ladies picked a hell of a place to have a circle of forgiveness party," Malachi commented dryly. There was tenderness in his voice, a warm glimmer in his amber eyes.

"It was you," I whispered. Malachi went still as a statue, the sudden and complete stillness almost unnatural. "My guardian, all those years ago."

"I'll just… wait in the car," Halia offered, dusting off her shoulders and making her way back. She smiled at us before disappearing inside the warm embrace of the running vehicle. The hazards blinked gold and red like a holiday display.

"This is your coat, isn't it?" I tugged on the lapels of the Marine issued peacoat. Malachi finally breathed. I only noticed because he had apparently been holding his breath.

"Yes," he replied softly. "I was back on leave for Christmas. Caught hell from my CO for losing my coat." Malachi grinned, this time it made it to his eyes. "Seemed like a fair trade in my book."

"Why?"

"Wes had gone to a party and was having a downer of a time. Asked if I could come get him," he began. "I realized whose house he was at as soon as I crossed the bridge. I don't know why he went. I walked in just in time to see you and Halia fight. I watched Jake follow you and I stepped between you."

"But why?" I couldn't wrap my fried brain around it. He didn't know me, didn't owe me anything at all back then.

"Jake has always been a jerk. But in high school, he was also incredibly impulsive and stupid. Entitled," Malachi said.

"I'm not sure he's improved much," I commented. His mouth quirked, but he remained solemn.

"Yeah, well. Jake and I are peers," Malachi continued. "We were in nearly all the same classes from freshman year on. I got to see his game play in real time. He never valued anything he had. Never had to work for it. I went into the Marines after graduation to pay for college. He just continued spending Daddy's money, refusing to grow up." He paused, leaning against the railing as if considering what to say next.

"That still doesn't answer my question," I pushed. "Why did you decide to step in?"

"If I'm being honest…" Malachi flushed, looking out over the river rather than at my face. "I might have had a mild crush on you. I hated that you were with him."

I barely caught myself before my mouth ran away with my self-righteous need to be an independent woman. No one else was saving me that night, least of all myself. If the Dark Lord wanted to rescue me, even from myself, because he had a crush? Well, I just needed to say thank you.

"It wasn't the only reason," he insisted, correctly reading my expression. "I'd have stepped between Jake and any girl that night. Even if you never knew it was me. I wasn't going to let him hurt you."

I didn't know what compelled me. Maybe the night. Maybe the last twelve days of cycling through repetitive days that never seemed to end. Maybe it was the right time and place. Maybe all the stars aligned. Maybe it was because I *really* wanted to.

I reached up and kissed him. He was tall enough I had to stand on tiptoes to reach. I rose up, arms snaking around his neck, fingers weaving into his hair. His lips were soft and warm, damp from licking off snow. He tasted like spiced cake and sugar. *God, I hope I taste anywhere close to as delicious,* my primary cortex hoped.

Malachi must have been startled because it took him a moment before he responded. One hand grasped my hip, the other tangled in my snow wet curls as he pulled my body against his. I felt my insides go liquid as fire coursed through my veins. Our breaths came in desperate rapid gasps.

I pressed tighter against him, hungry in the kiss. The air felt warm, a current of energy drifting through the snowflakes as we explored each other's bodies through kisses and traveling fingers. As though the barrier that had been holding us apart finally crashed to the ground.

A horn blared, and we startled apart. "It's about damn time!" Halia shouted. I looked over my shoulder. An inch of snow had coated her little SUV. She had her head half out the window as she flashed the headlights at us. She honked the horn again in celebration.

Malachi and I fell into laughter. He pulled me back for another kiss, softer this time. Inviting and patient. A tenderness so deep I shuddered. His arms held me firm, his warmth wrapping around me until I was dizzy. I'll tell you one thing, Malachi knew how to kiss. Malachi knew how to do a lot of things well.

He finally pulled his lips free, holding us together tenderly with his forehead pressed against mine. Clouds of mist billowed around our heads as our breath met the cold air in ragged pants.

"I have wanted to do that for a very long time," I sighed.

He blinked, tilting his head to one side. "Really?"

"I…" I laughed, nestling my nose against his chest. *Orange blossoms and cinnamon.* "Much longer than you know."

A distinctive *whoop-whoop* siren broke into our moment. I nearly growled at it until I realized a police cruiser had pulled up behind Halia, painting the snowy bridge in red and blue safety lights. The officer stepped out, a long white braid peeking out from under her red stocking cap.

"Alright, folks, what are you doing on the bridge? Can't you people see there's a blizzard?" the officer called over her microphone, a thick East Coast accent.

I shielded my eyes with a hand, peering through the falling snow and blazing headlights. "Mary Christmas?"

"And a merry Christmas to you, too, young lady," Mary said. "You folks need to come down from there. Before anyone makes any choices they'll regret." Sometime between the last time I'd seen her at Figgy Pudding and today, she had morphed from vaguely British Faery Queen into a Boston townie. So, that happened.

"It's my fault, Officer." Halia had exited the SUV, attempting to draw the attention to herself. "I parked us on the bridge."

"You stay with the car, ma'am. And you two! Get your feet on the ground, before I have to take you all into the clink," Mary threatened.

"To the what?" I couldn't believe this wicked winter faery was ruining my one day where I was finally, truthfully, feeling what Christmas could be. Wasn't this exactly what she wanted from me?

"We're coming, Officer," Malachi assured Mary. He offered me his hand to get down. I made the little hop down and we returned to the SUV.

"That's better," Mary clucked like a mother hen. "It's Christmas Eve!" She chastised.

"And has been for twelve damned days," I snapped.

Mary grinned. "And a partridge in a pear tree to you as well, miss." She climbed back into her vehicle, a final *whoop-whoop* as she raced off the bridge and out of sight.

"Well, that was almost the weirdest thing to happen today," Malachi said.

"Almost the weirdest," I laughed.

"Almost," Halia agreed.

I leaned back to admire Malachi's cognac eyes and marble cut jaw. Snowflakes clung to his eyelashes. "So… if you were in a time-loop, what would you do?"

"*Groundhog Day* or *It's a Wonderful Life*?" Malachi asked immediately.

"Well, with a nickname like Zuzu," Halia teased.

Malachi smiled broadly. "I'd find the people I loved most, and make sure they knew how I felt about them."

Marry me, I thought. "You know, in my family, it's tradition to watch *It's a Wonderful Life* on Christmas Eve."

"You're kidding," he said.

"Every year," I said.

His smile would have melted the arctic circle. I certainly became a puddle of feelings. "It's tradition in my family too," he said softly.

"Would you maybe like to watch it with me tonight?" I asked.

"I think I'm in love," he laughed, kissing me once more.

"Get a room," Halia coughed into her hand.

I smiled from the depths of my soul, leaning into the kiss, not caring about anything but this moment. I didn't even care if I made it to tomorrow.

This moment, this kiss, this was everything.

47

ZUZU'S PETALS

When we arrived at the Gatsby House, Malachi escorted me discreetly up the stairs. The door snicked shut behind him, the muffled chaos of the party falling away beyond the walls. He leaned against the door for a long moment, watching me. We were as close as we had been on the bridge. He tucked a loose hair out of my eyes, sweeping the stubborn tendril behind my ear. His touch sent butterflies fluttering through my stomach, and I shivered.

"Hi," he said

"Hi."

"So…"

"So…" I realized suddenly he was nervous. *Well, that makes two of us, sir,* I laughed internally. "Movie?"

He sucked in a breath and sighed in relief with something to do. "Movie, right."

He hurried to his computer, fingers flying as fast as any hacker as he closed windows and typed commands. While he worked, I got comfortable, kicking off my shoes under the bench and unbuttoning my coat. Before I could decide where to stash it, Malachi reached out and took it from my hand. He dropped our matching peacoats on the back of his computer chair.

He had taken off his work shirt in the minute or so I had been distracted and replaced it with a graphic tee. It was an amalgamation of the iconic Beatles Abby Road crosswalk, Ghost Busters, and Stranger Things crew. It was not a casual Hot Topic or Amazon find. He'd had that shirt custom made. And I loved it.

He noticed my own Disney Christmas Things shirt at almost the exact moment I noticed his. His wry smile broke into a broad grin. I grinned back until we both fell into a fit of laughter. The joy brought us closer together until our fingers found each other again and our mouths came together laughing.

His strong arms gathered me close, and I tucked in tight against him. I felt the heat rush through my body until I started giggling again.

"You're a nerd," I said, kissing the strong line of his jaw.

"So are you," he retorted, nipping gently at my ear. He lifted his head to look at me, fire and desire glowing in his eyes. It made my whole body shudder with an electric jolt. "Are you cold?"

"Oh, it is not the weather that is giving me shivers," I laughed.

He rubbed my arms anyway, pulling me toward the backless bench. He snatched up his red cable knit blanket he had neatly folded there, wrapping it around my shoulders.

"So…"

"So…" He kissed the top of my head. "Movie?" He asked.

"Movie," I nodded.

"Bench or…"

He gestured to the two spots one might watch a movie with

someone. The backless bench or the queen sized bed. It might be big enough for him by himself, but the two of us, as tall as we both were, the bed would be cozy.

"Bed," I decided. Two hours on a hard boned bench sounded unappealing for any occasion. Not to mention any cuddling or other activities that could arise.

Malachi set his computer at the foot of the bed and pressed spacebar. The Pass & Stow bell began to gong followed by the orchestral melody of *Buffalo Gals*. The peppy music faded into a chorus of prayers for George Bailey and the sound of falling snow as we settled into watch, stuffing pillows behind our backs.

A wave of emotion slammed into me as little Zuzu begged God to bring her daddy back. Tears welled behind my eyes and rolled down my cheeks. My breath hitched and my shoulders trembled as I struggled to keep it together.

"Are you okay?" he asked, shifting to see my face.

"Oh, I'm fine," I lied. "It's just…"

He had a tissue box in hand and was helping me blot away tears. It was just a stupid box of tissue, and it made me cry harder.

"We don't have to stay here if you don't want to." Of course he could tell I was not fine, because he was Malachi.

"No, it's not that! It's just… I haven't watched this movie since my mom…" I took a steading breath, wiping away a rogue tear and the hot mess of my nose crying had started. I tried again. "I haven't watched this movie since my mom died."

He hit the spacebar and paused the movie in the middle of blinking stars discussing how to help George Bailey. "We don't have to watch a movie at all," he said softly, offering me a fresh tissue. "Your company is more than enough. We can go back to the party if you prefer."

"I'd like to stay here. Finish one Christmas, if that's alright with you."

He tilted his head, puzzled. He still didn't quite believe this was my twelfth Christmas Eve this year. He didn't know it had been ten years since I'd had any Christmas at all. But tonight, if only for tonight, I really wanted to just believe that it was all going to be okay.

He settled back against the headboard and patted the open space beside him. "Come here," he said with one arm open to invite me to nestle in. I wiggled until I got comfortable. He wrapped an arm behind my back as he pulled me into the warmth of his body. I rested my head on his chest. He used his toe to press the spacebar and restart the film.

I woke up to the sound of little Zuzu's voice, the adorable chime of a bell reminding us how an angel got their wings. The black and white film continued rolling on Malachi's laptop. Had I fallen asleep? Malachi had propped us in the corner of the wall and the bed. He was sound asleep. I was hugged against his chest, the red blanket draped over our legs. I snuggled closer. Absently, he tightened his arms around me protectively.

"Merry Christmas," a gentle voice whispered.

My eyes snapped open, and my heart rate spiked to unsafe levels. "Mary?"

She was in her favorite naughty red dress, her bare feet kicked up on her green coat at the foot of the bed. She pushed aside Malachi's laptop.

"Well, who else would it be, my girl?" She tsked and shook her head with a smile.

"How did you get in here?" I asked. She started to speak, but I waved her off. "I know. Magic." I sighed and blinked sleep from my eyes, careful not to disturb Malachi as I detangled us and sat up.

She watched the sleeping Malachi, a grin spreading across her powdery face. Her white teeth gleamed in the light of the laptop, blue eyes glittering in delight. "Hang on to this one," she suggested. "He certainly believes in magic."

I rolled my eyes and slipped off the bed behind her.

"You did it. I'm so proud of you." She set aside the laptop and slid off the bed, slipping her feet back into her black boots.

"What did I do?" I demanded in a whisper.

"Oh, my girl." She draped her green coat over one arm, tossing long white curls over her shoulder. "You learned to believe in the magic of Christmas."

"I didn't do anything different. I've always—"

"You most certainly did so." Mary huffed in indignation. "For years, you've positively *raged* at Christmas. As if the holiday itself were responsible for your life problems."

"I've always believed in the magic of Christmas," I insisted.

Mary gave me a hard look.

"I just didn't think I deserved it."

Understanding seemed to settle over Mary. She dropped her coat on the ground and put one hand on each of my shoulders. "You listen to me, Zoë Marie Bly. Everyone deserves a little magic. Christmas is just a time and place to embrace the ones we love. To look to the stars and say thank you for this life."

I couldn't bring myself to look her in the eye. I was thankful, but so much had happened. A million memories swirled together. Some of it had happened, some of it hadn't. And I had to move forward with all of it. The bad and the good.

"We cannot see the light without the darkness," Mary said, somehow responding to my thoughts. She cupped my cheek with her hand. It was warm and soft. I leaned into her touch, and she brushed aside a tear with her thumb. "But you, my dear, will be just fine." She released me and headed toward the door.

"Did I make it? Did I escape the curse?"

Mary paused, one hand on the door knob, a knowing smile on her brightly painted red lips. "Oh, my dear girl. It was never a curse. It was simply an opportunity. And you did marvelously."

"But—"

"And yes. You broke the curse the way most curses are broken. With a kiss."

I glanced at the bed. Malachi slept, peacefully unaware of the faery queen showdown going on in his room.

"Oh, no. Not that kiss. Though, it was deliciously fun to watch you greedily take bites of one another," Mary chuckled.

"What kiss? I didn't kiss anyone but Malachi."

Had I? I mean, there was a whole lot of missing data between my first day on the job and the twelfth day of Christmas. There had been drinking and magic circles, outright insubordination, too. Had there been kissing?

Mary raised her eyebrows in a graceful arch. "When you forgave your friend, when you forgave yourself. That was the true magic, my dear."

I had given Halia a kiss of friendship, of true unconditional love to say I was sorry. Malachi had been an intoxicating kiss of perfection, but love? It was too new to know. Halia was and would always be my best friend in the world. My sister. A true love that would travel beyond time and places. And suddenly, I understood what Mary had been trying to do to me all this time.

It was only three quick steps across the floor before I reached her. I threw my arms around the batty old lady and crushed her into a hug. She smelled of cookies and hot chocolate. And reminded me of my mother.

"Thank you, Fairy Godmother," I said. I felt her soften and wrap her own arms around me.

"You are most welcome, child."

48

EVERY TIME A BELL RINGS

The sound of my "Jingle Bells" ringtone startled me awake.

No. *No.* Absolutely not. I had made it. I had done all the right things. Mary Christmas said I broke the curse. Why was it all—

"Good morning," a husky baritone of a voice said.

I cracked my eyes open. A pale golden glimmer leaked through the edges of the blinds and washed the room in a delicate light. I was warmly tucked into a bed in my Christmas Things shirt and USMC sweats that did not belong to me.

I collapsed into the world's most perfect pillows. Pillows that smelled like him. It was morning. I was still in Malachi's room.

I started crying.

Malachi stiffened, holding a tray with two steaming mugs and a plate of bagels and toppings. Worry creased his handsome face, frozen mid-stride, waiting for clarification.

"What's wrong?"

"Nothing, it's nothing." I flailed out of the bed and dove for my bag, furiously digging for my phone to quiet that screaming gremlin. I silenced the phone and dropped it on the floor with a sigh of relief. "Bad dream," I said with another weighted breath.

Malachi resumed his approach, folding his long legs under him and gracefully sinking to the floor beside me. He carefully settled the tray in front of us, then turned to face me. He reached out, gently wiping a stray tear away with his thumb. "Are you sure?" he asked, looking me solemnly in the eyes.

Nervously, I dropped my gaze to the tray between us. It was easy to spot the cup clearly meant for me. The one with all the creamy, sugary, swirling mouthfuls of deliciousness. I stared at it for a long moment, lost in thought.

"Zoë?" he asked gently, drawing my attention back to his face with a finger under my chin.

"You remember last night on the bridge when I asked you what you would do if you were in a time-loop?"

He laughed. "Yes. That's how we ended up here," he said, gesturing around his room.

"Right, well, what if I'd been serious?" His expression sobered, and his eyes searched my face.

I didn't have to guess how I might look. I was as serious as a chemistry test.

"Oh," he said in surprise. "Oh, you mean for real."

I nodded.

He exhaled a deep breath. So, I told him. Everything. Starting with the first whack-a-do day that ended with me and Mrs. Claus drinking tequila and eating nachos. And the second day where I got arrested. The fight with Halia. The magic circle. Even the part where I suspected him. All of it.

Every repeat all the way to the twelfth day where he and I caught Pecks. The final night where we were all on the bridge and I'd kissed him for the first time. Where Mary Christmas, and Halia for that matter, had purposefully interrupted us.

At some point, Malachi had claimed his coffee. Mine sat untouched on the tray. His was cradled in his hands, empty. When I finished talking, he set down his cup, stood, and paced around his room.

He paused every so often and made a gesture, working through his internal narrative in mumbled silence. After a long moment, he returned to the bed, offering me his hands and pulling me to my feet.

"I don't care," he said.

"What?"

"Time-loop, bad dream, good dream," he shrugged. "I don't care. Whatever happened ended with you here with me, that's what I care about."

"Even if it makes me sound crazy?" It was high on my to-do list to see a licensed therapist. Maybe a psychologist.

"You like your coffee with cream and sugar, right? Like, a lot of both?" He reached down, picked up my mug, and held it out to me. Through some sort of trickery, it was still warm.

I sipped and sighed. "Yes, it's perfect."

"How would I know that?"

Now, how did *he know to do that?* Sure, day one, day two even, he'd watched me make my coffee. Teased me about my milkshake parading as coffee. But after that?

My brain spiraled down a rabbit hole, wondering if maybe I hadn't been alone in my train wreck of a Christmas. "Are you in a time-loop?"

"No, no I'm not. At least, I don't think so," he hedged. "My point is that I knew. When I was making coffee downstairs, I just knew. Why would I know that?"

"Maybe some part of you remembers the twelve days too," I suggested.

He nodded and guided me to sit on the bed. It was comfy with just the right amount of support and softness. The blankets were a silken mess from the two of us sleeping. It was the most inviting thing I could think of at that moment, falling back into his perfect pillows and sleeping more.

"Maybe that's why all I can think about is this." Malachi interrupted my plans to sleep by pulling me to him, pressing his mouth to mine. My lips parted and welcomed his kiss with equal hunger. Heat shot through my veins like a wild storm, thrashing through my core until it was molten.

He carefully removed my coffee mug from my hands, setting it aside without ever taking his mouth off mine. I wrapped my arms around him in breathless bliss. His strong arm snaked around my waist and laid me down.

That's one way to snuggle into that perfect pillow, I thought with delight, only to be rewarded for my wisecrack by the banshee screech of "Jingle Bells." I cringed. "Sorry, that's mine."

Malachi laughed, ducking his head into my shoulder while his long arm reached blindly to the floor beside the bed.

"If it's my boss, tell him I quit," I said. He must have found the phone but instead of silencing it, he raised it for me to look at the call screen.

"It's my dad."

"Go ahead, answer it," he said softly, pressing his hands into the bed to lift his body off of mine. He nipped my nose with a kiss and rolled off the bed, striding to his computer to give me some privacy. I pressed answer.

"Hi, Dad."

"Merry Christmas!" my father said brightly. A clatter of something falling crashed through receiver. I jerked my ear away.

"Dad?!"

"I'm alright. Just knocked a bowl of carrots to the ground." He grunted as he presumably hurried to pick it back up.

"Are you cooking?" I didn't have many memories of him cooking. Mom had been the cook. After she died, it had been casseroles from the local Rotary Food Train club. Take out Tuesday had become a staple just to have something other than tuna fish.

"Sure! I'm getting pretty good, but this is a potluck Christmas. Lots of people need somewhere to go... I have this big house. It's a shame to not fill it with love."

I'd forgotten he did those. Mary Christmas had shown me and I'd already forgotten. How easy it was to forget people had lives outside of our own. That they continued to live when you weren't right there living beside them. The memory wrapped its greedy little fingers around my heartstrings and pulled.

Not gonna cry. Not gonna cry. I sighed. "Yeah, people need somewhere to go for Christmas."

"How's my Zuzu?" my dad asked.

I watched Malachi as his own fingers flew across his keyboard. He looked over his shoulder, head tilted in a question. I knew what he was thinking. Had I seen the game before? I nodded with a smile and thumbs up. It was going to be a great game when he finished it. He grinned and tapped a key to make the cinematic roll again.

"I'm really good, Dad."

"You sure? You're not just eating take out tonight in that lonely little apartment?"

"Dad!" I protested. "It's a *cozy* little apartment."

"Not if you're the only person there, Zoë," he said stubbornly. "Christmas is supposed to be a time to be with people. It doesn't have to be me. I understand why. I just wish you'd spend some time with people outside of that building."

I had hurt him. All the years, I'd ignored him. Not because he was a bad dad. He was a great dad. But I had been running away so hard I'd forgotten to see what was waiting for me at home.

"Dad?" I asked softly.

"Yes, Zuzu?"

"I'm in town, and I have this friend…" Malachi turned at my tone. Humor tugged at the corner of his lips. 'Friend' was a subjective term for the path we were treading. His eyes sparked with lightning and whiskey. A heady feeling washed over me, and I felt a tingle from my head to my toes. "Do you have room for two more?"

49

OVER THE RIVER

My family home was in the middle of a block that took Christmas *very* seriously.

The average home had a well-manicured yard, bursting with snow drifts and glittering themed lights. Rudolph and Frosty frolicked between candy canes and sweeping arches of light. Every house was expected to participate, to some degree or another.

It was not uncommon growing up to have caravans of cars cruising through the neighborhood at all hours of the night. Eventually, the city put in an ordinance that allowed people to walk the block, but limited actual vehicle traffic to residence only. Which was why we had to park near the elementary school and hoof it all the way back through the snow.

Anchored in the middle of the block sat two warring holiday houses. One modern IKEA flat-pack turned McMansion was covered with millions of perfectly symmetrical lights. Military perfect patterns gave the overall impression that the holiday had been hand-picked and shipped over by Amazon.

The contrasting gingerbread Victorian house across the street had bows of fir and ribbons of red twisting around every arch, tree, limb, and rail in sight. There was a to-scale sleigh, complete with eight reindeer and a life-like Santa, perched precariously over the roof in take-off positions. The yard held giant glowing spheres of ice cut to look like oversized snow globes. The glittering garlands of light mimicked the stars. A true holiday spectacular.

I shuddered to think what the electric bill for the block was every year.

Malachi, bless him, trudged beside me in quiet solidarity. His hand would periodically reach out to steady me when my shoe would slip on ice.

"I told Halia heels were a stupid idea," I groused.

Malachi chuckled softly. I had allowed Halia to dress me in one of her sleeveless Audrey Hepburn pieces. A red with black lace number, complete with festive embroidery in varying degrees of ugly sweater that still somehow managed to be chic. There was even a clock stitched at five minutes to midnight. I'd growled at the insufferable thing. Malachi's face had lit up like a kid on Christmas morning when he saw it.

"I know women don't like to be told they're adorable," he said. "But that dress is absolutely charming on you."

He was so damned good at just *noticing* me. It scared the hell out of me. It also melted my insides to liquid fire, turned my knees into mushy blobs of goo. You know, balance.

At that exact thought, I tripped on a tricky patch of road. Malachi caught me around the waist without even missing a step. He guided me up the front steps, allowing me to walk the last few on my own. I didn't know why I was so nervous to knock on the door. But there I was, arm raised, hand closed in a fist to rap on the door. And I hesitated.

"Are you okay?" Malachi asked.

Over my shoulder, he stood with a box of treats and a bottle of wine. He was wearing his Navy coat and black jeans. He'd wrapped his lean muscles in a green Aran cable knit sweater that made most women start drooling and fantasizing about Highland Games.

Stop it, Zoë, I scolded myself. If I'd wanted to play, I should have stayed in bed. Instead, I was here in the cold pretending twelve days hadn't just repeated themselves. Ready to see my dad and have a real Christmas. But I was a bad daughter. I'd run away and never faced the hard truths. Truths Mary Christmas had forced me to revisit. *Rotten, meddling faery.* If I was honest with myself, I was terrified.

I reluctantly nodded. "It's just been… a while," I said with a resolute sigh.

Malachi took the last step and crossed the freshly shoveled porch in one easy stride. He rested his free hand against my hip and buried his lips in my hair. His warm breath tickled my ear and sent a delicious shiver down my spine. "You don't have to do anything you don't want to."

"I know," I said softly, turning my head enough to find his mouth with my own. But before I could claim his lips, the door burst open with a mighty force.

"If you two are finished necking, the cider could use a fresh toddy," Mary Christmas tsked.

I whipped my head forward so fast I'm almost certain the bones in my neck cracked. "Mary?"

There she was. Perfectly ridiculous in her utterly fabulous red cocktail dress, the garish gold reindeer belt and black boots no sane women should be wearing on icy walkways. I speak from personal experience.

"Well, don't just stand there in the cold," she scolded. "Come and give your godmother a squdge."

She held open lace covered arms, her arctic blue eyes twinkling in the waning sunlight. Before I could gather my jaw off the floor, Mary had me in a crushing embrace. She smelled pleasantly of cookies and popcorn, of all things.

"You must be Malachi," she said over my shoulder. "Lovely to meet you. Shall we?"

Without waiting for a reply she swept us both over the threshold and into the house. She tugged me out of my coat and flung it against the coat rack. By some sorcery, it settled magically on a hook. Malachi tilted his head to the side curiously and slung his coat on the hook next to mine.

"What are you doing here?" I asked when I finally was able to get my brain back in alignment. "I thought–"

"Would I ever miss your father's Christmas dinner?" She pish-poshed me, dragging me into the chaos of strangers. "It was this or dinner with Mrs. Nesbitt. You know how I feel about her."

"Mrs. Nesbitt?" I had vague memories of a deplorable woman who loved to terrorize children and harass adults about ordinances as if we were in a proper HOA. Which we were not, but that didn't stop the busy body from melding.

"I believe your word for her would be Cascade Karen," Mary said distractedly. The nasty woman who wanted four tickets flashed in my mind. *No way!*

"Everyone, Zoë's here!" Mary announced, drawing me back to the moment. "Someone find David."

The house looked exactly as it had when Mary had showed it to me in… a dream, I suppose. The long table with my mother's mismatched china was full of people I'd never met. People my father knew from one walk of life or another. They laughed and teased, enjoying each other's company and the seasonal festivity with casual joy. My father was not among the strangers. It shot a pang of sadness right into my gut as their cheers crescendoed in greeting.

"Just put those anywhere in the kitchen, kind sir," Mary ordered Malachi, who obediently snaked through the crowd to deposit the wine and cookies he had brought.

"You look absolutely ravishing, my dear," Mary continued on. "The holidays can be such a drain on one's energy. You must learn to protect yourself or time will just get away from you."

Seriously? I opened my mouth to blast the rotten fairy with whatever damage my words could do.

"Hello, Zoë," the velvety bass of my father's voice floated through the ambient sounds of Christmas dinner.

He looked exactly like I remembered. His eyes were the same Kelly green of a shamrock as my own. He'd grown his beard, an annual tradition starting November 1st where he raised funds for the local library. He looked more like Santa today than he had when I was a child, white threading through his beard and full head of hair.

He wove through the crowded space and pulled me toward him, wrapping strong arms around me in a firm embrace. I returned the favor, twining my own arms around his waist. I was afraid to let go.

"I missed you, Zoë," he murmured.

"I missed you too, Dad," I replied. "I'm so sorry for all the time we've missed. I should have come home sooner."

"You're here now," he said. A tear escaped his beautiful green eyes. I reached to wipe it away. He leaned his cheek into my hand.

"We have a lot to catch up on."

"Yes, we do," he agreed. "I want to hear all about the other Washington, work, life… love?" He must have noticed I was alone because he suddenly looked around as if someone were missing. "Where's your friend?"

I searched unfamiliar faces for Malachi and spotted him near the fire place, talking to Mary. She had a box of cookies. My insides coiled into knots.

"Excuse me."

I briskly rushed through the crowd, weaving like a ribbon between people. Mary popped the tin lid free, a golden glow shining like a beacon, the cookies glittering like fireflies.

"I promise, you've never had anything–"

I snatched the cookies out of Mary's hands before she could finish her sentence and tossed the lot of them into the fire, Christmas tin and all. The waxy paper and powdery dough burst into a multitude of colorful flames. The flimsy metal began to warp. I dusted the surgery crystals from my hand, satisfied in their destruction. *Those were no ordinary cookies.*

"Well, that was unexpected," Malachi said, eyebrows raised, amusement on his lips.

"Hands down the worst cookies in existence," I grumbled.

"Zoë!" My father balked at my vehemence. "Is that anyway to treat your godmother?" My father had found us and was staring in horror at the burning pile of wasted sugar and twisted metal.

"Come now, David, I can always make more." Mary smiled wickedly.

"Absolutely not," I growled. "You will not be giving anyone here cookies today. Is that clear?"

Malachi tilted his head as though it might help him see better. He looked from Mary to me and back again. Sudden understanding had him grinning like a fool.

"I don't know," Malachi said. "Her cookies got all of us to the same place at the same time. Maybe they were just the right sort of magic."

I blinked at him several times. My head swam with overlapping memories that threatened to overwhelm me. Malachi laced his fingers through mine, gently calling me back to myself. He leaned in, touching his forehead to my own so I could just breathe. I nodded, inhaling the precious citrus and cinnamon I'd come to associate with him. Warm and gentle.

It was true, the cookies had started with a nightmare. But they also ended with my true friends and family. Still…

"Next time, I'm making the cookies," I said stubbornly.

The End

MRS. CLAUS' CHRISTMAS COOKIE

A 3-ingredient shortbread.
Will not trap you in a time loop. Probably.

❄ 2 Cups Butter ❄ 1 Cup Brown Sugar ❄ 4 1/2 Cups Flour ❄
❄ OPTIONAL: 1-2 TSP ground nutmeg ❄

Directions: 1) In a large bowl, combine the butter & sugar until creamy. 2) Add 3 1/2 C flour & mix until well combined. 3) Scrape sides of bowl onto a board and knead by hand. Add flour a little at a time until play dough consistency. It is ok to not use all the flour. Stop adding flour when it is soft but not sticky. 4) Chill dough for 20 minutes. I recommend you chill the bake sheet. 5) Preheat oven to 325º while dough chills. 6) Form dough into balls or 1/2" discs & set on a lightly greased bake sheet. 7) Bake 15 - 20 minutes or until edges start to crisp for a soft center. 8) Cool to serve.

❄ Enjoy! ❄

ACKNOWLEDEGMENTS

This is the part where I tell you everyone who helped make this novel possible.

It has been a long, arduous journey to publication. I started writing during my chemotherapy treatments because I needed to find the joy in Christmas. I used voice to text on my phone and then spent the next four years recovering and working a little bit at a time.

To my husband Collin, for carrying our family when I couldn't. For supporting me through this process even when book girlies sometimes confused you. And for sticking by me through chemo, writing, resting, and recovery. That may seem like a given but it's not and I want to say thank you. I could never have done it without your love and support.

To the doctors at Cancer Care Northwest who walked me through each step of the process with understanding and empathy. To the nurses at Cancer Care Northwest who hooked me up with sweet treats and cozy blankets while I sat through day long sessions of chemotherapy. Your team saved my life.

To my friends who have listened to me talk about this story for a long time now, read early drafts, have given feed back, this story took shape because of you. Amy, Chelan, Alex, and Christie. You ladies helped me believe in myself and make it possible.

To my editor Whitney, and my copy editor Terry, it would

have been so much easier to cut and paste or change my work, but you didn't. You made it better. Thank you for polishing my brain-goo into a novel and letting my personality shine.

To my beautiful daughters, you are the magic that makes life worth fighting for. You were both so little when I was diagnosed. Life changed so much that I'm not sure either of you even have memories of what it looked like before cancer. Before this book. Thank you for motivating me to finish. For encouraging me to tell stories and create magic. You are always and ever my why.

ABOUT THE AUTHOR

Lions, and tigers, and… elephants? Erin Hemenway was raised backstage at the MGM Grand showcase, *'Hello Hollywood, Hello'* where she   sewed sequins onto, ahem… costumes, at age four. She lived a wild and varied life which included riding for the Historic Pony Express and touring the musical *'Oklahoma!'* in Europe.

She settled down in the Pacific Northwest where she began making racing documentaries and independent adventure films. With two kids and a breast cancer diagnosis, Erin transitioned into a full-time writer to keep her sanity during chemotherapy.

Erin lives in the Pacific Northwest with her family and their flat-coated retriever Ellie.

Love what you read?
Join my newsletter and be a part of my crew!

www.eringowrite.com

SUBSCRIBE TO MY NEWSLETTER

SCAN THIS CODE

www.eringowrite.com

  @erin.go.write

Made in United States
Troutdale, OR
11/12/2024

24701691R00192